In an endearing modern-day prodigal son story, with a sweet romance entwined throughout, author Martha Rogers has crafted a tale that carries the reader from page to page with both gentle passion and heart-pounding tension. *Love Finds Faith* is more than a romance; it is a lesson in love and faith that will enthrall readers of all ages.

—KATHI MACIAS

Award-winning author of
more than forty books, including
The Doctor's Christmas Quilt

www.kathimacias.com

Once again Martha Rogers has given us a heart-warming story filled with compelling true-to-life characters whose family struggles are as dangerous as the Texas wilderness they seek to tame.

—LOUISE M. GOUGE

Author of *A Lady of Quality*

In *Love Finds Faith* Martha Rogers deftly captures the fluctuating emotions of a prodigal son who returns home. Rogers skillfully crafts the harsh reality of life on a Texas ranch, and the nettlesome problems of sibling rivalry are realistic. The faith and love of a kind woman makes this a romance to savor.

—VICKIE MCDONOUGH

Award-winning author of 27 books and novellas, including *Whispers on the Prairie*, book 1 in the Pioneer Promises series

A charming modern-day telling of the prodigal son with a twist, plus the addition of a young woman who feels she is too flawed for any man to love. If a gentle read with hope built in is what you enjoy, *Love Finds Faith* will fit the bill for you.

—GOLDEN KEYES PARSONS

Author of the highly acclaimed
Darkness to Light series

Love Finds Faith

Love Finds Faith

THE HOMEWARD JOURNEY
BOOK TWO

MARTHA ROGERS

REALMS

Most CHARISMA HOUSE BOOK GROUP products are available at special quantity discounts for bulk purchase for sales promotions, premiums, fund-raising, and educational needs. For details, write Charisma House Book Group, 600 Rinehart Road, Lake Mary, Florida 32746, or telephone (407) 333-0600.

LOVE FINDS FAITH by Martha Rogers
Published by Realms
Charisma Media/Charisma House Book Group
600 Rinehart Road
Lake Mary, Florida 32746
www.charismahouse.com

All Scripture quotations are from the King James Version of the Bible.

Cover design by Bill Johnson

Visit the author's website at www.marthawrogers.com.

Library of Congress Cataloging-in-Publication Data:

Rogers, Martha.
  Love Finds Faith / Martha Rogers. -- First edition.
     pages cm. -- (The Homeward Journey ; Book Two)
  ISBN 978-1-62136-546-4 (trade paper) -- ISBN 978-1-
  62136-547-1 (ebook)
  1. Homecoming--Fiction. I. Title.
  PS3618.O4655L65 2014
  813'.6--dc23
                                             2013023605

First edition

14 15 16 17 18 — 9 8 7 6 5 4 3 2 1
Printed in the United States of America

"But seek ye first the kingdom of God, and his righteousness; and all these things shall be added unto you."

—Matthew 6:33

CHAPTER 1

Stoney Creek, Texas, June 1877

WHERE WERE SALLIE and Manfred? They were supposed to meet her here at the station. Hannah Dyer patted her damp brow with a handkerchief and tapped her good foot on the wooden platform where moments before she had stepped down from the afternoon train.

That her brother-in-law, Manfred, might be delayed she could understand, as doctors had emergencies arise all the time, but her sister, Sallie, didn't have such an excuse. Well, maybe Sallie's four children did give her an excuse. One of them must be delaying her. Hannah looked forward to seeing her nieces and nephews. It'd been almost eight years since Sallie and Manfred had moved to Texas, and over four years since they'd been home to Mississippi.

Hannah breathed in and then exhaled in a puff of air. The train whistle blew, and others now boarded the train. Waving away the soot in the air, she hobbled over to the luggage cart. Her baggage sat neatly stacked, ready to be picked up.

Mercy, the men had already unloaded the baggage car. Sallie should have been here by now. Resisting the urge to sit on her trunk, Hannah stood with her weight on her good left leg, resting the toe of her heavy, thick-soled boot on the platform. No matter how hard the cobbler tried when making her special shoes, her legs were never quite the same length, and the shoe for her shorter leg was always heavy and cumbersome. Even this new pair carried enough weight that it sometimes added an awkward gait to her walk.

1

Someone shouted her name. Hannah shaded her eyes against the sun to find Sallie pulling up with a wagon. Sallie hopped down, picked up her baby, and ran to Hannah.

"Oh, my, I'm so sorry. I couldn't get the children together, and Manfred is delivering Mrs. Fairchild's baby, and..." She stopped to stare at the trunk and other bags. "Goodness, is all that yours? How will we ever get it into the wagon?"

"I'll be glad to help you with it, Mrs. Whiteman. That is, if you'll introduce me to the lovely young lady here."

Hannah turned her head to gaze into the warmest brown eyes she'd seen since leaving Mississippi. The young man removed his light tan cowboy hat and grinned at her. His coffee-colored eyes now sparkled and creases formed to fan out from the corners. A tingle started at her toes and spread upward to engulf her heart.

Sallie shifted her baby on her hip. Her brow furrowed and she bit her lip. "Micah Gordon, I didn't know you had come home."

"Just got in. I was on the same train with this young lady."

"Oh, goodness me. Micah, this is my sister, Hannah Grace Dyer. She's come from Mississippi to help the doctor as his nurse. Hannah, this is Micah Gordon. His father has one of the larger ranches around these parts. Um...he's...he's been gone awhile."

Hannah smiled at the cowboy. His boots, hat, tan shirt, and string tie fit him perfectly, and she had to tilt her head back to meet his gaze. Funny she didn't remember seeing him on the train. Certainly she would have noticed this handsome face. Heat rose in her cheeks. "It's very nice of you to offer to help with the baggage."

He picked up two of the valises. "I take it you want them in the wagon over there, Mrs. Whiteman."

"Yes, yes, of course." Sallie scurried back to the wagon and the two children there.

Six-year-old Clara said nothing but stared with clear brown eyes at the aunt she most likely didn't remember, as she'd been a toddler the last time Hannah had seen her. On the other hand, eleven-year-old Molly stood in the bed of the wagon with hands on her hips. "Auntie Hannah, it's about time you got here. I've been waiting and waiting for you to come."

Even at a young age Molly showed signs of the beauty her mother possessed. Two stiff plaits held her red hair in check, but strands still escaped around Molly's heart-shaped face and blue-green eyes. Hannah crossed to the wagon, trying to minimize her limp so her heavy shoe didn't thump on the hardwood platform, but the thump still echoed across the boards.

"I'm so glad I'm finally here too, Molly. You've grown so much since your last visit to Mississippi." She had grown several inches, and Hannah remembered how much she had liked to hear such praise when she'd been Molly's age. Sure enough, a wide grin split Molly's face.

Hannah waved her hand toward the trunk. "I brought everyone gifts from Mama and Papa. They wanted to come, but Papa said it was too far right now. They'll try to come for Christmas." She cast her gaze to Micah, who handled the trunk with ease. Such broad shoulders he had. No wonder her bags and trunk presented no problem for him.

Micah stepped back and swiped his hands together. "There now, it looks like you're all set for the ride, Mrs. Whiteman."

"Thank you, Micah. I'm glad you decided to come home. Your ma and pa are going to be so happy to see you." She patted Hannah on the back. "You go ahead and climb up, then I'll hand Daniel up to you."

Hannah stared at the wagon wheel. How did one get up to the seat? Sallie had used the wheel to step down, but where was a foothold? She might balance on her heavier boot and step up with her good one, but what if she lost her balance? At home they'd always ridden in a carriage with a step stool to help. She bit her lip as a hand landed on her arm.

"Here, let me assist you, Miss Dyer. If you're not used to wagons, they can be difficult to maneuver." Micah offered one hand for support and pointed to the wheel with the other one. "Put your foot right there and I'll boost you up."

"Oh, dear, Hannah, I'm so sorry," Sallie apologized. "I didn't even think how difficult it might be for you to climb up on a wagon. Thank you, Micah."

Hannah had no choice but to pick up her skirt with one hand and set her normal foot on the little projection that jutted out from the wheel. Once her foot hit the wheel, Micah's hands went around her waist to hoist her up to the seat. *Thunk!* Her heavy boot hit the side of the wagon, and she almost lost her balance. She glanced down at Micah only to find him wide-eyed, staring at her feet. The tingle in her heart disappeared to be replaced with resignation for her deformed leg and foot.

His facial expression was no different from all the others when they first saw her ugly shoes. Her words wanted to stay lodged in her throat, but she forced them out. "Thank you, Mr. Gordon. I'm all right now."

He stepped back and shook his head, pity lacing the brown eyes that had been smiling and friendly only minutes earlier. Hannah bit her lip again. Why couldn't people just see who she was inside and not look only at her deformity?

Stoney Creek would be no different from all the other places she'd been. She might as well have stayed in Mississippi with Mama and Papa or in Louisiana with Grandma Woodruff. At least people there knew of her disability and had stopped shaking their heads with pity in their eyes.

Sallie handed baby Daniel up to Hannah then sprang up onto the wagon seat with little or no effort. Would Hannah ever be able to move like that? So far she hadn't, but maybe here she'd have more opportunity to exercise and be less of a cripple. She'd endured stares and ridicule for all of her twenty-four years of living, so she would manage with them in Stoney Creek as well.

Sallie flicked the reins, and the wagon moved away. Hannah so wanted one last look at Micah, but as much as she desired to see his handsome face, she had no desire to see pity there. "Micah seemed like a nice young man. You say he lives on a ranch?"

"Yes, but Micah's been gone for the past five years. From what I've heard, he told his pa he was tired of ranching and wanted to see what else life had to offer. I do believe there was much more to it than that, but I didn't pry or listen to gossip. I hope he's come back to make amends with his pa. Both his parents grieved terribly when he left. Broke some young ladies' hearts too."

A prodigal and rogue. How intriguing. Of course, with his handsome face and those penetrating eyes, he'd have the girls pursuing him. Not likely she'd have a chance with him after he'd seen her foot. That sent most young men the opposite direction right away.

She moved her skirt a bit and stared down at the special shoe that helped her stand straight. The shoes she'd worn as long as she could remember now became a burden she didn't want to bear. If only she could be normal, she might attract a young man and marry and have a family like Sallie. God had been good in not letting the problem keep her from pursuing her dream of becoming a nurse, but He hadn't answered the other prayer for a man in her life.

She hugged little Daniel to her chest. Instead of feeling sorry for herself, her heart should be full of thanksgiving for this opportunity to help her family.

Her sister chattered on about the town and those who lived there, but Hannah only half listened. She'd come here for a purpose. Manfred needed help with his medical practice, and she'd be the best nurse he'd ever had. If God wanted to send along a young man for her, then He would. But it would certainly be nice if that young man happened to be as handsome as Micah Gordon.

Micah stood in the middle of the street to gaze after the wagon stirring up dust as it headed for the doctor's home. What a pity for such a beautiful young woman to be burdened with a deformity like that. Golden hair laced with red framed a face set off by eyes so blue they defied a color description and were made even more intense by the blue of her dress. Not that her looks should matter, because courting a cripple, or any other woman for that matter, didn't come into his plans for his future.

What that future might be remained his number one concern at the moment. Those who'd known him before would think he'd been up to no good after the way he'd left town, and they'd be right. He had spent too much time and money on women and fun in the past years. After hitting rock bottom, he had no place to go. But to come home begging was not an option he had wanted to face.

He'd finally pulled himself out of the muck and mire a few months ago and found a job cleaning the livery stable in a small town. When the livery owner had trouble keeping track of his money and who had paid what, Micah called on his talent for arithmetic and numbers to take on the book-keeping for the livery. The man had upped Micah's wages but not changed his main job title. If Micah had to muck stalls, he could do that just as well at home. So once he had enough money saved up for the journey, he headed home.

As much as he hated ranching, here he was back seeking forgiveness from his parents and a chance to prove himself useful on the ranch. Roping, branding, and rounding up lost strays were not his idea of living. He'd much rather take care of the business end and keeping records, but Pa probably didn't want to hear that.

Micah headed for the hotel to get a room for the night. After he cleaned up, he could still make it out to the ranch in time for supper. A good shave wouldn't hurt either.

A glance up and down the main street revealed not much had changed. The bank and general store still sat across from each other on opposite corners, and the hotel stood in the middle of the next block. A larger building across from the station bore a painted sign declaring the building to be Brunson's Livery and Blacksmith. Old Willy Brunson must have hired a smithy, since Willy didn't have the strength it took for that job. If his father didn't welcome him home, per-haps he could find work with Willy here at the livery until something better came along.

A midsummer afternoon on a weekday drew few people into town. Most would be at home resting or escaping the heat. The few who walked along the boardwalk stared at Micah then nodded, but no one showed real signs of recognizing him. That didn't surprise him, since he was taller and more filled out than he had been as a wayward son leaving home. At twenty-four he had become a man.

When Micah opened the door to the hotel, the clerk looked up, and a grin spread across his face. "Well now, if it ain't Micah Gordon. Good to see you. What's it been? Three or four years?"

Micah laughed and dropped his valise to the floor. "More like five, Charlie. Got a room for me?"

Charlie swung the register around for Micah to sign. "Sure do, but ain't you going out to see your folks?"

"I am later, but I want to be in town tonight." He picked up the pen and signed his name on the book. No need to tell Charlie the real reason for not going home first. Without knowing how his parents would greet him, he figured staying in town was the better option, but he only had funds for a few nights. After that he'd be back out on the streets again.

"Sure thing, Micah. Here's your key. Your room's at the head of the stairs, then the second door to the right. Looks out over the street. It's one of our nicest rooms."

Micah gripped the key in his hand and bent to pick up his bag. Next thing in order after a good bath and shave would be renting a horse. That would go over big, what with his pa having some of the best horses money could buy in his stables, but Micah wasn't at the ranch and had no horse here in town.

Charlie continued to grin and shake his head. "Can't believe it's really you. Your folks are going to be mighty glad to see you." Then his grin turned to a smirk. "Know a few young ladies who'll be glad to hear you're back too."

Micah shrugged and headed for the stairs. He doubted Charlie's last statement. The girls he'd known must surely be married by now with families of their own. Pretty women didn't stay single in a town like Stoney Creek, where there were more than enough men for them.

After a bath and clean clothes Micah was ready to face his parents and whatever future may be out there for him. Pa would say his elder son needed to settle down, take over the ranch, and marry a nice young girl, but rounding up cattle and breaking horses wasn't on Micah's short list of things he wanted to do with his life. It hadn't made the long list either. Not that he didn't love horses, but he didn't want to spend all of his time on the back of one. However, he'd do whatever it took now to regain Pa's trust and convince him that his elder son's interests and talents lay in business and not cattle herding.

After one last glance at the mirror Micah closed the bag with his few belongings in it. No need to unpack until he learned what kind of reception he'd receive at the ranch. He locked the door to his room and pocketed the key. May as well get the trip over with now.

Downstairs, Charlie greeted him again. "Hey, there, Micah, you clean up nice. Bet your sister will be happy to see you. Maggie, I mean Miss Margaret, is always talking about you when she comes into town."

"I'll be glad to see her too." So Margaret no longer wanted to be called Maggie. A smile creased his face. Just like his little sister to decide to use the longer version of her name. She'd be twenty now.

He wondered how his other siblings would greet him. At twenty-two, his younger brother, Levi, probably had more knowledge of the ranch by now than Micah would ever have.

Levi had always loved being out on horseback, working the cattle, and couldn't wait to put school behind him. Micah, on the other hand, rather enjoyed school, though he never dared admit it aloud. He'd never quite seen eye to eye with Levi, and their differing perspectives had caused more than one disagreement between them.

Micah especially looked forward to seeing his little sister Rosie. She'd been only eight when he left, and now she'd be a young lady of thirteen. Would he still be her hero, like he used to be? He rather doubted it.

He crossed the street to the livery, curious as to whom Willy had hired as blacksmith. He must be new in town, because Micah didn't remember any boys with the strength of a smithy. Of course they could have grown up by now.

Willy greeted him with a huge grin splitting his face. "Why, if it ain't Micah Gordon. Didn't know you was coming home. Come on in, boy. You wantin' a horse? Where's Red Dawn?"

"Had to sell her, Willy, so now I need one to get out to the ranch." A clanging noise rang out from the back. "I see you've hired a smithy."

"Sure 'nuff have. Come on and see. I think you may know him."

When Willy approached the new smithy, Micah's eyes opened wide, not at the size and strength of the man, but at the color of his skin, dark as midnight. Micah remembered him as the one who had come with the Whiteman family years ago.

Micah stuck out his hand. "Good to see you again, Burt. This town sure needed a good blacksmith."

The man grinned, his white in sharp contrast to the black surrounding it and grasped Micah's hand in an iron grip. "Good to see you come home, Mr. Gordon."

Willy led a horse to Micah. "Let me get this one saddled and you can ride out of here. His name is Gray Mist."

Burt grinned again. "He picked you out a good one. I put those shoes on him myself."

Micah grabbed the saddle and helped Willy finish up with getting the horse ready to ride. A few minutes later Willy handed him the reins.

"Thanks. I'll have him back tomorrow if not tonight." Micah swung up into the saddle, tipped his hat, and turned his horse to the northwest and the road out of town. As he rode down the street, the bank door opened and an older man and beautiful young woman stepped out. He recognized the man as Horace Swenson, the owner, but who was the young woman with him?

She turned toward him, and her smile froze on her lips. Her eyes opened wide and her hand grasped her throat.

Camilla Swenson. If not for that sunny blonde hair and almost violet eyes, he'd never have recognized her, but she had recognized him right away. Camilla had grown up. Suddenly, returning to Stoney Creek became the best idea he'd ever had.

CHAPTER 2

THE WAGON WITH Hannah's belongings had been hitched to the post at the back of Sallie's home. She had explained that it would be easier to get the baggage upstairs from there because the door was wider and the stairway closer than from the front door where Manfred had his office and examining room.

Sallie had jumped down as easily as she had boarded the wagon and took a now sleeping Daniel into her arms. "I'm taking him up for his nap, then we can get your belongings. Do you need help getting down?"

The girls had already hopped down and raced each other to the house. "No, I think I can manage." Getting down from the wagon proved easier than getting up on it, and once on solid ground, Hannah stood outside and admired the two-story white clapboard box house with green shutters at the windows revealing lacy curtains behind them. Nothing as fancy as their brick home in Mississippi, but very nice by some standards, and it fit a doctor's family.

When she crossed the back door threshold, Molly and Clara were seated at the table waiting for their snack. Sallie pushed through the swinging door from the other room. "Welcome to our home. We're so glad you're here."

Hannah glanced around the kitchen and gasped. "Oh, Sallie, it's wonderful." Her gaze swept around the pale green walls with bright red accents and sturdy pine cabinets. A pine table sat in the center surrounded by eight spindle-back chairs. "Are you sure I won't be taking up too much space with four children here?"

Sallie laughed and reached into her cupboard for two glasses. "Of course not. Clara and Molly share a room, and the baby's cradle is still in our room. Tommy has his own room, but Daniel will move into it in a few months. Even with that we have extra ones for guests."

"Five bedrooms? That's as many as we had at home. I'm surprised."

Sallie nodded. "We were fortunate that the doctor Manfred replaced had six children, so they had plenty of rooms for our family."

Hannah glanced around the kitchen again. "Where is little Tommy?" She'd almost forgotten about the eight-year-old nephew who had been a child of four the last time she'd seen him.

"He's with Doreen Weatherby, our preacher's wife. She has a boy Tommy's age, and they love to play together. She'll bring him here before supper." Sallie set the two glasses now filled with milk on the table then laid a napkin beside each. "I'm certainly glad homes out west always have had kitchens indoors and not out in a separate building like Grandma Woodruff's was. I can't imagine why folks in the South thought they had to do it different when they built their homes before the war."

Sallie could speak lightly of the war now, but at the time it ended, they both had seen the worst side of it, and Hannah hoped and prayed nothing like that would ever happen again. She shook off the memories and smiled at her nieces. "Those cookies look mighty good. Maybe I'll have one with you later."

Clara held up hers. "You can haf' mine, Auntie Annie."

Sallie bent to kiss the child's head. "It's Hannah, sweetie, not Annie."

Hannah laughed and covered Clara's hand with hers. "That's all right. If you want me to be Annie, I will be Annie. Thank you for the cookie, but I'll wait until we've put things away and then have one."

Clara's broad smile revealed one tooth missing in the center front. Hannah squeezed her hand. How fast she'd grown in the years since they'd been back to Mississippi. Her brown hair hung straight down her back with a fringe of curls about her forehead. They framed a round little face with brown eyes just like her father's. Living here with the children would be much more exciting than being back home with just Mama and Papa, since Tom and Will had gone their own ways.

Sallie picked up two of Hannah's satchels. "Molly, you stay here with Clara and have your cookies and milk while I help Aunt Hannah." She headed for the swinging door. "Since Daniel's down for a nap, we can get your things up to your room. We'll save the heavy trunk for Manfred to bring when he gets back."

"That's a good idea. I sure don't want to try to carry it." Hannah picked up another bag and followed her sister into the hallway.

Sallie nodded toward double doors on her right as she headed up to the second floor. "That's Manfred's office. He should be back soon unless the Fairchild baby has complications. She wasn't due until next month, but that baby had a mind of its own and decided to come into this world right now."

That had happened often in Hannah's nurse's training at Bellevue Hospital in New York. Whether it was the first baby or the fifth, they came when they decided. Papa had wanted the best schooling for her, so she'd gone north to the new nursing school. She'd only been there two years when Manfred said he needed a nurse, so she'd jumped at the chance to put her new skills to use. A look at the office would come later when Manfred could give her a tour, so for now she let her curiosity concentrate on her new bedroom.

Sallie opened the door and stepped back, smiling widely. "I hope you like it."

Hannah squealed and clasped her hands to her chest. "It's perfect. How did you get Grandma Woodruff's quilt here without my knowing?" She hurried to the bed and ran her hands over the log cabin design quilt that had been on her bed when she stayed with her grandparents.

"Mama decided the room would feel more like home with it, so she sent it as soon as you told them you were coming. She sent a few other things too."

"I see. Oh, it's just wonderful." Hannah touched her fingers to the rose print bowl and ewer set on a side table with a mirror above it. "This was in our room at Grandma's too."

She retraced her steps and wrapped her arms around Sallie. "You've made me so welcome, and I love it. Thank you."

"Well, you deserve it, coming all this way to help Manfred with his patients. He has his hands full." She stepped back from Hannah and held her hands.

"Speaking of hands full, I'd better get back downstairs to the girls. You do what you can to settle in until Manfred brings up the rest of the things when he gets home. I need to put the horses in the stable too." She headed out then stopped at the doorway. "I'll get supper started shortly, but soon as you finish, come join me in the kitchen. I want to hear all the news from home."

Hannah nodded. "I'll be down soon as I freshen up, and I can't wait to share news with you."

Sallie laughed and waved her hand at Hannah before closing the door behind her and heading back downstairs.

Such a lovely room, and it was all hers. Hannah plopped on the bed and ran her hands across the quilt again. Mama always knew what would please her girls, and she'd done a good job this time. Hannah undid the clasps on one of the bags and began removing a few of the items. A chest stood against the wall next to the washstand. She stowed some of her things there and then opened the wardrobe to find pegs and wooden hangers for her clothes.

The laughter of the girls and a man's deep voice drew Hannah out into the hallway. She leaned over the railing to find her two nieces greeting their father in the lower hallway. Manfred was home. She rushed down the stairs to greet him, only to almost be run over by a bundle of energy.

Manfred grabbed at the boy. "Whoa there, buster, you almost knocked over Aunt Hannah." His voice scolded, but his eyes and smile only held love for the rambunctious eight-year-old.

Two blue eyes under a shock of red hair stared at her. "Aunt 'Annah? From Mis-sippi?"

"One and the same." She extended her hand. "And you must be Tommy. What a fine-looking young gentleman you are."

He grinned, revealing a fine set of snowy new teeth. "Thank you." Then he ducked his head and ran to the kitchen.

Manfred wrapped one arm around Hannah and the other around Molly. "Now what have you two ladies been up to this afternoon?"

Molly began telling her father about all of the luggage Hannah had brought with her. When they reached the kitchen, Molly slipped from her father's grasp and ran to throw her arms around Sallie's waist. "And Auntie Hannah's going to stay for a long time, isn't she, Mama?"

With the warmth of love from her nieces, nephews, and her sister, Hannah would indeed stay a long time in the Whiteman household. Who cared whether she attracted a young man? Nursing was what she'd come to do, and she planned to do it with all her heart.

Micah picked up the pace of his horse as he neared the ranch. The overwhelming desire to see his mother and sisters pushed aside the worries about the greeting Pa and Levi might give on his arrival.

The high-arched entry and gate with the Circle G brand at the top welcomed him at the bottom of the rise where the house sat overlooking the thousands of acres making up the ranch. He rode through the open gate and up the path toward the two-story house with its wraparound front porch. Ma's roses bloomed in a riot of yellow, pink, and red. How she managed to keep them so full and green in the heat of a Texas summer never ceased to amaze him.

As he approached the house, Lasso, the family golden retriever, raised his head then stood alert and curious until Micah drew closer. The dog barked twice and raced at Micah, nipping at the horse's legs and trying to jump up at Micah.

The front door opened, and two women and a girl appeared on the porch. The youngest of the three flew down the steps. Micah dismounted and reached out his arms to brace himself against the body hurtling in his direction as well as the jumps of Lasso around his legs.

"Micah! Micah! You're home." Two arms wrapped around

his midsection and squeezed hard. "I knew you wouldn't stay away."

Lasso barked and pranced around the two, trying to get his paws on Micah's hips. With one hand he reached down to pat the dog's head, and with the other he disentangled Rose Ellen's arms. "Look at you, Rosie. All grown up, and pretty as a picture." Not only had she grown in height since he'd left, but she'd begun to fill out in all the right places and at thirteen years of age had become a most attractive girl.

Her cheeks flushed red, and she blinked her eyes to clear away the tears. Ma and Maggie now stood beside him. Ma reached for him and hugged him, her head resting on his chest. He inhaled the familiar rose water scent she used as well as the aroma of cinnamon and sugar. Home. He'd come home.

"Oh, my son, I've missed you so." She raised her head and placed her hands on either side of his face then stood on tiptoe to kiss his forehead. "It's been so long. Welcome back."

"Thank you, Ma. It's good to be home." And that was the truth, no matter what his father and Levi had to say or how they felt. Ma and his sisters had drawn him back. They were the ones he'd missed the most in the years he'd been gone.

"Yes, Micah, we have missed you." Maggie crossed her arms at her waist. "You could have at least written and let us know where you were and what you were doing. For all we knew, you could have been dead somewhere."

Her mouth skewed into a frown that pierced his heart with guilt. Dead he could have and probably should have been. He had no real reason to give her, and even his excuses sounded lame now that he actually had to explain. "I'm sorry, but I was angry when I left, and by the time...never mind. I'll tell you about it later after I've spoken with Pa." He'd almost revealed too much, and around his younger sisters he didn't care to tell much about what had happened, especially in those early years. He wrapped his arm about his mother's shoulders.

"I detect a hint of cinnamon and sugar. Does that mean you've been baking?"

Ma swatted her hand at his arm. "Of course it does. Now come on into the house. Pa and the others will be back soon, and they'll all be hungrier than a bear after hibernation. Grubbs is down at the bunkhouse fixing supper for the hands, and ours is almost done too."

Micah sauntered up to the house with Ma. Maggie and Rosie followed behind, their heads together in conversation, no doubt about his last statement. Their furtive glances in his direction indicated that curiosity guided their words.

When he stepped through the door, the years rolled away, and he became the nineteen-year-old young man who sought answers to questions that had no true answers. He was no closer to knowing what he truly wanted out of life than he had been when he walked out of this house and into the unknown world.

"The place hasn't changed a bit, Ma." The fireplace still dominated the large room where the family spent most of their time. At the back, a stairway led to the second floor where he, his brother, and his sisters slept. How would Levi feel about sharing a room once again? Probably wouldn't be too happy about it. If that was the case, Micah would return to the hotel and stay there as long as the little money he had left held out.

Micah plopped down onto the dark blue upholstery of the pinewood sofa. He ran his hands over the arm supports, worn smooth by years of handling by Gordon children. He gestured to Maggie and Rosie. "Come sit down with me and tell me all you've been doing these years. I can see how much you've grown, Rosie. You're not a little girl anymore. You turned into a young lady while I've been gone. And Maggie, you're a woman now."

Rosie sank onto the sofa beside him, but Maggie stood with her mouth in a firm line and her hands curled into fists by her side. "My name is Margaret, if you please, and Rosie is Rose Ellen or just Rose. We've outgrown those childhood names." She glared at Rose. "You can sit and visit if you like, but I'm going to help Ma with supper."

She turned with a swish of her skirts and marched to the kitchen. Rose covered her giggle with her hand. "I love Margaret, but she's always so prim and proper. I'm sure she's glad you're home."

"I hope so." He reached over and touched his sister's shoulder. "You're a very pretty girl, Miss Rose Ellen Gordon. I bet you have boys clamoring all around you at school."

A deep flush tinged her cheeks, but before she could answer, horses' hooves pounded the ground outdoors. Micah's heart lurched, and the bitter taste of fear filled his throat. Pa and Levi had arrived. He stood and wiped his hands down the side of his pants to dry the moisture now coating his palms. Footsteps thundered across the porch, and the door swung open.

Pa stepped through, his head bent toward Levi with some bit of information. He turned and his eyes opened wide when he spotted Micah. Levi's brown eyes darkened and his jaw clenched.

Micah stepped forward. "Hello, Pa, Levi. I've come home."

CHAPTER 3

FOR A MOMENT or two no one spoke a word. The only sound to reach Micah's ears was the pounding of his own heart. Pa removed his hat, and a veil dropped over his eyes as he narrowed them to peer at Micah. The tension in the room lay thicker than a slab of beef, and no one appeared ready to slice through it.

Micah locked gazes with his pa. "I'm sorry, Pa. I should have written."

Pa's hands gripped the brim of his hat until his knuckles turned white. "Yes, you should have. Five years and not a word. Then here you are on our doorstep."

Levi jerked his head. "He's right. You could have been dead for all we knew. Why did you come home now?" He waved his hat. "Never mind. I don't want to hear your sorry excuses. I need to take care of the horses." Levi slapped his hat back on his head and strode through the door.

Ma and Maggie had come from the kitchen in time to witness the scene. Ma's hand clasped her throat, and her eyes glistened in the lamplight.

Micah had hurt them all, and no matter how much he wanted to or how hard he tried, he couldn't take back those years. He lifted his chin. "I'm sorry, Pa. I'll leave now if you don't want me here."

"No, no. It's such a shock. None of us expected you to come back like this." He furrowed his brow. "You and I have some serious talking to do. I want to know where you were and what happened, and why you've come back."

Hope planted a seed in Micah's heart. One baby step,

but it could be the beginning of reconciliation. "Yes, Pa. I understand." If only Levi had stayed around for that talk. He couldn't do anything about his brother, but maybe Pa would understand. "I'd like that. I have much to tell you."

Pa's hand gripped Micah's shoulder. "We can talk after supper. No need to let Ma's hard work get cold." He turned to Rose. "Go get your brother and tell him to come for supper now or go without."

"Yes, sir." She scurried away to do his bidding.

Pa hadn't smiled yet, but the expression on his face had lost some of the chill exhibited earlier. Trust would be hard to rebuild, but Micah intended to do everything he could to do just that.

Rose returned to take her place at the table. "Levi said he'd eat and sleep with the hands in the bunkhouse tonight."

Pa's jaw hardened. "Very well. Let's eat our supper before it grows cold."

They all sat down, and Maggie reached for his hand. "I'm happy you're here, Micah." After witnessing that scene with Levi, she must have decided to drop her own misgivings and smooth things over, for Ma and Pa's sake.

He squeezed her fingers and bowed his head for Pa to say grace. It'd been a long time since he'd heard words bless food, and even longer since he'd asked God for anything at all.

At the end Pa said, "Thank You for bringing our son safely home. For whatever reason, he's here, and we give thanks for that, no matter how long it may be. Amen."

That last sentence gripped Micah's heart, and the seed of hope planted only moments earlier began to grow. He'd be here as long as it took to come to an understanding with his family or until they ran him off.

Hannah sat at the kitchen table while Sallie put finishing touches on the evening meal. Supper tonight would be light to keep the heat from overwhelming the preparations. Daniel sat tied to his chair with a large dishtowel knotted through the slats. He banged on the wood surface of the table with his tin spoon and added to the dents and scratches already there.

"Looks like your family spends a lot of time around this table." Hannah traced one of the scars with her fingernail.

"Oh, we do. Manfred is one who believes in things being used. If it's too fragile for the children to handle, then it's not for our family. The exception being the lamps, but the children have strict orders about those." Sallie removed a pan of cornbread from the oven and set it on a folded cloth on the table. "Do you mind cutting this for me and putting it on that plate?"

Hannah picked up the knife beside the pan. "Of course, but I should be helping you more."

"Don't worry about that. You're a guest tonight, and we'll be eating in the dining room. Besides, I did most of the cooking earlier in the cooler hours of the morning. I hope you don't mind cold ham and cold pickled beets. The only hot dishes are the cornbread and the black-eyed peas I boiled earlier today." Sallie sliced ham onto a platter and grinned at Hannah.

"Sounds perfect for a summer evening." She turned the cornbread out of the cast iron skillet and cut the golden crusted bread into squares. "It's nice that Manfred entertains the children while you fix supper."

"Oh, he loves it, and they do too. Sometimes there's an

emergency, and he has to leave before supper or in the middle of it, so he cherishes the time he does have with them." She ladled peas into a pottery bowl. "I'm so glad to hear that Grandma Woodruff is feeling better. Mama's last letter said she was not up to her usual busyness around the house."

"She's fine now, but she sorely misses you and the little ones. I hope we can all make it home for Tom's wedding in the fall."

Laughter erupted from Sallie as she set the bowl on the table. "I'm amazed that Laurie Bevins was finally able to snag our wayward brother. From all his talk the past few years, I figured we'd have an unmarried brother on our hands for the duration."

"She's a beautiful woman, and she absolutely adores Tom." Hannah stood with the plate of cornbread. "Shall I put this on the dining table?"

"Yes, go ahead. I'll bring in the rest. Oh, by the way, I almost forgot. Lettie and Burt are coming by after supper. I thought you might like to see them and their two children."

"That's wonderful. I haven't seen them in years since they didn't come to Mississippi the last time you visited." Hannah had loved the servant girl, and Lettie had been through some really dangerous and rough times with the family during the war. She had married her sweetheart, Burt, when the war had ended just like Sallie had married Manfred.

Hannah headed for the dining room, making the effort to keep her shoe from clumping against the floor. Would she ever have the opportunity to marry someone, just as Sallie and Lettie had, and experience the love of a man and a family of her own?

When the children spotted Hannah and Sallie with food, they cheered and squealed and ran to the table. Clara and

Tommy climbed onto their chairs and settled on one side. Molly shook her head and shrugged her shoulders before easing down beside her sister. Hannah bit back her giggle. Molly's disapproval of her siblings' antics reminded Hannah of dinners with Tom and Will when they were growing up. They had created a stir at every meal, and Sallie had frowned at them exactly as Molly had done.

Mealtime in the Whiteman household brought back memories of dinners around the table back home in Mississippi. Laughter, teasing, and love filled their voices and eyes. Hannah sat back and enjoyed the meal and the fellowship with her family.

After they finished dessert, Molly headed upstairs with Clara to entertain her, and Manfred took charge of Daniel and Tommy. Such a wonderful family. Hannah picked up two plates and sighed. Staying here with Sallie and Manfred would give her the chance to be around little ones and enjoy watching them grow and change.

As soon as the dishes had been washed, dried, and put away, Hannah followed Sallie to the parlor. The brass knocker on the front door clunked twice.

"That'll be Lettie and Burt. They'll be so happy to see you." Sallie rushed to the front door to greet her guests.

When Hannah greeted the couple in the parlor, she grinned at the young woman who hadn't aged any more than Sallie had. They both were more mature, but they could have been back in Grandma Woodruff's parlor twelve years ago when they waited for Manfred to come home from the war. "I'm so glad you and Burt decided to come to Texas with Manfred and Sallie."

"Now you know I wouldn't let Miss Sallie come all this way without me. We were together too long to separate." She poked at her husband's arm. "I'm just thankful Burt here was agreeable to the trip."

"Humph, I wasn't about to let you get away from me." Then he grinned at Hannah. "Glad to see you made it safely here, Missy. Doc needs a good nurse to help take care of the people here in Stoney Creek."

Burt shook her hand with the firm grip befitting a blacksmith. Even the long sleeves of his homespun shirt couldn't conceal the bulging muscles of his forearms and his broad shoulders. Hannah tilted her head back to look into his dark eyes. At well over six feet tall, he towered over her.

Lettie wrapped her arms around Hannah in a hug that transported her back to Mississippi, and Hannah blinked back tears. "It's wonderful to see both of you. I'll be less homesick with you here." She stepped back and turned to the boy and girl standing beside their father. "And you must be Yancy and Dorie. It's good to meet you. I've known your pa and ma a long time."

Their dark faces beamed with delight. Sallie nodded toward the stairs. "Molly is upstairs with Tommy and Clara. You two go on up and join them. We'll have some cookies in a little while."

The two young ones scampered up the stairway, their voices audible as they greeted their friends. Sallie untied her apron and laid it across the back of a chair. "Y'all come on into the parlor so we can sit and visit a spell. Hannah has told me a little about home, but I wanted to wait until you two were here to hear more about what's going on in St. Francisville and Woodville."

Once they were all settled, Hannah began with her report from home. "Mama is busy with plans for Tom's wedding. Of course she doesn't have near the work she had with yours, Sallie, but she's helping Laura and Mrs. Bevins with the flowers and table decorations for the dinner after the ceremony."

"Of course Mama would have to be involved. She didn't have much opportunity with Will's last year, so she's making up for lost time. I'm hoping we'll be able to go back for Tom's since I had to miss Will's because of Daniel, not that I minded, you understand, but this wedding should be fun, and I don't want to miss it."

Talk continued for another half hour or so until Sallie rose from her chair. "I think it's time for some coffee and sugar cookies."

Lettie jumped up. "I'll come help you. Hannah, you stay here and enjoy yourself a little while longer. Knowing the doc here, you won't have much time to sit in the days ahead." She took a few steps then stopped and turned back with a crease across her brow. "I heard tell that Micah Gordon has come home. Sure would like to know what he's been doing all these years he's been away."

Burt shook his head. "Nary a word to his family in all that time. Strange if you ask me." He glanced at Hannah. "Now that's one young man you might ought to steer clear of, Missy. Most likely he's up to no good and will cause his ma and pa grief."

Hannah pressed her lips together. Micah had been so helpful earlier today. How unlike Burt to make such a statement, especially in light of all that he'd endured with criticism and prejudice in past years. She certainly didn't intend to make any judgments against Micah until she knew him better. That is, if she ever had the chance to even get to know him. His facial expression when he saw her deformed foot and cumbersome boot didn't bode well for any type of friendship, no matter how good or bad the young man may be in the eyes of others.

After dinner Pa led the way to his office and closed the door behind them. Micah's stomach churned, but this was something that had to be done, and the sooner the better. He swallowed several times to get rid of the bitter taste on his tongue as he waited for Pa to be seated behind the desk and indicate he was ready to listen.

Pa opened a drawer and pulled out a sheet of paper and a pen. Puzzled for the moment, Micah stared as his father began writing. After a minute or so he stopped and peered up at Micah.

"Have a seat and tell me what the past five years has been all about." He leaned back from the desk and folded his hands with his elbows on the chair arms. "Spare me the details and specifics. I don't need to know it all, just the basics and why you're back now."

Micah sat down. He breathed deeply to calm his nerves and exhaled long enough to clear his head. "After the big fight among the three of us, I just couldn't take any more, even though you stood up for me against Levi. In my heart I knew he was right about my not pulling my weight. Ranching isn't in my blood like it is yours and Levi's."

Pa said nothing, but his eyes bored into Micah's soul. He'd hurt his father and left without a word of explanation or apology. That his father even listened now was a miracle.

"Where did you go?"

"I had planned on going up to Dallas and see what I could find there. I had some money saved, and that took me about halfway. I did odd jobs to earn a little money, but I…I lost it all in a card game. Never could get ahead and never made it to Dallas."

"I see. You didn't think enough of us to write and let us know where you were and that you needed money?"

The steel in Pa's voice cut Micah to the bone, but he deserved it. His chin dropped to his chest. "I was too ashamed to let you know what had happened."

Pa's eyes narrowed and his mouth worked in that way it did when he fought anger. "So you let Ma, me, and the rest worry about you, wondering where in thunder you could have gone and why we heard nothing."

"I'm sorry. I came back because I saw what I did was wrong. My life was headed nowhere, and when I finally realized it, the only thing I wanted to do was come home."

"So what now? Are you ready to settle down here and take on the responsibility of helping Levi and me with the ranch?"

"Pa, my heart is with business and numbers, not riding herds and branding cattle. I know that's all a part of running a ranch, but it isn't what I want to do with my life."

"But it's your legacy. I've worked hard so you'd have something after I'm gone."

"But what about Levi? Doesn't he deserve an interest in the Circle G? He's the one who's been doing all the work."

"You're the eldest, and as such the ranch will pass to you. I've taken care of Levi. He'll get a large acreage and stock to start his own spread. He'll marry and have a good start for a life of his own." Pa's jaw set in a firm line, one that meant no argument.

Micah ignored the warning sign. He had to make Pa understand. "That's well and good, but I believe Levi would be happier running the Circle G and continuing what you've built." Why were they even talking about who would inherit the ranch? Pa still had a lot of years left.

"Tarnation, boy, what was the sense of your even coming back if you dislike ranching so much? If you want to stay around here, you have to pull your weight." Pa's hand went to his chest and rubbed over his heart.

Micah's fists clenched at his sides, but he noted the gesture and the fact his father's face had paled. "Is something wrong, Pa?"

"No." He waved a hand in the air. "I ate supper too fast is all." He glared at Micah. "You didn't answer my question."

Warning bells clanged in Micah's head, but what could he do? Pa always denied when he was sick. So he answered Pa's question. "I have what it takes to ride herds, but I don't want to do it full-time."

"Just what do you plan to do or think you can do if you don't want to ride herd?"

In light of what he'd just witnessed, Micah put his own desires on hold. "I will ride herd until I can show you what else I'm capable of." Pa deserved at least that, in light of what Micah had done to him.

"And how long will that be? Will you up and decide to run off again and leave your ma and the rest of us worrying about you?" Again his hand massaged the left side of his chest.

Micah had no choice now. "No, I wouldn't do that again, I promise. All I'm asking is for a chance to prove what I can do, and what I'm best at."

After a moment of silence Pa stood. "All right, if you'll give me a month, we'll talk again after that."

At least Pa was giving him a chance. Now he had to convince Levi they could work together. Besides, he wanted to keep an eye on Pa. He didn't like the pallor of his face or the fact he had massaged his chest several times. "Agreed."

Pa came from around the desk and extended his hand. "Then that's settled for now. In spite of everything that's happened, we're all glad you're home."

Micah grasped Pa's hand. He doubted Levi joined in with being glad, but at least Pa had listened. He'd stay a month or more just to prove himself and be sure Pa was all right.

CHAPTER 4

WEDNESDAY MORNING LEVI joined the other ranch hands around the table for breakfast. The talk centered around everything from rounding up strays to mending a few fences, but no one mentioned Levi's presence at their gathering rather than his family's. Most of them didn't know Micah, and even if they had, they didn't dare talk about him in front of Levi.

Grubbs, the cook, finished frying the potatoes and drained off the grease. The look he sent Levi's way relayed displeasure. He'd been around the ranch longer than Levi could remember and had scolded him on more than one occasion. Grubbs would most likely give Levi an earful later, but he'd say nothing in front of the other men.

Randy, one of the younger hands and close to Levi's own age, punched Levi's arm. "When are you coming into town with us to have some fun? Could have had yourself quite a time last night at the saloon."

What was this boy thinking? He had no business in a saloon at his age. He didn't begrudge the older men their time off or how they spent it, but he hated to see one as young as Randy start down that path.

"Most likely I won't be going with you at all. The saloon's not the place for me." He wanted to add *nor you either*, but he'd best keep his mouth shut for the time being.

One of the others guffawed and slapped the table, making the tin plates jump. "Don't you know the boss and his son here is teetotalers? Besides, Levi is sweet on Miss Bradshaw, the schoolmarm."

Heat rose in Levi's face. How did Lucky know about Miss Bradshaw? They'd only been together a few months and that mostly on Sunday afternoons. He planned to ask her father about marrying her, but no else knew that. "What gives you that idea, Lucky?"

A smirk crossed the man's face. "I seen you at the general store when we were there for supplies last week. She come in, and suddenly you was all thumbs and rosy cheeks."

The incident replayed itself in his mind. Seeing her that morning had sent his heart to racing, but he'd been too surprised to say anything intelligent to her. "She's a very nice lady and a good teacher far as I've heard." Better to keep them talking about Ellie Bradshaw than his attitude toward Micah.

Grubbs set food on the table. "Time for you to quit your jawin' and get to eatin'."

They didn't need to be told twice to dig in for their meal. All talk ceased as the cowboys filled their stomachs with Grubbs's food.

After the meal had been eaten and dishes cleaned, a group of the men headed for the stables to saddle their horses for the day's work. Fences needed mending and strays rounded up. Levi started that way to join them, but Grubbs's hand grasped Levi's arm.

"Wait a minute, son. You and me need to have a few words."

Here it came...the scolding. Levi didn't want to stay and listen, but respect for the long-time ranch hand bade him stay put.

They sat down at the deserted dining table. Nothing the old man said would change Levi's mind or attitude, but he'd let Grubbs have his say.

"Levi, son, I'm near twice as old as you, and I've been

around long as you've been born. It sorely grieves my heart to see you acting this a way towards your brother. You two is different as day and night, but you're both Gordon boys. That means somethin' in these here parts. People like and respect your pa because he's an honest, hardworking man. What you're doing is going to break his heart as well as your ma's."

Grubbs paused, but Levi had no comment. He narrowed his eyes and waited for the old man to continue.

"I know my thinkin' don't make no difference to you, but you think about what the good Lord says you should do. Jesus done told a story about a son that went away then came back. His pa welcomed him home too, but the other son didn't like it one little bit. You've heard that story, and it jest might do you good to read it again." He pushed back from the table and stood. "That's all I'm a gonna say about it. It's between you and the Lord now, son."

Levi's jaw clenched at the truth in Grubbs's words, but it still didn't make right Micah's coming back and thinking he could just take up his old life without any consequences for abandoning them.

He rose from his chair and strolled out to lean against one of the railings on the bunkhouse porch. The smell of frying steaks and the chatter of his sisters as they dressed spilled from the open windows of the house across the way. Soon his family would sit down to breakfast without him. Remorse nibbled at his soul, but it'd take a heap more than missing a few home-cooked meals to change his mind about Micah.

Ruth Gordon wiped her hands on her apron and reached for a towel to remove a pan of biscuits from the oven. The aroma of frying meat and hot bread filled the air as she opened the oven door. She looked forward to serving her long-lost son Micah a hearty ranch breakfast. Homemade strawberry preserves would top the biscuits to perfection.

"Mmm, that smells heavenly." Joel wrapped his arms around his wife's waist. "What else are we having?"

She nudged him away with her elbows. "Nothing if you don't let me get it finished." She turned a smile his way. "Hug me again, later, and I might return it."

Joel stepped back with a grin. "Hope that's a promise." He leaned around to snag a warm biscuit.

Ruth swatted at him. "Keep it up and you won't get anything." She glanced over her shoulder as she spooned scrambled eggs into a large bowl. "Where are the girls?"

"They're coming. I heard them fussing over their hair. I guess they want to make a good impression on Micah this morning."

Ruth chuckled. "I'm not sure Micah will notice." She wiped her hands on a towel. "I just wish Levi would get over his resentment of Micah and try to make amends. Those two didn't even acknowledge each other last night, much less speak. I do think Micah would have, but Levi didn't give him the chance. Walked right on out of here like Micah didn't exist. What's gotten into that boy?"

"I don't know, but it needs to get resolved soon if they're going to work together." Joel had told her in bed last night about his conversation with Micah. She had been relieved to hear that Micah planned to stay at least for a month. Perhaps in that time they could all rebuild their relationships and put the past behind them.

"They'll work it out eventually. You know how boys can be." She handed Joel a stack of plates. "Here, make yourself useful until the girls get here."

"We're here now, Ma." Margaret entered the kitchen and donned an apron then took the plates from her father. "Why don't you go call in Levi? Apparently he slept in the bunkhouse last night."

Ruth, Margaret, and Joel shared a sober look before Joel shrugged. "I'll see if he's willing to come, but I won't push it. Besides, I don't have the strength for an argument. My stomach can't stand the deprivation much longer." He grinned and scurried from the room when Ruth swatted a towel toward him.

Rose came into the kitchen. "What was Pa doing in here? Sampling the food?"

Ruth laughed and moved the steaks to a large platter. "He tried, but he'll have to wait like everyone else."

Rose looked around. "Where's Levi? I saw Micah upstairs getting ready, but not Levi."

Ruth pursed her lips. "Levi slept out in the bunkhouse. Your pa is calling him in right now."

Ruth began stirring flour into the fat from the steak to make gravy. Her heart ached with the pain of the separation between her two boys. So different they'd been growing up. Micah liked to have a good time and got out of work whenever he could to go into town, while Levi roamed the outdoors and worked the ranch with his pa. Perhaps she needed to have a talk with Levi. It had helped in the past, but now that he was older, he might not be as prone to listen.

Margaret handed Rose the bowl of eggs and some

silverware to take out to the table in the dining room. Then she scooped the biscuits into a bowl and covered them with a towel to keep them warm. Before she followed Rose to the dining room, Margaret leaned over and whispered, "What are we going to do about Micah and Levi, Ma? What if Levi won't accept Micah's return at all?"

Ruth blinked back tears. "I don't know anything we can do except pray for them to make peace with each other. Your pa wants them both working with him. That's always been his dream."

"And he never gave up on Micah's coming home. I heard Pa praying so many times for him to come home." With a sigh, she left the kitchen to deliver her food to the dining room.

Ruth stirred the gravy to remove all the lumps of flour, but nothing could dissolve the lump in her throat. She loved her two boys with a depth they would never understand until they had children of their own.

The difference in the two that bothered her more than their personality traits was their attitude toward God. Micah had never been one much for church and had to be all but forced to go each Sunday. Levi, on the other hand, loved the Lord and didn't miss any opportunity to worship Him whether at church or at home. With both their personalities and ill feelings keeping them apart, she'd have to be on her knees in prayer even more in the next few days or weeks or however long it took to reconcile them.

Margaret poked her head through the door opening. "Is that everything?"

Ruth finished pouring the gravy into a bowl and handed it to Margaret. "This is the last. I'm coming." She untied her apron and hung it on the hook by the pantry door. One returned face would join with her and Joel at the table today, but the latest missing son grieved her soul. *Lord, touch his heart today. Levi loves You, and only You can melt his heart of stone toward Micah and make it again a heart of love.*

She straightened her shoulders and pushed through the door to the dining room. The matter lay in the Lord's hands, and that meant she'd be praying every day for reconciliation and forgiveness. It would happen even though it may take time, because her Lord was bigger and stronger than any disagreement between two brothers.

After washing and shaving, Micah gazed around the bedroom he once shared with Levi. His brother's bed sat empty, all neat and tidy. Levi had not come back to the house last evening, choosing to sleep in the bunkhouse instead.

That rejection gnawed at Micah's insides this morning. Last night Pa had listened to his story and then in his own way had welcomed his wayward son back into the fold. The fact that his father didn't condemn and throw him out gave Micah hope for reconciliation with Levi. He hadn't quite made his point strong enough, but he'd have a month or more in which to show his father the skills he picked up the past five years and how they could be used on the ranch. He also hoped to observe Pa to make sure his health wasn't as bad as it appeared.

Even his sisters' warm reception and love failed to alleviate the pain of Levi's rejection. The main goal for Micah now would be to regain the trust of his brother and assure him that he would help run the ranch, but not take over. Since Micah had no desire to take control, he must somehow make Levi see and believe that.

He had dug around in the cedar chest and pulled out an old shirt and a pair of pants from years ago. They were a mite short, but his waist had stayed trim, so they should button up with no trouble. He'd promised Pa to ride with him this morning and see the changes that had been made on the ranch in his absence.

He pulled on the boots he'd worn here last night. Now he looked more the part of a ranch hand and would be more comfortable in the hot sun that beat down on summer days in Texas.

He sniffed the air, and the aroma of frying meat filled his nose. Ma must be frying steaks for breakfast. She'd have gravy and biscuits along with eggs, more than likely. A hearty home-cooked breakfast was a treat he'd missed all these years away.

He sauntered into the dining room where Margaret and Rose finished placing food on the table. Ma came in just as he sat down, and her smile warmed his insides. "Whatever you fixed, I can hardly wait to eat it." He stood and slipped his arms around his ma's waist and kissed her cheek.

Her face, still rosy from the heat of the stove, flushed even more as she tilted her head. "Go on with you, boy. Compliments won't get you an extra helping." Then she grinned. "But maybe the kiss will."

Margaret poured out mugs of piping hot coffee. "And you didn't miss us, your sweet sisters?" Her eyes sparkled with mischief and her face glowed with love, but it wasn't necessarily for him. He'd learned last night that she and the mercantile owner's son were courting.

"Hmm, you weren't so grown up and nice back then. You gave me more trouble than necessary if I recall correctly." He grabbed Rose in a hug. "And this one was not much more than a baby when I left."

"I was not a baby. I was already eight years old, and I'm thirteen now." She swatted his arm with her dish towel.

Pa came through the kitchen door. "Now this is what I like to see, my family having a good time." He leaned toward Ma. "Levi's already eaten."

He spoke low, but Micah still caught the words and his stomach lurched. No peace could come to his heart until he talked with Levi and made amends. He'd see that it happened this morning. Ma's eyes revealed the hurt Levi's absence caused, but she attempted a smile as she clasped Micah's hand for the blessing. He gave hers a squeeze to let her know he understood and it was all right.

Pa completed the prayer and passed around the platter of fried steak after helping himself to a piece first. Very seldom had they served anything but beef when Micah had been at home before, and from the looks of things, that hadn't changed. Pa always said that those who raised and sold beef should always have it on their table to support their business. After all, who would want to buy a product the producer didn't eat? The only exception was Thanksgiving, when Ma insisted on a turkey because that was the tradition of her family.

Conversation during the meal steered away from Levi, but Micah enjoyed the talk about their activities. One thing he'd learned in a hurry last night, he needed to call his sisters Margaret and Rose. Calling them by their given names would not be easy, but he'd promised them he would try.

After breakfast Micah followed Pa out to the corral where their horses waited. Pa's horses were some of the finest in all of Central Texas, known for their ability to round up cattle and for their endurance on the cattle drives to market.

Regret for having sold Red Dawn filled Micah, but the payment for the horse and odd jobs had brought enough to live on until he found the job at the livery. If he decided to stay on the ranch for any length of time, he'd have to pick out a new mount and return Gray Mist to the livery in Stoney Creek.

Levi sat atop his own horse and glared at Micah. Somehow he'd have to get his brother to see how sorry he was for leaving them. And he was eager to talk to Levi about the future of the ranch and their relationship. If Pa would trust Micah with the business end of buying and selling cattle and keeping the books, Levi could take care of the branding, roundups, and cattle drives. It seemed like an ideal setup, but if Pa and Levi didn't agree, Micah would have no choice but to leave and find work elsewhere. He had no desire to be a hands-on rancher. A businessman, yes. But a cowboy—never.

CHAPTER 5

HER FIRST FULL day in Texas Hannah awakened late to sunlight streaming through the window. Her sister must have known she would be tired from her long journey and let her sleep in. She stretched as joy and anticipation filled her soul. Today she'd begin her new life working with Manfred in his office. She threw back the covers and planted her good foot on the braided rag rug next to her bed. She stood, balancing on it until she could limp across the room to wash the signs of sleep from her face and eyes.

Leaning against the washstand, she used the toes of her shorter leg to help stabilize her stance. If she walked too much without the built-up shoe, her hips and toes ached with the effort of balancing. In the last few years she had learned to ignore her disability until Micah Gordon saw it for the first time and pity filled his face.

With a sigh and a shrug of her shoulders, she dried her hands and hobbled back to the bed for her stockings. After pulling them on, she slipped her feet into the black lace-up boots. They were more comfortable than they looked because of the special cushions Papa had the cobbler insert in each shoe. The heaviness of the right shoe was the only drawback. Someday maybe someone would invent a way to make the shoe lighter.

Hannah finished dressing in one of her new uniforms and hurried down to the kitchen. The aroma of frying bacon and something sweet filled the air and caused her stomach to growl. After that huge dinner last night she shouldn't be hungry, but her stomach said differently. She had planned to help this first morning here, but Sallie was already at the stove when Hannah arrived.

"I'm sorry I'm late. I should have come to help you sooner."

Sallie waved her hand. "Don't worry about it. I see you're all dressed for your first day. That's good. Manfred will be pleased." She turned back to the frying pan. "I fix breakfast like this every morning. Well, maybe I don't make cinnamon buns every morning, but I do the rest. One more plate won't make a difference."

"You made Grandma Woodruff's cinnamon buns! I can't wait to eat them. It's been a long time since she fixed them at home. Mama tried, but they just didn't turn out the same." The fragrant smell of cinnamon coming from the oven already teased her taste buds, and her mouth watered with the anticipation of eating one. "I hope you made plenty."

Sallie's laughter caused Daniel, in his chair by the table, to bang his spoon on the table and babble his own brand of language. Hannah knelt beside him. "How's our big boy this morning?" She leaned in and inhaled his baby fragrance of powder and soap. Her lips touched his forehead before she sat back in a chair next to him.

"Is there anything I can do to help? I see the table is all set and ready for us." How long had Sallie been up? She must not have slept long last night after their late bedtime.

"Here, the bacon and eggs are done, and the rolls are ready to come out of the oven. Take these to the dining room while I get the rolls." She handed Hannah two platters. "Oh, and you might give a call up the stairs to let the children know breakfast is ready."

Not five minutes later the family had gathered around the table, the blessing said, and food was served. Hannah devoured hers as though she hadn't eaten just yesterday. If she kept this up, the new clothes made for her new life wouldn't fit. She'd brought home one of the uniforms she'd worn in nursing school, and the dressmaker in Woodville had made two more of blue cotton along with several aprons in white cotton. Mama had starched them and packed them to bring to Texas along with a few nicer dresses for Sunday church.

Molly swallowed a gulp of milk and wiped away the stain left on her upper lip. "You look nice in your uniform, Auntie Hannah. I like to help Pa, but he says I have to wait a few more years."

"That's wise of your pa because you might catch something from a sick patient." Of course she didn't need to see the kinds of injuries that would come into the office either. It had taken Hannah a few tries before she became accustomed to seeing blood.

Hannah saved her cinnamon bun for last, and when she bit into it, memories of mornings in Grandma Woodruff's kitchen swept her back to her childhood. They were perfect. She allowed the cinnamon sugar mixture to coat her mouth with its goodness before swallowing and taking the next bite. "These are so good. You have the gift of Grandma's culinary skills, and I envy that."

"Maybe so, but you can stitch up a cut on someone's head or body, and I could never do that. You have a gift like Manfred, a gift of healing."

Manfred laid his napkin on the table. "And along those lines, it's time for me to show you the office." He pushed back his chair and stood then reached over and placed the palm of his hand on Molly's head. "I'm sure you're going to be big help to your ma today. In another year or two I may allow you to help around the office."

Molly smiled and nodded, her eyes bright with the love she had for her pa. "I will take good care of Clara and Tommy today. Auntie Hannah can tell me all about what she does to help you, so someday I can too."

"That's my good girl. Now, come, Hannah, it's time to start our day." He strode from the room and into the hallway leading to the room where he saw patients.

Hannah swallowed the last bite of her cinnamon bun then patted the crumbs from her mouth. What an exciting day this would be. Her first day as a real nurse working with a doctor. She tweaked Molly's nose. "I'll tell you about everything this evening, Miss Molly."

She followed Manfred to the front of the house where he had his office, an examining room, and one room for patients who needed an overnight stay or more in-depth care. The doctor who had lived here before had built the house with a family in mind as well as a medical facility. Manfred had been fortunate to land such a good practice when the older man had become ill and he and his wife moved away to live with their oldest daughter.

Manfred pointed to the cabinet with a large bowl and ewer sitting on top. "Cleanliness is extremely important to me. You'll wash your hands after every contact with a patient. You will use only clean instruments and use them once. Soon as you finish with anything, it goes into that bin and then is washed with hot soapy water. I saw enough of what dirty, unsanitary conditions can do to sick and wounded during the war. That's not going to happen here."

She'd heard about his ordeal in a Yankee prisoner camp and could understand and agree with his philosophy of cleanliness. She gazed about the rest of the examining room. Two beds sat against opposite walls with partitions that could be pulled around them to give more privacy. In addition, two glass-enclosed cabinets lined the other wall with the table for washing one's hands between them. Sallie had cleaned the room thoroughly yesterday, and the odor of antiseptic and cleaning supplies lingered in the air. That would be Hannah's job from now on, and she intended to keep the room sparkling clean and ready for new patients every day.

Micah retrieved his saddle from the stables where he'd left it the night before and checked out the corral. Half a dozen horses milled about. One of them stood out from the others and caught Micah's attention. "Pa, does that smokey gray colt belong to any of the hands?"

"No. He's just been broken and was slated for sale, but if he's the one you want, he's yours."

"Does he have a name?" Micah picked up his saddle and headed for the colt. Less than two years old, the young horse tossed his head and mane as Micah approached.

"You called it with his color. Rose named him Smokey. She said he reminded her of the smoke coming from chimneys on cold days. You can rename him if you prefer."

Micah grinned and slid the bridle into the horse's mouth. "Nope, that suits him fine." He finished saddling the horse and joined his father.

"Let's get started so I can see what you've done while I've been gone." Micah turned his horse in the direction the other hands had taken. Levi had raced away before Micah could speak to him, but a chance would come today, of that Micah was certain. The uncertainty lay in how the discussion would end.

Micah spent the morning rounding up strays on the south side of ranch, one skill he hadn't lost in the years away. At the noon break Micah watched as Levi filled his plate and moved to a spot under a tree at a distance from the others. Micah grabbed his tin plate of beans and bread and ambled over to the same area. Now was as good a time as any. He made his way to the side and came up from the back before Levi had a chance to spot him and get away.

"It's time we had a talk, Levi."

Levi's face hardened and he set his plate on the grass. "I don't want to talk to you."

He started to stand up, but Micah gripped Levi's arm. "I don't care. It's going to happen now if I have to tie you up like a calf."

"Nothing you say is going to change anything." Levi's jaw clenched and the muscles there twitched.

"Listen to me and find out."

When Levi didn't respond, Micah breathed deeply then exhaled. "Look, I'm sorry I left the way I did, and sorry I never wrote. I was thoughtless and selfish."

"You can say that again."

Micah ignored the remark and changed tactics. "How do you think the ranch is doing?" Maybe he could warm up his brother with a little shop talk.

Levi's eyes narrowed. "So you came back just to check out your inheritance? See how much money you'll get so eventually you can go blow that too?"

"That's not what I mean." Micah frowned. Apparently his

brother thought he was just a gold digger. This was going to be harder than he thought.

"Yeah, I just bet. You knew that Pa planned to leave the ranch to you, but you don't care about it or you wouldn't have run off."

"I do care what happens to it, but I don't want to run it. That should be your job—"

"Sure, leave all the work to me while you go gallivanting to town, drinking and charming all the young ladies—"

Micah interrupted. "How's Pa? I'm worried about him."

Levi's mouth popped open then he frowned. "What do you mean?"

"I mean I don't think Pa is in good health right now."

"Ha, that's a good one. Pa's as strong as an ox. If you think he's ailing, that's just wishful thinking on your part."

Levi's derisive laugh cut Micah to the core. At this rate nothing would be settled. But Micah had to keep trying. "I'm serious. Last night when we talked he kept rubbing his chest. Said it was something he ate, but I don't think so."

"So what'd you tell Pa during your talk?"

"I apologized. And I promised to stay a month to prove what I can do to help him and you."

Levi's hands clenched into fists. "You think you can come in and take up with running things without a by your leave? You're mistaken, and I won't stick around and let you boss me around. I've been giving the orders the past two years, and I take orders from no one, especially you."

Levi raised his fist and landed a punch on Micah's jaw that sent him reeling backward. "That's what I think of your coming home." He spun around and stalked away.

Micah nursed his jaw. Trying to call Levi back now would do no good. By the set of his shoulders and the firmness of his step, his brother would not listen. Besides, Levi twisted any little thing Micah said until Micah couldn't tell up from down or forward from backward. In Levi's mind, Micah was the most selfish, self-absorbed creature on the planet. And maybe he was. Once.

Micah hunkered down and poked at the beans on his plate. Maybe he could wait a few days until Levi cooled off some and then try again to reason with him. Something was wrong with Pa, he was sure of it, and now that he was back home, he needed to convince Levi to face facts and work together. The future of the ranch could well depend on it.

CHAPTER 6

THURSDAY MORNING MICAH rose early to pack up his belongings at the hotel. He'd returned last night with the promise to bring everything back to the ranch. Going home to live may not be the best idea, but Ma had insisted, as had his sisters. He'd never been able to resist their charms, so now he planned to check out of the hotel and head for the ranch. Helping out at the ranch gave him security for the moment, but at what price?

He and Levi had never seen eye to eye, but their youthful battles had never reached this extreme. He'd hurt his brother more than he'd realized. The resentment he'd seen in Levi's eyes yesterday pained Micah, but he deserved every bit of it, even the sucker punch at the end of their argument. Micah rubbed his jaw as he remembered their conversation.

Even after Micah had walked out and disappeared for five years, Pa hadn't changed his will. Why he hadn't remained a mystery. Levi deserved the ranch all the way, not just a parcel of land and a small herd. If Pa's health hadn't become an issue as well as his promise to stay, Micah wouldn't be headed to the ranch now. He'd keep his end of the bargain and help take care of the herds, mend fences, and whatever else needed to be done for at least a month. But Micah could make no guarantees as to how long he'd stay after that unless he, Pa, and Levi reached some agreement for the future.

After checking out of the hotel, Micah headed for the livery where he'd returned the rented horse and left Smokey for the night. He may not like to herd cattle and break horses, but he loved to ride. He'd even raced a time or two in earlier years when they had competitions at the Independence Day celebrations. Maybe they'd have a race again this year and he could see if Smokey had the speed of the horse he'd sold.

Camilla Swenson exited the bank, spotted Micah, and hesitated. Smiling, he swept off his hat and crossed the street to her side. "Good morning, Miss Swenson. I assume that is still your name?"

She raised her eyebrows. "Yes, it is." She gazed at him speculatively. "What brings you back to these parts, Mr. Gordon?"

"I decided it was time to come home. I see I've missed a few changes while I've been gone, including you. You're not the same gangly young girl who hung around with my sister at school, and that's a nice change."

Camilla's cheeks turned a bit pink. "Thank you, Mr. Gordon." She tilted her head to one side and grinned, revealing the dimple in her right cheek. "Will you be coming to church on Sunday? We'd be pleased to see you there."

"Thank you, Miss Swenson. If you are there, I promise to make a point of attending."

Micah shifted the bag to his other hand. Nice as it was talking to Camilla, the quicker he got out to the ranch, the quicker he could get to work. No sense in giving Levi any more reason to fuss at him. He smiled at Camilla and placed his hat back on his head. "Now, if you'll excuse me, I must get to the ranch."

He turned toward the livery but caught her words following him. "See you Sunday, Mr. Gordon."

Her words of anticipation filled him with contentment as he rode out of town. Camilla was fun to flirt with, and he enjoyed her company. She could be the exact diversion he needed to take the edge off the tension at the ranch and add some pleasure to the next few weeks.

Only eight in the morning, and already the Texas sun beat down and caused beads of perspiration on his brow. He mopped it with his neckerchief then stuffed it in his back pocket. When he got to the ranch, he'd tie it proper around his neck.

The ride consumed less than half an hour, but at this time of day Pa and the others would already be out in the pasture. He'd join them later, but first he wanted a look at Pa's ledgers. Pa would never admit a problem with the ranch, but something didn't sit right in Micah's mind. His business experience, as well as learning to read people, gave him reason to be concerned. If the ranch was doing poorly, that could explain the stress and be the cause for the pain in Pa's chest. Levi may not see it, but Micah had. Pa's stubborn streak would prevent him from admitting a problem even if Micah asked. Most men tended to lie, at worst, or gloss things over when it came to business. Micah preferred to see the plain and simple truth now and find ways to help than to be in the dark.

The books would be easy to find since his pa was a creature of habit. They'd be in the same drawer, locked, but with the key in the usual place under the lamp on his desk.

The house lay quiet when he entered. Ma and the girls must be upstairs. He headed for Pa's office and opened the door. With a glance over his shoulder to see if Ma had come down, he stepped into the room then closed the door behind him.

The extra large oak desk sat in front of two bookshelves filled with all types of books, from how to take care of sick cattle to the latest in literature. The collection of Shakespeare volumes still filled one shelf to the left of Pa's chair. Pa may be a range-hardened cowboy, but he had a keen mind and enjoyed reading classics.

Micah settled into the leather chair behind the desk and picked up the Bible lying there. If his memory served him right, another, smaller one lay on the nightstand near the bed in Ma and Pa's room. Micah fingered the rough binding. Pa put such great store in following what the Bible said about living. He believed in the Lord and the promises of Jesus found in the Bible.

A bookmark lay between the pages, and Micah's fingers trembled as he opened the thick black book. The silk ribbon rested on a page from the Psalms. Verses were underlined, and many had side notes written in his father's hand in the margins. Micah gulped and blinked his eyes before closing the book with a thud.

Whatever Pa believed, he'd taught to his children, but Micah had no use for the verses. God had never done him any favors, and the promises spoken in the Bible were only empty words with no meaning to Micah. He shoved the Bible aside and reached to open the drawer. Locked, as he'd thought it would be. Micah lifted the oil lamp and there sat the key.

He smiled and picked up the key to unlock the desk drawer. One thick ledger lay on top, and he removed it. When he opened the pages and thumbed through them, he found rows and rows of numbers listed under expenses and income. Some glowed red and shouted a loss. Pa's steady handwriting continued as Micah turned the pages.

Toward the end the numbers were black, but one number stood out. A deposit noted a loan from the bank. Upon closer inspection, Micah discovered the profits in the past few months barely covered the expenses. If this kept up, another loan would be in order. What had happened to the prosperity of five years ago?

Micah went back through the numbers and spotted places where poor decisions had cost the ranch money. Something must be wrong for Pa to lose money like that. If things kept on the way they were headed, the end of the year would show great loss. He grabbed a sheet of paper and a pen to start taking notes and adding figures.

When he closed the ledger, Micah had enough notes to show his father ways to cut costs and save money. The business end of the ranch excited Micah and whetted his appetite for making things come out even. He folded the paper and stuffed it into his vest pocket. Now he had to convince Pa of the changes needed to keep the profits coming in and pay back that loan.

He opened the door and listened. Voices came from the direction of the kitchen. Tantalizing aromas of cinnamon and nutmeg filled the air. Ma and Margaret must be baking for the evening meal. He closed the office door behind him, making sure it didn't thud or click. Then he slipped out the front door and headed for the barn, where he had left his horse.

Pa had said last night they were going to work rounding up strays in the hills to the west. That's the direction Micah headed on horseback, his mind filled with numbers and ideas. Now all he had to do was convince Pa to trust him with taking care of the books instead of rustling cattle for the ranch.

Hannah plopped into a chair and blew out her breath. What a day it had been. Nine-year-old Kenny Davis had fallen from a tree in his yard and broken his arm. He'd been quite the little trooper while Manfred set it. Meanwhile Mrs. Phillips had brought in both her boys with fever and vomiting. And Jay Barnes, a rancher, had needed stitches on a cut in his hand, which Hannah had done while Manfred was busy with Kenny.

Manfred appeared in the doorway to the examining room, wiping his hands on a towel. "Well, we've had ourselves a busy time. It's a good way to start off your time here. Now you'll appreciate the lulls even more."

"Yes, I will. Of course the hospital kept me busy, but so much of that was routine care. This is much more exciting."

Manfred smiled. "This first week will be exceptionally busy, what with people coming in just to meet the new nurse."

Yesterday and today many patients had come in out of curiosity with no real medical problems. "I like the people I've met so far."

"We're a nice town, and it appears like they've accepted you without any question. Jay Barnes isn't one to let just anyone stitch him up, but he looked happy with your work when he left, and thanked me for the time. Not sure when or how he'll pay his bill, but he'll come up with something for it."

"I noticed that many of your patients didn't pay you right away. Is it usually like that?"

"Most of the time. Those who can pay up front do, but the others take care of it as they can, and sometimes it's with food, or a chicken, or some other thing they have. I'm happy to accept whatever they have to offer, and so is Sallie."

"One thing I can say for my sister is that she can make more out of less better than any other woman I've met, even Grandma Woodruff, who was the best at it. Sallie inherited that trait from her." No matter what Sallie started with, something good always came from it. This she admired in her sister, but it wasn't a trait passed on to Hannah.

Manfred nodded toward the door. "No patients are waiting, and Sallie won't have dinner ready for another hour. Could you do me a favor and run down to the store and restock a few items? We need more bandages and tape. And I need to catch up on my bookwork."

"All right, but I think I'll change out of this uniform first. Don't think the store patrons would appreciate seeing Jay's blood on it while they shop."

Fifteen minutes later Hannah strolled up the main street of town toward the general store. The bell jingled when she entered, and Mr. Hempstead nodded a greeting as he finished wrapping an order for another customer.

"Be right with you, Miss Dyer."

"No hurry. I'll wait." Hannah glanced around, enjoying her first trip to the store. Colorful bolts of fabric filled a wall, inviting her to explore someday, and canned goods lined another group of shelves. The bell jingled again, and Hannah glanced up to see a beautiful young blonde, about her age, but tall, with a confident bearing. Hannah swallowed hard. With a girl like that around, who'd ever pay attention to any other female in the room?

The young woman's gaze met Hannah's. "Hello, you must be Miss Dyer. I'm Camilla Swenson, and my father owns the town bank. Are you taking a break from your nursing duties?" A smile graced her lips, but Camilla's eyes held a look that spoke nothing of friendship or cordiality.

A chill skittered along Hannah's spine. Never had she seen eyes so cold and unwelcoming. Surely she didn't see Hannah as any competition for the attention of young men in town? "Hmm, yes, my brother-in-law needed a few supplies for the clinic."

The woman at the counter picked up her package and turned to leave. She gave Camilla a quick smile but didn't speak and hurried from the store.

Camilla stepped up to Mr. Hempstead and handed him a sheet of paper. "I'm in a hurry, so could you take care of this order for me?"

Mr. Hempstead raised his eyebrows. "Miss Dyer was here first. I'll just take care—"

"I said I was in a hurry, Mr. Hempstead." Camilla drew up her shoulders and lifted her chin.

A young man appeared from the storeroom. "Don't worry, Pa. I'll take care of Miss Dyer." He smiled at Hannah and held out his hand for her list. "Welcome to town, Miss Dyer. My name is James Hempstead, and I work with my father here at the store."

"Thank you, Mr. Hempstead. I'm not in any hurry, but I do appreciate your help." Hannah followed the young man to the back of the store. His manners as well as good looks piqued her interest.

James reached up to a shelf and extracted a box of bandages. "Don't pay that Miss Swenson any mind. She always wants to be waited on before anyone else. That's just the way she is."

He stated it in such a matter-of-fact way that Hannah glanced again at the young woman. She stood tapping her fingers on the counter as though impatient for the time Mr. Hempstead took with her purchases. She glanced in

Hannah's direction, and before she could look away, their gazes locked. Again a veil slipped over her eyes, and they held no warmth at all.

Hannah shuddered and turned back to James. "I need to pick up some tape for the doctor as well." She waited while James located the necessary supplies.

"Here's all you ordered, Miss Swenson."

Hannah glanced back only to see the young woman grab up the parcel and turn without a word of thanks and swish her way back outside. The rudeness of people who thought their position and standing more important than courtesy was inexcusable to Hannah. She picked up what she needed and headed back to the front.

"I'm sorry for that, Miss Dyer." Mr. Hempstead reached for his pad and pencil to write down the items she placed on the counter.

"You don't need to apologize. I'm fine, and there's no rush." She smiled in hopes it would help him feel better. Rudeness, while it had no place in her world, evidently fell naturally to Camilla Swenson. Hannah made a mental note to pray for the woman. She was sure she had not seen the last of the lofty Miss Swenson.

CHAPTER 7

WHEN MICAH HAD finally caught up with his father and ranch hands midmorning, Levi was off rounding up strays on another part of the ranch. Pa had welcomed Micah's help. They'd kept busy moving part of the herd to a new feeding ground, so he had no opportunity to talk with Pa.

Now as he washed up for supper, Micah went over in his head again exactly what he wanted to say. He'd promised at least a month's work on the ranch, but if Pa listened to Micah's proposition, the stay would last much longer, and that would please Ma and the girls. It might not go over with Levi, but in his present mood, no plan would be to his liking if Micah was a part of it.

Margaret greeted him when he entered the house. "About time you came in. I was just fixing to call everyone to supper."

"I washed up outside instead of trekking more dirt into the house." He glanced at the table, still set with only five places. "I suppose Levi isn't coming in for supper."

"You supposed right. With him hiding out at the bunkhouse, I haven't had a chance to talk to him since you came home. Ma hasn't seen him either, and I can tell it grieves her."

"I'm sorry about that, Margaret. I tried to talk to him yesterday, but he wanted no part of what I had to say. I'll try again. He deserves the ranch much more than I do."

Margaret's eyes opened wide. "Does that mean you plan to leave us again soon?"

"No, it means...I'm not sure what it means, but I'm going to talk to Pa again tonight about it after supper."

"Talk to me about what?"

Micah spun around to find himself face-to-face with Pa. Heat rose in Micah's face, and he swallowed hard. "Some things about the ranch, but it can wait 'til after supper."

"Well, it'll have to." Ma stepped through the kitchen doorway with a platter of meat in her hands. "I'm not letting supper get cold. Where is Rose?"

"I'm right here, Ma. I smelled the meat and onions cooking." Rose hurried to her chair.

After the blessing, chatter around the table between his sisters allowed Micah to tune them out and concentrate on his food and what he'd say to Pa. His father sat at the end of the table, and although he served his plate and ate, his hard gaze stayed on Micah.

Pa probably thought Micah had decided to leave. Maybe that would help. Pa might be persuaded to let him run the business end if he thought Micah might leave otherwise.

They had finished eating and Ma was dishing up cobbler for dessert when she said, "Micah, did you stop by the house this morning before you went out to the range? I thought I heard you, but when I looked, you were getting on your horse to leave."

"Yes, I did stop by, but since Pa wasn't here, I didn't stay." He didn't lie, but he chose to leave out the details.

Pa narrowed his eyes and pushed back from the table. "Might as well get this over with right now." He stood and glanced at Ma. "I'll have coffee and some of that cobbler later."

He strode toward his office, and Micah had no choice but to follow. The anger in his father's eyes didn't bode well for the meeting, but Pa needed to know the truth. Whatever happened after that would determine the future.

Pa stood behind his desk with the palms of his hands flat

on top. "Why did you come by the house? You knew we'd be out on the range already."

Moisture coated the palms of Micah's hands, and he itched to rub them on his pants leg, but kept them still at his sides. Although they stood eye to eye, his pa's heftier build still created a prick of fear. "I wanted to check on something first."

Still that narrowed-eye glare. "And what would that be?"

Might as well tell him the truth. Pa didn't cotton to liars, and Micah didn't need that mark against him. "I thought I should see how the ranch is doing. I wanted a look at your ledgers."

Pa said nothing, but his jaw worked in a way familiar to Micah. The vein in Pa's temple throbbed blue, and his mouth set in a firm line. His attempt to control his anger failed as he slammed a fist on his desk.

"I knew it. When I came in a while ago, I could tell something was different. What gives you the right to go through my private business?" He jammed the key in the drawer lock and yanked it open. Then he slammed the ledgers on the desk. "And just what did you think you'd find?"

The old fear of reprimand threatened to take over, but Micah stood firm even as his nerves tensed tighter than a rope around a tied-up calf. "Since you plan to leave me the ranch, I figured I had a right to know where it stands. I found about what I expected to find. You're barely making ends meet with the cattle. You had a few bad months, but you're not getting back into the black quick enough, and you owe the bank."

The muscles in Pa's jaws worked again, but after a few moments they relaxed and he slumped into his chair. "Times have been hard, and the market was down on our last drive.

I haven't told your mother or the others." Then his eyes narrowed at Micah. "And it's not your place to go telling them either. I can work this out myself."

"I have some ideas about ways to save some money and to make more at the same time." Micah grabbed a ladder-back chair and pulled it up to the desk. "I'm real good with figures, and if I had a chance to study these ledgers more carefully, I believe I could really help."

Pa's shoulders slumped before he straightened up with the old fire in his eyes. "Just because you were always good at ciphering doesn't mean you know anything about the business end of a ranch. I can take care of the books. I need you riding and taking care of the herd and helping with the horses. That's your job until the ranch is yours."

All the air flew out of Micah's lungs with the weight of denial pressing hard. "Pa, Levi's done a good job with the herds and the ranch hands while I've been gone. I don't *want* the whole ranch. I just want to help you make it like it used to be. I can do that better here in the office and out with the buyers and sellers than I can on the range. Levi told me he's been giving the orders to the hands for the past several years, so why can't we let that continue?"

Pa drummed his fingers on the desktop for a few minutes. Again his eyes narrowed and his jaw tightened. "Yes, he has, but you're back now. My father left this land to me, and I've built it and added to it so that it's one of the best in the state, and now that legacy falls to you as the oldest son."

"But it's not going where it should with all the debt you have. Let me help in turning it around. Besides, how can I do anything if Levi won't take orders from me?"

"We can fix that, but this business of your poking your nose where it doesn't belong—" He stopped and rubbed his right arm above the elbow. Beads of perspiration dotted his forehead.

Concern gripped Micah even tighter than it had before. His voice lowered and softened. "If you're leaving it to me, I have a right to know where it stands and what to expect in the future. I ask you again. Let me take over the job of running the business end of ranching by managing the books and taking over the buying and selling and talking to the other owners at auctions and cattle sales."

Pa nodded his head as though to concede the issue. "Maybe, but I don't want your ma or sisters to know how the ranch is doing. It's as good as it always was for them. Do you understand? Can I trust you to keep this between us?"

"Of course. The last thing I want to do is to hurt Ma or the girls. Why haven't you talked with Levi about it?"

"It doesn't really concern him either. He'll get his inheritance when the time comes."

If there is anything left to inherit. "Will you at least reconsider the terms of your will and divide the ranch between the two of us, or even give Levi the larger share?"

Pa picked up the ledger book and placed it back in the drawer then locked it. "I'll consider it, but until I decide what to do one way or another, you are to stay away from my desk. In addition, you and Levi need to work out your differences."

He waved his hand in dismissal. "Now go on about your business for the evening."

"I will, Pa. I really do want to help, and Levi deserves to know that at least a half interest in the ranch will be his."

"I'll pray about it. Now go, and tell your ma I'm ready for my coffee and dessert." He picked up a stack of papers and began reading them.

Micah said nothing, but just before he closed the door,

he glanced back and found his father once again massaging the left side of his chest with his right hand. Micah leaned against the now closed door. What he'd witnessed disturbed him more than he could admit.

If Pa was in poor health, getting the ranch back to solvency was a priority. The sooner Pa turned the bookkeeping and deal making over to Micah, the sooner that could happen.

After Ruth dished up a bowl of cobbler with fresh cream for Micah, she filled one for Joel and set it on a tray with a mug of coffee. From the look on her son's face and his lack of talk, things between her two men must not have gone well. Her heart ached for her oldest son. He'd never had a love for the cattle and ranching like his Pa or Levi, but he did love to have fun. Now even that seemed to have drained from him, leaving a very unhappy young man in its wake.

She carried the tray across the main room and knocked on the office door before turning the handle and peeking in. "I've brought your coffee and dessert."

Joel glanced up from his papers and smiled, but it didn't quite reach his eyes. "Come on in. I need the distraction of your pretty face right now."

"Compliments will get you anything you want, Mr. Gordon." Ruth balanced the tray with one hand and closed the door behind her, praying the lighthearted comment would relieve the sadness she detected in her husband's eyes.

This time his smile did go to his eyes, and Ruth grinned with satisfaction. Mission accomplished. Still, the pain from a few minutes ago concerned her. She bit her lip and set the tray before him. "How did the talk with Micah go?"

A long sigh escaped from Joel as he picked up his coffee. "Not well, I'm afraid." He sipped the brew then set it down. "Ruth, why do I always wind up making a mess of things when I talk with Micah?"

So it was Micah troubling him and not Levi. "You don't mean to, I know, but there's something about our oldest child that sets him apart from the other four. He's never enjoyed life here at the ranch. We probably should have sent him off to school somewhere rather than trying to keep him at home."

"I think you're right about that. That boy came in here, unlocked the drawer, and went over the ledgers without asking me."

Ruth sat down hard in the chair vacated by Micah. "He did what?" That must have been the noise she heard earlier this morning.

"He went over the ledgers I keep for all the ranch business. He says he wants to take over the bookkeeping and the buying and selling of the cattle at auction."

Not only did the boy possess good looks, but he also had book smarts and the personality it took to charm people and make business deals. She smiled. "With his wit and charm, he would do a good job. Suits him better than rounding up cattle and branding them."

"Oh, so I'm not charming and witty?" The twinkle in his eyes belied his tone of voice.

She waved her hand through the air. "Of course you are, but Micah is younger and he does have a way with people. What did you tell him?"

"Nothing except that I would pray about it." He paused a moment, and furrowed his brow. "I suppose Levi is the logical one to take care of the herds and be the boss of the ranch hands."

"Yes, he is. I'm glad you told Micah you'd pray about it instead of saying a flat no." She braced her hands on her thighs. "Now eat your cobbler and drink your coffee. You have some business with the Lord." She stood and turned to leave.

"Wait a minute, Ruth." When she stopped, he came around from behind his desk and embraced her. "I don't know what I'd do without you. Depending on how things work out with the boys, what would you think if I changed the will and left the ranch to Micah and Levi, with the idea that Micah would be the business manager and Levi the trail boss?"

She leaned back to search his face. "I think that would be a very smart thing to do."

He pulled her back to his chest and kissed the top of her head. "I'm still going to pray about it and watch how Micah conducts himself over the coming weeks. He may be smart and personable, but I haven't seen true repentance for all those years and what happened during that time. God doesn't appear important to him, and if he doesn't have godly character, then maybe he isn't the one who should be running things after all."

"Give him time. He's still young. God has time to do a work on him."

He leaned down and kissed her. "How did I ever manage to marry such a smart woman, and a pretty one at that?"

"You're not so bad looking yourself." She pushed away from him. "I have to get back to the kitchen now. You take care of your business, and I'll take care of mine." At the door she stopped and turned to him. She smiled and winked. "If you're nice later, maybe we can take care of some business of our own."

A loud laugh warmed her cheeks and heart and followed her through the door and on to the kitchen. The great room sat empty, so everyone must have gone upstairs for the evening. She hummed to herself as she tidied up her kitchen and set things out for tomorrow. She glanced out the window and spotted a lone figure walking across the yard. Levi! She whispered, "Oh, Lord, please help me to find a way to reach his heart so he can forgive and accept Micah."

A solitary tear slipped down her cheek. Her family may think she only knew about cooking and cleaning, but she knew more about what was really going on than she'd ever let Joel know.

CHAPTER 8

O
N SUNDAY HANNAH hastened to finish her preparations for attending church with the family. The preacher and his wife had come to visit yesterday and had welcomed her to Stoney Creek. Since meeting them, Hannah had looked forward to attending the service this morning.

When she had mentioned the name for the town and the nearby creek, the reverend informed her it had been named for Rayford Stone, who had built the first house in the settlement and started ranching. His love for the country and his aggressive nature had brought others to the area, and when the settlement became a town, they decided to name it for Mr. Stone.

Sallie had then laughed and said the creek had enough stones in it to be named that regardless of the founder's name. She promised to take Hannah there for a picnic one day soon.

Hannah stepped to the window to draw the curtains against the morning sun and spotted a familiar figure on the street. Micah Gordon strode with purpose in the direction of the church. In spite of the warnings from Burt to be wary of Mr. Gordon, Hannah's heart did a little flip-flop, and she admired from afar his broad shoulders, purposeful stride, and handsome face.

Her hands held the edges of the curtain closed a moment as she inhaled deeply and attempted to push all thoughts of him out of her mind with little success. Of course, he'd most likely be in church this morning with his family. Sallie mentioned he'd been in the mercantile Friday to purchase a shirt and tie. Hannah had been out helping Manfred at one of the ranches where a horse had thrown a cowboy and severely injured him. Hannah sighed, wishing she'd been at the store when Micah had come in, even if he didn't pay any attention to her. Maybe he'd be courteous and speak to her today at church. She hated to admit it, even to herself, but she was eager to meet the young men of the town, like James Hempstead and Micah Gordon. Especially Micah.

She grabbed her Bible. If she didn't stop thinking about men and get downstairs, Manfred and Sallie would go off and leave her.

When she entered the hallway at the top of the stairs, Sallie's voice called from below. "Hannah Grace, we're ready. Are you coming or not?"

"I'm coming now." Her shoe thumped harder on the stairway as she hastened her way down. The faster she tried to walk, the clumsier the shoe became. She'd have to remember to go more slowly down the stairs. At the landing she tucked her Bible under her arm and reached out to embrace her niece Molly. "You look especially nice this morning."

A grin spread across her face. "Thank you, Auntie Hannah. Ma made the dress for me." Molly slipped from Hannah's grasp and whirled about so that her skirt flared out around her.

"Now don't be showing off, Molly. It's not becoming." Sallie herded her two younger ones ahead of her with one hand while holding Daniel in her other arm. "Papa's waiting with the carriage, so we must hurry along."

Hannah suppressed her grin at Molly's pout as they headed out the door. Perhaps Sallie needed reminding of how she once preened and whirled in front of the mirror in their room back home. Having a beautiful sister like Sallie had been difficult at first, but as they grew up, Sallie always managed to find a way to make Hannah feel special. Now Hannah could pass that encouragement on to Molly.

They all climbed into the carriage Manfred had obtained for his growing family. With Tommy and Daniel in front with their parents, Clara and Molly clambered up to sit on either side of Hannah. Both girls chattered all the way to the church. As soon as one paused, the other picked it up. Such little magpies, but they were precious, and Hannah didn't even try to add to their talk.

Although she only half listened, Hannah learned about Molly's and Clara's friends they'd meet at church. As soon as the carriage halted in the church yard, both girls jumped down to join those friends under the trees.

Manfred assisted Hannah from her perch on the seat. She smoothed her skirts and glanced toward the entrance. Her heart jumped then thudded when Micah appeared on the steps. A beautiful woman joined him, and Hannah's throat tightened. Camilla Swenson, the banker's daughter, laughed and placed a hand on Micah's arm.

Hannah stiffened, remembering her earlier encounter with Miss Swenson on Thursday at the general store. The graceful, blonde woman had let Hannah know she didn't quite measure up to Miss Swenson's social standards. Although the attitude hurt, Hannah shrugged it off. She hadn't come to Stoney Creek for its social life.

Her gaze darted to Micah. How handsome he looked in his dark suit. Except for the boots and string tie, he could have been a banker himself. Hannah regained control of her emotions, resigned to the fact that a man like Micah Gordon would never be attracted to her. He might be polite, but pity would most likely lace his demeanor.

Sallie touched her arm. "It's time to go inside. I want you to meet some of the other people who don't live in town."

Hannah blinked. Camilla and Micah had disappeared into the church. "Yes, of course. The more of them I meet, the more confidence they'll have in me if or when they come into Manfred's office." She walked beside Sallie up the steps and into the sanctuary.

Sallie made her way to the fourth row from the front, where Molly had already sat down with Clara. Several couples stopped, and Sallie introduced her both as her sister and Manfred's new nurse. Friendly smiles welcomed her before they headed to their own places. She'd heard so many names in the past few days that her head swam with them, but give her time and she'd learn them all. She'd make sure of it.

The pianist began the first hymn, and the congregation rose to sing. She resisted the urge to turn and see where Micah would be sitting. He'd probably be with Camilla, so forgetting him would be the best route to take.

At the end of the music Reverend Weatherby stepped to the pulpit. "We're happy to welcome a new resident among us today. Miss Hannah Dyer has come to live in Stoney Creek and serve as a nurse with Dr. Manfred Whiteman. We're pleased to have you, Miss Dyer, and look forward to knowing you better, although I do hope it's not in a professional capacity."

The congregation tittered, and a few chuckles filled the air, but the welcome warmed her heart. Then he welcomed back Micah Gordon, and this time heads simply turned or craned to get a look at him. A tight smile and quick nod of his head acknowledged the greeting.

After a seemingly endless sermon and final prayer, Reverend Weatherby stood at the door to greet the members as they departed. Hannah grasped his hand. "Thank you for the welcome. I look forward to meeting here each Sunday." She meant it, but she hoped the sermons would be somewhat shorter than today. Back home the services never ran more than hour or so. Things were so different in Texas.

She started across the yard but stopped short. Camilla and Micah stood by the carriage conversing with Manfred. Taking a deep breath, she set out the rest of the way. At least she could be cordial.

Micah itched to get away from the church. The only reason he'd come today had been the invitation of Miss Swenson. If he hoped to impress her, he had to show interest in her activities. He'd had no use for church since the day he'd left home. After all, God sure hadn't done much for him these past five years. If it hadn't been for Micah's own determination, he'd still be in the mud of his former life.

"Good morning, Mr. Gordon, Miss Swenson. It's nice to see you again."

Once again Miss Dyer's beauty struck Micah. He'd had no opportunity to get acquainted with her other than the brief encounter at the train station. She stood a few inches shorter than Miss Swenson, who stood straight and tall as though she were the queen of Stoney Creek.

The contrast in coloring struck him even more as he compared Miss Swenson's pale features and light blonde hair to Miss Dyer's glow and spun-gold hair that shone with red highlights. Most men likely wouldn't notice such things, but

those few years before he gave up the wild life had him com-
paring women to decide which one to grace with his company. If not for the deformity of her leg, Miss Dyer would be
tops on his list of women to charm.

Micah grinned and acknowledged Miss Dyer's greeting,
but Camilla merely sniffed and raised her head a little higher.
Anyone below her status didn't deserve recognition. A chill
coated the warm air, and Miss Dyer's crestfallen features
replaced the smile with which she'd greeted them. Pity rose
in his heart. Rudeness wasn't necessary, but then it wasn't his
place to correct Camilla's behavior.

A hand tugged at his arm. "Come, Micah. Your parents
won't like to be kept waiting."

"Of course, Miss Swenson. After you." He swept his hand
to the side for her to pass. He tipped the brim of his hat.
"Have a pleasant afternoon, Doctor and Mrs. Whiteman and
Miss Dyer."

Camilla waited beside the buggy he'd borrowed from
her father to take them out to the ranch. Micah hadn't been
happy when Ma told him she'd invited the banker's daughter.
The invitation seemed a little precipitate, but Camilla had
jumped at the offer, so he couldn't exactly play it down.

He left his horse with her father and helped her up to the
seat, then he pulled himself up beside her. She opened her
parasol and balanced it on her shoulder. "You may call me
Camilla, Micah. After all, we are old friends, and my father
gave me permission to ride with you today."

"Yes, he did, and I'd be delighted to call you Camilla." Most
likely her father had agreed because Pa was one of the bank's
best clients, and Micah stood in line to inherit the ranch.
How gracious would the old man be if he knew Micah had
no interest in the ranch? Then another thought struck him.

As the banker, Mr. Swenson should know exactly where the ranch finances stood, especially with a loan pending. So what was the banker's motive for allowing Camilla to accompany Micah out to the ranch today? Did he want a firsthand, eye-witness account of the state of affairs?

He might spend some time with Camilla, but he made no plans beyond the next month or so. She may be beautiful to look at, but he had more pressing issues to deal with right now than the choice of a wife.

On the way to the ranch, as the heat rose, Camilla dabbed at her forehead with a lace-edged handkerchief. "I can't believe it's so warm already in June. What will it be like in July or August? I shudder to think."

"It's Texas, Camilla, and if I remember correctly, summers are always hot and dry." That had been one of the things he'd wanted to escape, but he hadn't traveled far before he'd gambled away his money. He'd never been able to leave the state.

"Yes, but it could at least rain once in a while. Papa is afraid the lack of rain is going to harm the market for cattle and keep the farmers from having a decent crop. That will affect their holdings at the bank."

Her matter-of-fact tone raised Micah's eyebrows. How did she know so much about her father's opinions? "I can see how he'd be concerned. Do you discuss such matters with him?"

Her laughter rang out. "Oh, yes. Since Papa has no sons, he's decided I should follow in his footsteps as the town banker. Of course, if I should marry, that would change." She turned her head slightly and peered at him through lowered lashes.

Beautiful, coy, *and* smart. Camilla was more intriguing than he'd remembered her to be. "I found I enjoyed working with numbers and keeping accounts when I worked at a livery stable last year."

Her smile accentuated the dimple in her left cheek. "I do believe we have more in common than our ages, Micah. I'm looking forward to spending more time with you."

"That will be more my pleasure than yours, Miss Swenson."

She tapped him on the arm with her laced gloved hand. "Now, Micah Gordon, I told you it's Camilla. We've known each other far too many years to be anything but Camilla and Micah."

Courting Camilla might be a way to his dreams after all. Despite any ulterior motives the banker might have in allowing Camilla to accompany him today, he'd enjoy the afternoon, She did look nice on his arm, and her intelligence and influence could go a long way toward his dream of becoming a wealthy, successful businessman. Perhaps marrying for a position at the bank would solve any problems with Pa and Levi as well.

His mother's spotting him with Camilla this morning at church might turn out to be one of the more fortunate encounters of his life. Now her invitation for Camilla to join them for dinner became the opportune time for him to get to know her better.

As Camilla chattered away about the town and her likes and dislikes concerning it, Micah tried to listen, but his mind still raced ahead to the afternoon. If only he could make contact with Levi and try to get him to understand the ranch could be his, the weeks ahead would go much more smoothly.

Camilla grabbed his arm. "Micah Gordon, you're not listening to anything I've been saying for the past half hour."

Micah's brain went into action and drew on lines he'd

used in the past with other women. "I was so charmed by your beauty, Camilla, that I became completely engrossed. Please forgive me."

She batted her eyes and a wide grin spread across her lips. "Of course I will forgive you."

It had worked again. As long as he remembered what impressed young women like Camilla, he'd do well. And it didn't hurt that she actually was a beautiful young woman with a fine figure and a rich father. The day ahead looked brighter and brighter. Only one person could ruin it. Levi.

Hannah retired to her room to rest after playing a while with the children following Sallie's wonderful Sunday dinner. She removed her clumsy shoes and lay back against the pillows on her bed.

Church had been pleasant this morning. She had been pleased by the welcome from the people. Lucky for her not all the town's residents were as unfriendly as Camilla Swenson.

Her thoughts turned to Micah. She'd noticed the Gordon family and saw that Micah had a brother close to him in age. Even she, a virtual stranger to the town, had noticed the iciness between them. At first it appeared Micah intended to speak, but his brother had walked by without so much as a nod. The two had acted like they didn't even know each other. Whatever could have happened to cause that much dislike between brothers? She couldn't imagine snubbing Will or Tom no matter how angry she might ever have been with them.

Something powerful must be going on for the behavior she saw. Sallie had told her about Micah's wayward life before he left Stoney Creek, but he didn't appear to be that kind of man now that he'd returned. What had happened to love and forgiveness in a family?

"Hannah, it's Sallie. May I come in a minute?"

"Sure, come on in." Hannah sat up on the bed and tucked her shorter leg under her body and dangled the other leg over the edge of the bed.

Sallie stepped in and closed the door behind her. "I don't mean to intrude on your private time, but we haven't had much time for talk with the clinic being so busy. What did you think of church this morning?"

"It was different from home, but the people are friendly except for Camilla Swenson. Even Jay Barnes stopped and talked to me, and I was glad to see Kenny there with his mother and father. His arm must not be hurting him."

"I imagine he'll be in a few more times in the next months. He's a rambunctious little boy and doesn't seem to be afraid of anything. And I wouldn't worry about Camilla. She's the only child Mr. Swenson has left, and her widowed father dotes on her. She's had everything her way for so long that none of the rest of us bother fighting it."

They continued with small talk about others in the congregation. Hannah asked about the pretty young schoolteacher, Miss Bradshaw. "She looks about my age and someone with whom I could be friends. Do you know her?"

"Yes, her family has lived here for years. Ellie went away to school then came home to teach when the other teacher decided to go back East. Word has it that she is seeing Levi Gordon. I think they would be a good match."

Hannah picked at the design on the quilt covering her bed. What she really wanted was to know more about Micah Gordon. A deep breath bolstered her courage. "How do you think things are going with Levi and Micah? I noticed how Levi treated Micah at church and thought it was rather sad. I could never do that to Will or Tom."

Sallie shook her head. "There's a lot going on there that we know very little about. Micah left under a cloud, and Levi was very angry with him. I imagine that anger has grown stronger in the years Micah's been gone." Sallie absent-mindedly smoothed the quilt where Hannah had wrinkled it.

"That's so sad for two brothers to feel that way. I'm glad his mother and father and sisters appeared to welcome him." A sigh escaped, and Sallie shot her a glance.

"Do I detect some interest, little sister?" A cloud of disapproval came into her eyes. "Depending on who Micah has become, you might steer clear of him, like Burt suggested. In the three years I knew him before he left, he had become quite the ladies' man. He broke more than a few girls' hearts. I'm surprised Camilla has taken up with him. Maybe she sees him as a challenge."

Hannah shook her head, glad that the topic was out in the open. "I must admit I do find him intriguing. With Camilla around, I won't have much chance to get to know him better, unless he breaks a leg or something."

Sallie laughed. "I have an idea that might help you out. I would like to give you a welcome party. That way you can get to know everyone a little better, including Micah Gordon. What do you think of that?"

"I think I'd like that. Maybe it will help me to remember names and faces. I did get rather confused this morning at church." Hannah dipped her chin. "I...I don't think it will make much difference with Micah, though. He seemed quite smitten with Camilla. If she's at the party, he'll never notice me, and most likely none of the other men will either."

Sallie frowned. "Hannah Grace Dyer, you stop that kind of talk right now. You are a very attractive young woman and a talented one as well. Give it time. Men will see what a delightful person you are and will take notice. You didn't let your deformity stop you when you were younger, so don't start it now."

Hannah cringed, but then Sallie's frown disappeared and a smile appeared. "Let's see what happens in the days ahead." She slipped from the bed and reached for Hannah's hands. "We have a party to plan, and it's going to be the best party this town has seen in a long while."

She leaned over and kissed Hannah's cheek, much like she had when they were children. "You'll see. It'll be fine."

At the doorway, Sallie stopped and turned back to Hannah. "When you've rested, come on downstairs for tea and cookies."

When the door closed behind her sister, Hannah thrust her short leg from under her skirt. All her life she'd coped with disability and had gone her own way with confidence in her abilities to study, learn, and be whatever she wanted to be. That feat had been accomplished and bolstered her belief in herself, but it had done nothing for her social life. The party may be fun, but Hannah didn't plan to get her hopes up for any recognition from Micah Gordon—or any other man for that matter.

CHAPTER 9

OR A WEEK now Micah had helped Pa with the cattle, mended the west fence, helped break in two new horses, and cleaned stalls, but still Levi would not talk to him. The discussion last week had turned into an argument and had done more harm than good. Since then Micah had approached his brother three times on the range, and each time Levi rode off in the opposite direction. He'd even tried to talk to him out in the bunkhouse, but Levi would have no part of it.

Meanwhile Pa did nothing to intervene, just stood back and gave orders and watched him work. He suspected both Pa and Levi were waiting for him to prove himself, and he couldn't blame them for that. But the hostility from his brother and the worry in Ma's eyes bothered him. At times he wanted to up and leave again, but his promise to stay and the image of his father rubbing his chest would not allow that.

Tonight Micah would have dinner with Camilla, as they had arranged after their lunch on Sunday. But tomorrow he'd confront his brother and lasso him like a wayward calf if he tried to walk away again. They'd both inherited Pa's stubborn will, but that could be good in the long run if Levi would listen and cooperate.

Dinner at the hotel with Camilla would be a good diversion from the problems with Levi and Pa's silence. Not only was she pretty to look at, but Camilla also had a good mind for business and carried on an intelligent conversation, unlike many of the women he'd known.

As he tied his string tie under the collar of his shirt, the image of Hannah Dyer crossed his mind. Where had that come from? He hadn't seen her since church last Sunday, and he certainly had no interest in her. Her attractiveness couldn't hide the fact that she had a limp, and her shoe made a loud noise when she walked across a wooden floor. If only she didn't have that deformity, he might be more inclined to befriend her, and perhaps more. Ma would say his thinking was rather shallow and that there was more to a person than outward appearance. But he'd seen the difference a pretty woman could make in a man's social life and business prospects.

He shoved her image from his mind and grabbed up his hat. He flicked off a piece of lint and brushed the dust from today's ride from the crown. Someday he'd have an entire wardrobe of hats from which to pick and choose and could leave behind the one he wore for ranching.

At the foot of the stairs he met Margaret. She sniffed the air, and a wide grin split her face. "I do believe I detect the scent of bay rum. Must be a very special evening you have planned. You're even wearing your best white shirt."

Her teasing reminded him of old times, and he chucked her shoulder. "It's the only white shirt I have, but I'm taking Camilla to dine at the hotel. Is James coming to call?"

Red tinted her cheeks, and she ducked her chin. "Yes, he is. Rose has promised to stay upstairs while I entertain him in the parlor."

"I see, but I can assure you, Pa won't be far away."

"You're right, but he's going to be in his office and will keep the door open just a bit. We'll have some privacy to talk."

Micah tilted his head and studied her a moment. Her eyes held a sparkle he'd noticed every time James was around or his name mentioned. Her tone of voice changed even now as she spoke of her suitor. "Tell me, little sister, are you in love with James?"

"That's a question for Pa, not my big brother, but I am in love with him." She wrapped her arms around her chest in a hug. "He makes me feel so special when we're together, and I think of him all the time when we're apart."

Laughter burst from Micah. "I do believe that's love." A lot he knew, but it sounded right. He reached over and hugged her to his chest. "He'd better be good to you, or he'll have both me and Pa to answer to." He stepped back and gazed into her eyes. "You are a very special young woman, Margaret Sue Gordon, and don't you ever let anyone tell you or treat you otherwise."

Her eyes moistened, and she smiled. "Oh, Micah, I'm so glad you've come home. I really missed my big brother."

Again he laughed. "You used to be a nuisance, and I loved teasing you and getting you into trouble, but now you've become a beautiful young woman, and I want to make sure no one hurts you or causes you pain."

Margaret hugged him again. "Thank you, and I love you."

"Good, but now it's time for me to get out of here. I have the buggy all ready to go, so I'll be leaving for town." Dishes rattled in the kitchen, and he turned his head that direction. "Bye, Ma. Don't wait up for me."

"I won't." Her response came from the open door. "Give Camilla my regards."

With a nod of his head Micah headed out the door and to the corral where he had hitched the buggy an hour earlier. He made sure the two lanterns he'd attached were secure as he'd need them on the return trip home later that evening.

On the way into town Margaret's words about James gave

him pause to think. He'd have to treat Camilla that way and make her feel special so that she'd be more interested in him. If he could charm her into falling in love with him, he'd have a better chance of landing a position at the bank if he needed it.

Micah drew to a stop in front of her home and dropped the weight from the carriage to tether the horses. Before stepping down, he gazed at the two-story home before him. It rose from the grass like a stately queen with a trimmed yard and rose bushes on either side of the steps leading up to the porch.

Such a large home for only two people may appear unreasonable to some, but it had once housed a family of five. He'd learned only this week of the death of Mrs. Swenson and her two sons in an influenza epidemic three years ago. Pa had quarantined his family at the ranch and didn't allow any of them or the ranch hands to come into town until the epidemic had subsided.

He approached the fine oak door inlaid with leaded glass then raised the brass knocker to announce his presence. The housekeeper opened the door and welcomed him. "Miss Camilla is in the parlor with her father."

Mr. Swenson rose from his chair to greet Micah. "Good to see you, my boy."

Micah shook the man's hand. He stood at least four inches shorter than Micah, and his balding head shone in the light of the nearby lamps. They made small talk for a time, then Micah said, "I've come for Miss Swenson, Mr. Swenson."

"Yes, yes, of course." He reached for Camilla's hand and helped her from her position on the sofa. "You take care of my girl."

"I will, Mr. Swenson." He offered his arm to Camilla. "Shall we depart?" How grateful he was now that Ma had insisted that her children learn proper manners. He hadn't used them for a while, but they would serve him well in courting Camilla.

On the short ride to the hotel Camilla said very little but to comment on the weather and the need for rain. Micah agreed as he helped her from the carriage and walked her into the hotel. After they were seated and their order given, Camilla pulled off her gloves one finger at a time and gazed at him with an unreadable smile.

She tilted her head to one side. "Tell me, how are things at the ranch?"

Micah gazed at her trying to determine her purpose for bringing up the ranch. She must know that Pa was in financial trouble, but why spoil the evening before it even began? "They're running right along. Levi still isn't speaking to me, but I plan to take care of that tomorrow."

"I see. Have you lost any cattle to the drought?"

"No, but we will if it doesn't rain soon." He furrowed his brow. "Why bother your pretty little head with such dull business?"

"Oh, it's not such a dull business. I'm always concerned about our customers at the bank and how they are faring."

Of course she would be, and with all the money Pa owed, she'd take special interest in the Circle G. "And is that all I am to you? A customer of your father's bank?"

Pink tinted her cheeks. "No, of course not." She reached across to grasp his hand. "You're much more than that, and I pray I am more than the banker's daughter to you."

He covered her hand with his. "You are. You're a beautiful woman, and I'm pleased to be in your company. I hope it's the beginning of a much longer relationship."

Her eyes opened wide, and her free hand rested on her dress just below her neck. "How sweet of you to say so."

Micah smiled and reached for his glass of water. His throat had become as parched as the land at the ranch. The smooth liquid slid down his throat as easily as the smooth words he'd just spoken. Margaret had always said he could charm the horns off a cow with his sweet talk. Maybe after tonight he'd have a prize worth much more than a pair of horns.

Levi waited until Micah and the carriage disappeared around the bend before leaving the bunkhouse. Grubbs's supper had been good, but nothing like Ma's. Maybe he could wangle a piece of her pie in a while. He sank into a chair on the bunkhouse porch and tilted it back against the wall.

He'd spent a lot of time and energy avoiding Micah on the range this week. Micah had tried several times to get him to talk, but Levi wanted no part of it and so far had managed to skirt the attempts by taking off with several of the other cowboys.

The anger that flooded his heart at Micah's return had slowed to a stream, but forgiveness hadn't made an appearance yet. Micah had never shown an interest in the ranch and got out of the hard work as often as he could to go into town. As the oldest, Micah had pretty much done what he wanted even when it displeased Pa.

No matter what Levi did, Pa never gave him the praise and attention that he'd lavished on Micah. Pa never spoke about the argument the night before his brother left five years ago. He'd finally complained to Pa about Micah not pulling his weight. Even with Pa taking up for him, Micah had stormed out of the house, and that was the last they'd seen of him. He could have been dead for all the family knew. To come back like he did and act like those five years never happened riled Levi. Then having Ma and Pa accept him back as though nothing had ever happened hurt Levi to the core.

A tall figure marched across the yard from the house. Levi let his chair down with a thud. Pa! He was the last person Levi wanted to see, but Pa had already spotted him.

"Levi, stay right there. I want to have a talk with you."

The strength behind those words stopped Levi in his tracks. He'd never defied Pa in the past, and this wasn't the time to start. He waited until his father reached the steps. "What do you want to talk about?" As if he didn't know.

Eyes as sharp as flint bored into Levi. "You know exactly what it is, and I plan for you to listen to every word. Understood?"

"Yes, sir, but not here on the porch." He didn't want the other hands hearing what his pa had to say. Levi stepped off the porch and headed toward the corral. Once there he stopped and turned around. "All right, what do you have to say?"

The muscles in Pa's neck stood out taut as the wire in their fences. His eyes grew even darker than usual, and his hands clenched at his sides. "This has gone on long enough. Your brother is home, and it's time you acted like you're glad he is."

How could he get Pa to understand without making him even angrier than he already was? Levi moistened his lips and inhaled a deep breath before letting it out. "I've worked harder the past five years than I ever have in my life to make up for Micah's absence. I am better with the cattle and horses than Micah ever was or could be."

"So, I won't argue with that. What else is there?"

Courage rose in Levi's chest. Would his father really listen to him now? "In all that time you've never shown any appreciation for my work. You always talked about Micah returning and inheriting the ranch someday. That hurt, Pa."

"You know I love you and I'm proud of what you've done, but Micah is the firstborn, the oldest, and it's his right to inherit the ranch. You'll have your share to start your own spread."

That wasn't what Levi hoped to hear. It all came down to more rejection by his father. Pa didn't understand at all. He started to brush past his father, but Pa grabbed his arm.

"I'm not done yet. I expect the two of you to act civil toward one another. You're going to be working together no matter what either of you may want. There are some things you don't know, and I'm working through them now. Until that's done, you'll do as you're told. I won't have this animosity between the two of you."

"And if I don't?" The words hung in the air, and Levi wanted to reach out and grab them back. Why had he made his thoughts verbal?

Pa narrowed his eyes. "If the two of you can't get along and work together, then one of you doesn't need to be around here." He turned on his heel and strode toward the house without a backward glance.

Pa's ultimatum rolled like thunder in Levi's head. He had no choice now. He'd have to leave the ranch, Ma, and the work he loved. Never would he give in and let Micah be in charge of the ranch. Not after the way he'd left with no mind to his family.

Levi spun around and ran back inside the bunkhouse. In a few minutes he had his saddlebags packed and a bedroll ready. The other men simply stared at him, not one of them saying a word.

Grubbs stood with hands on his hips, shaking his head. "You're making a big mistake, boy."

Levi grabbed his gear and headed out. "I'm sorry, Grubbs. I don't have a choice." He didn't expect the old man to understand. He'd been with Pa since their days of just starting out, and his loyalty would always be with Pa, and rightly so.

"Everybody's got a choice, son, and you're making the wrong one." Grubbs followed Levi to the stable where he saddled his horse.

With his knowledge of ranching and all the spreads in Texas, he shouldn't have trouble finding a new place to start over. It pained him to leave Ma, but for his own sanity and to prevent another major blowout with Micah, he had to do this. "Grubbs, don't you say a word to Ma or Pa until tomorrow. If you do, I'll go so far away no one will find me."

At the old man's nod, Levi slapped the mare's hindquarters and raced down the road. He'd made his choice, and now it was up to him to do something with it.

CHAPTER 10

ICAH SQUINTED HIS eyes against the morning sun beaming through his window. He opened one eye wide enough to peer at the watch on the stand beside the bed. The time appearing there made him sit up and shake his head. How had he slept so long? Then he remembered how late it had been when he'd returned home last night.

He raked his hands through his hair and grinned. He may have missed breakfast this morning, but dinner and an evening with Camilla had been worth it. By the time he'd left her, they had made plans to meet after church tomorrow for dinner at her home and for more time together the next week at the Independence Day Festival.

A few minutes later Micah had dressed and headed downstairs to see if Ma had any leftover biscuits in the pantry. An eerie silence greeted him when he reached the parlor. On Saturday Ma would be in the kitchen deciding what she needed in town for the next week, and the girls would be chattering away about what they would purchase at the store.

In the kitchen he found the coffee pot still hot on the stove. He poured a cup and frowned. Where was everyone? The quiet set his nerves on edge. Something had to be wrong.

Noise from outside flooded him with relief. It was late so everyone was outside ready to leave for town. He needed to stop Levi and talk with him this morning before he left. Micah set his cup on the counter and rushed outside to stop his brother before he could get away.

The scene that greeted him stopped him in his tracks.

Instead of the wagon with Ma and the girls, they all stood around the bunkhouse. Ma still wore her apron but her hands twisted it into a mess of wrinkles. Rose and Margaret held each other, and Rose cried onto Margaret's shoulder. Where was Pa?

He strode to his mother's side. "What happened? Where's Pa? Was he hurt?"

Ma dropped her apron and reached out to take his hands. "Oh, Micah, Levi's gone. Grubbs said he packed up his bag last evening and left after he and your pa argued." Tears filled her eyes and spilled down her cheeks.

Micah's jaw tightened. Levi had run away because of him. His return had brought more grief to his family. Remorse for his behavior took a backseat as anger against Levi rose. Didn't he see that he had done the same thing Micah had done? If only that stubborn boy had stopped long enough to listen, none of this would have happened, and everyone would be going into town today for their regular Saturday errands.

"Pa left to go into town to look for him. He's hoping Levi only went that far last night and stayed at the hotel." Ma clung to Micah, her fingers twisting themselves into his.

"Did Pa say what they argued about?" Fear twisted Micah's gut into a mass of tangles.

"No. I didn't even know Levi had gone or that they'd argued until Grubbs told me right after Pa left."

They must have argued about him and the ranch. Pa must have put down an ultimatum, telling him to get along with Micah or else. That would have been insult enough to rile Levi, but where would he go? Micah had headed for the first saloon and card game he could find out of town, but Levi never gambled or stepped foot in a saloon. At twenty-two he may be a man, but he wasn't hardened like Micah had been. No telling what could happen to him.

Fear wrapped itself tighter about his heart, but he had to stay calm for Ma. He hugged her tight with his cheek against her head. "It'll be all right. Pa will find him and bring him home." He didn't believe his own words, but he had to speak them for Ma's sake. He glanced over her shoulder to find Margaret staring at him with narrowed eyes and a frown.

He should never have come home. His return had brought grief to the ones he loved. If he hadn't given Pa his word that he'd stay a month, Micah would have left once he realized Levi would have nothing to do with him. But a Gordon's word was worth something in this town, and he wouldn't shame Pa by breaking it now. He'd done enough damage without that.

Rose pulled on his shirt. "Micah, you have to do something. Go help Pa find Levi and make him come home."

Micah released Ma and cupped Rose's chin in his hand. "Levi wouldn't listen to me. He's hurting over an argument with Pa, so Pa needs to talk to him."

Tears coursed their way down her cheeks. "Please, Micah. Go help Pa find him."

Her plea stabbed him with more pain. He glanced again at Margaret, whose mouth was set in a firm line. Her nod sent another plea to his soul. Micah stepped back from Rose and Ma. "All right, I'll go. Not that it'll do much good, but I'll try. Let me get my horse saddled."

Ten minutes later he rode toward town without any idea as to what he'd do once he got there. Finding Pa should most likely be first. Maybe he'd already found Levi and was headed home with him now. Micah had his doubts, but he could at least hope for the best as he rode.

Once he drew near Stoney Creek, he made his first order of business finding Pa's horse. When he didn't find him at any of the hitching posts along the boardwalks, he dismounted in front of the livery and sought out Burt and Willy. Micah found the smithy at his fire, shaping a horseshoe.

Burt glanced up. "Micah Gordon. You're the second one in your family I seen this morning. You looking for Mr. Levi too?" He laid aside his hammer and dipped the still glowing shoe into the water that sizzled and sent up a thread of steam.

"Yes, I am. Have you seen him or my pa or know where they went?" He had to ask, but his gut told him he had come too late.

"Yeah, your pa came by early a lookin' for him. I heard he'd come into town last night, but I haven't seen him for myself."

Willy stepped up behind Micah. "I saw him come into town, but he didn't stay here. Took off for the south."

At least he hadn't gone to the saloon, but of course Micah hadn't really expected him to do that. That was a place he would've chosen, not his little brother. "What about Pa? Did you see where he went?"

"Nah, but I told him what I told you about Levi heading south. He may have gone that way after your brother." Willy scratched the stubble on his chin. "'Pears to me like you boys done had another fight."

That was none of Willy's business, but Micah shook his head. "He and Pa had a little misunderstanding." He turned his horse toward the road back home. He'd wait until Pa either brought Levi home or told the rest of them his whereabouts. Ma would be disappointed, but the highway south covered a lot of territory.

Hannah held the invitation envelopes in her hand and stepped onto the porch. She and Sallie had spent the last two evenings writing and addressing them. Hannah still wasn't sure if a party was the right thing to do to get know Micah, but Sallie loved entertaining. Nothing would probably come of it, but it would be nice to meet more of the townspeople in a social setting.

When she reached the end of the walkway to the house, a horse barreled around the corner headed out of town. She gasped and swirled around to watch the rider disappear in the dust. Where in the world could Micah be going on a Saturday morning in such a hurry? If he'd been coming into town, she might understand, but it seemed that he had been in town already and now wanted to get somewhere else fast.

She waited until the dust settled before crossing the street and heading down to the general store where she'd leave the invitations to be delivered by the lad who worked for Mr. Hempstead. Sallie's ideas for the welcome party had grown bigger by the day. Of course it'd be nothing elaborate like they would have had at home in Mississippi, but she had already reserved the town hall for Saturday, July 14, just two weeks from today. Hannah hoped to meet some of the eligible men in town, but from what she'd seen already, not many prospects twenty-five or older lived around here. To her dismay, even James Hempstead was already spoken for by Margaret Gordon.

With her birthday coming up in August, she'd be twenty-five soon, and most people would consider that to be on the road to becoming a spinster. She may not have a man in her life, but her nursing would take most of her time and give her plenty of excitement. A sigh escaped her lips. Who was she fooling? Ever since Sallie and Manfred's wedding she'd longed to have one of her own.

Best to put that idea out of her head and stick to the present. She pushed through the door of the store and the bell jangled. Mr. Hempstead glanced up and smiled at her then returned to helping the customer at the counter.

Hannah gazed around at the store, which had turned out to be much larger than she first thought. Shelves lined two walls and were filled with everything from piece goods to lanterns. Cans of snuff and tobacco mingled with bags of coffee beans, molasses, and dried beans on another set of shelves. The scents blended to give a distinctive aroma to the store that was not at all unpleasant.

The woman at the counter turned, said hello to Hannah, then left. Mr. Hempstead stepped from around the counter. "Now how can I help you today, Miss Hannah?"

"Mrs. Whiteman would like for these invitations to be delivered if Lenny has the time." She set the stack of invitations on the counter. "They're divided so that they can be delivered more easily without backtracking."

"I see." He picked up the one on top. "Mrs. Whiteman must be planning a big party by the looks of this stack." Mr. Hempstead grinned and replaced the envelope. "I'll have Lenny get these out this afternoon, Miss Hannah."

"Thank you, my sister will appreciate it." She pulled a list from her reticule. "I have a few other things she wants me to pick up too."

After purchasing the items Sallie requested, Hannah made her way back to the street. The livery sign across the way caught her attention. A visit with Burt would be nice this morning, and maybe he would know why Micah had been in such a hurry. She crossed the wheel-rutted street and entered the stables.

Burt held a horseshoe and stooped to pick up a few nails. He turned and spotted Hannah. "Good morning, Missy. What can I do for you?"

"Nothing really. I wanted to stop and say hello since I haven't seen you since the night of my arrival. How are Lettie and the children?"

"They's fine, Miss Hannah. Those two is growing so fast, I can scarce keep up with them."

Hannah laughed and nodded her head. "I know what you mean. I can't believe how much Sallie's children have grown." She bit her lip then moved to the real purpose of her visit although it was really none of her business. "I saw Micah Gordon take out of town like the devil himself followed. Is there a problem at the Gordon place?" After all, a doctor might be needed and she could send Manfred.

Burt laid down the shoe and nails then wiped his hands on a cloth rag hanging on a hook by the forge. "T'ain't my business to spread rumors, but I do think somethin' happened out there last night that sent Mr. Levi into town. Then Mr. Gordon came into town this morning looking for him. Willy told him he'd seen him heading south, so Mr. Gordon must have headed that way. Then Mr. Micah came in looking for Levi. Told him the same thing, but he hightailed it back to the ranch instead of heading out after his pa."

Hannah bit her lip again. She'd seen at church how those two brothers treated each other. Whatever had happened between them now must be powerful to cause Levi to leave the ranch. His poor ma. First one son leaves then comes home and then another son runs off. What were those two thinking, if thinking at all?

"Thank you, Burt, and I do hope you and Lettie can come over for a visit again soon."

"We will, Miss Hannah, we will." He picked up the shoe. "Now I got a horse that needs new shoes, so if you'll excuse me, I best be getting to work."

She waved to Burt and stepped back into the sunshine. Such a beautiful day for a family to be out of sorts with each other. Why did boys create such problems? Tom and Will had their arguments and once even resorted to fisticuffs, but neither one had ever been so angry as to not speak to the other.

As she walked toward home, a plan began to formulate in her mind. Perhaps if she and Sallie were to ride out for a visit, they might create a diversion for Mrs. Gordon. Friends were a comfort when trouble reared its ugly head, and Sallie knew all the right things to say to encourage others.

With that idea planted firmly, Hannah's heart became lighter. Then it sank and became heavy once again. What if Sallie considered her idea to be meddling and not helping? Out here people may not welcome others into their private affairs. And Hannah didn't really know the Gordons, so they were unlikely to confide in Sallie with Hannah nearby. With her thoughts now weighing heavily in her heart, Hannah dismissed the idea of a visit and trudged the last block home.

CHAPTER 11

FOUR DAYS AND no sign of Levi, and no knowledge of his whereabouts had reached the ranch. Pa figured he'd gone to one of the nearby ranches seeking work, and even though begging for a son to come home wasn't a part of Pa's character, he planned to speak to some of the ranchers who would be in town today for the festivities.

Micah rode into town hoping Levi would show up at the Independence Day celebration. Couldn't that fool-headed boy see he was doing exactly the same thing Micah had done five years ago? If Ma was as distressed then as she was now, he'd have found some way to make Pa understand. Now she had to go through it all over again.

What he'd seen the past few days clamped his heart with remorse and guilt. If he hadn't come home, they wouldn't have this problem, but if he'd never left in the first place, things might really be different. He shook his head. No way to know what would have happened, and thinking about what he should have done or could have done didn't solve the problem of the here and now.

The weight of Levi's absence fell heavily on Micah's shoulders, but he wouldn't disappoint his family again. He'd do what had to be done until someone could persuade Levi to come home. Of course Micah would like to wring his brother's neck or tan his hide right now, but he'd forget all that if Levi would come home.

The sight of the red and white buntings and decorations about town shoved thoughts of Levi to the back of Micah's mind. Camilla would wonder if he'd forgotten their plans for the day if he didn't show up soon. He nudged his horse to go a little faster and headed straight for the Swenson home.

As he wrapped Smokey's reins around the hitching post at the Swenson house, he glanced up at the second floor window that was Camilla's. She must have been watching for him because she parted the curtains to wave down at him. He grinned and waved back then headed up the walk.

Camilla opened the door before he had a chance to use the large brass knocker. "Come in, Micah. We can be on our way soon as I say good-bye to Papa."

A few minutes later they strolled back down the walk and toward town. "Are you sure you don't want to use your pa's buggy?"

"No, it's a beautiful day for a walk, and it's only a few blocks to Main Street." She hooked her hand under his arm and leaned close. "Did you see all the decorations when you came into town? Mrs. Thornton and I were in charge of them, and even if I do say so myself, they look a lot better than last year."

"I wouldn't know about that since I wasn't here." He placed his hand over hers as they walked, and more people began to join them as they headed for the main festivities. Despite the problems out at the ranch, being here now brought pleasure to his heart. He hadn't missed these festivities until this moment as he walked beside Camilla.

"What events do you plan to enter today?"

"I've entered Smokey in the race already. He's fast, so we'll see how he does against the others today." Even if he didn't win, he planned to enjoy the day. He hoped the rest of his family could do the same.

At breakfast they had talked about coming into town, but Ma hadn't shown much enthusiasm until Pa suggested that Levi might not be far away and might come back for the festivities. James had picked Margaret up right after breakfast, leaving Rose to complain about having to help with the dishes.

Camilla's pull on his arm drew him back to the moment. She smiled up at him and arched an eyebrow. "Are you going to enter the shooting contest? I remember you won it once."

"No, I'm too rusty for that. I haven't really handled my gun much at all in the past few years."

"I'm sure you would do well with some practice." Camilla batted her long lashes at Micah and smiled.

His pulse sped up under the gaze of this beautiful woman. "I'd like to think so."

They stepped up onto the boardwalk lining the streets of Stoney Creek. Every store and place of business had gone all out to make their contribution to the celebration. Red, white, and blue streamers, banners, and flags decorated doors and posts all along Main Street. Mr. Hempstead had even tied patriotic bows on some of his merchandise in the windows.

The sun shone bright and the temperatures rose as the morning progressed toward noon. He and Camilla made their way around the exhibits of items townspeople had for sale. As they left the booth showing a neighbor's wood-working skills, he spotted the family carriage at the hotel hitching post. Ma must have decided to take Pa's advice and come into town. She stood across the street talking with the doctor's wife and Hannah Dyer.

He glanced down at Camilla, who had stopped to admire a hat in the dressmaker's shop. He'd like to go across and speak to Ma, but with Miss Dyer and Mrs. Whiteman there, it might not be a good idea. Too many times he'd noticed the looks of disapproval Camilla gave Miss Dyer. Those two ladies should be friends, not enemies, but then he'd never understood the workings of a woman's mind.

"Micah, it's almost noon. At one o'clock the mayor will be giving his speech and telling us about the surprise he has for our town. Let's eat at the hotel now and get out of the heat so we'll be done in time for the speeches and entertainment."

"If you say so. I'm always ready to eat." He led her across to the hotel and noticed that the ladies had disappeared. He'd have to wait and speak to Ma later.

After they had ordered, Camilla toyed with the linen napkin. Finally she peered at him with a hint of a frown on her lips. "Levi's leaving has altered things at the ranch, haven't they?"

"Yes, but why should that concern you?" The hairs on his neck bristled. From what he had gathered from their previous conversation, Camilla knew as much about Pa's business as Micah—and probably much more, which would include the financial problems.

"You were so set against being a rancher and rounding up cattle, but now with him gone, that's exactly what you're doing."

"Not so much. We have plenty of ranch hands who can take care of the herds. I help out where I can when I have to." He sat back to see where this conversation might be headed.

"I see. With the storm and all last year, has your father been able to recoup from the losses?"

Micah's hands clenched into fists, and he dropped them to his lap. She did know all about their situation. "I haven't been that deep into the ledger books." He had, but she didn't need to know that. Was she that concerned with how Pa would repay last year's loan?

"Oh, well, I thought you would know more about his

finances and how things are at the bank." She bit her lip and frowned.

"And just how are things at the bank?" He mentally scanned through what he remembered from checking the ledger books, and could only surmise she meant the bank loan last year.

"I think you should let your father be the one to tell you those things." Then she glanced up and smiled. "Here's our food. Let's not talk about business anymore and enjoy our lunch together."

She may not want to talk business any longer, but someone had explaining to do, and right now it appeared that person would have to be Pa. The conversation had tarnished the edges of what started out to be a beautiful day with a woman he admired. Any joy he held earlier took a backseat to the concern that arose in his gut about the ranch. If only Levi hadn't chosen to leave. Somehow he had to be found and brought home.

Levi pulled his hat down low on his forehead and stood in the shadows to watch the crowd for any sign of his family. He'd taken a risk coming into town like this, but he didn't want to stay back at the Hudson ranch alone. He'd sworn Mr. Hudson to secrecy about his presence on the ranch. The two ranches bordered one another, but Levi made sure he went nowhere near the outer boundaries of either one. Mr. Hudson urged Levi to go home but continued to give him work. Levi suspected that Mr. Hudson gave him a job out of concern for his ma and pa, whom he'd always respected, but Levi worked hard to earn his keep.

So far he'd been able to avoid the crowds strolling the streets by going through the alley ways behind the stores then edging up to the front to take a look around. No one had recognized him so far, but he'd have to stay away from the livery and the stables. Willy would run and find Pa soon as Levi made an appearance anywhere near there.

The only ones he'd really miss today were his ma and sisters and Ellie Bradshaw, the schoolmarm. He had dreamed of marrying her and partnering with Pa on the ranch. Now that Micah had returned, little chance he had of that happening. Micah may be the rightful heir, but he'd done little if anything to prove himself worthy of that inheritance.

Camilla and Micah came out of the hotel together. Anger swelled to a roar against his brother. Here he was back for only a few weeks, and he not only had the ranch but also a wealthy, beautiful woman at his side. He hated Micah for coming back and spoiling everything. Levi clenched his fists at his side and pushed the anger to a place where it could smolder. Somehow he'd get even with his brother.

He moved closer to the street, staying well behind the crowds. People began heading for the town square and the bandstand where Mayor Thornton would make his annual speech to the town. Rumors had it that the mayor would make a grand announcement today. What it could be roused Levi's curiosity and pushed Micah and Camilla aside for now.

He blew out his breath and willed his anger to subside. Skirting around the crowds, he got within good hearing distance but out of sight. Across the way he spotted James and Margaret, but before he turned his head, he and James locked gazes. Levi shook his head, and James frowned but turned his eyes toward the bandstand without saying anything to

Margaret. He may tell her later, but by then Levi would be gone again.

Ellie Bradshaw must be furious with him for leaving without saying good-bye to her. They had planned to be together for today's festivities, and breaking that promise hurt more than he dreamed it would. With her raven black hair and brown eyes, she was one of the best things in his life. Somehow he must let her know he was sorry to let her down. He wouldn't blame her if she never spoke to him again, but at least he'd try to seek her forgiveness.

Mayor Thornton's voice captured Levi's attention, and he concentrated on the man on the podium. After welcoming everyone and praising the country for once again being united and Texas for its grand and glorious history, he began talking about the town of Stoney Creek. With Ellie and Micah pushed to the back of his mind, Levi settled in to listen.

CHAPTER 12

HANNAH LISTENED AS Mayor Thornton announced the plans to build a new courthouse and introduced the young man who was to be the county attorney. The sight of the young man on the platform grabbed Hannah's breath and stole it completely away. As tall if not taller than Manfred and with dark brown hair that curled at his neck and around his ears, Alexander Hightower made quite an impressive appearance. The mayor beamed with satisfaction as the crowd applauded and cheered the new attorney.

Mr. Hightower may not have the rugged good looks of a cowboy like Micah Gordon, but his black pants and gray jacket fit him to perfection and spoke of the city of Dallas from which he'd just arrived. Only a man accustomed to the ways of city life could wear a suit with such bearing and ease.

Hannah bit her lip and tilted her head. He was likely near her in age, and the young women in the crowd certainly took notice and giggled with each other, pointing toward the young attorney. Let the others act like silly schoolgirls over the new man, because he assuredly wouldn't cast a second glance in her direction.

A nudge in her arm caught her attention. Sallie's eyes twinkled with amusement. "Listen to the twitter among our ladies. I can see why. He's certainly a handsome young man."

"Yes, I will give him that... in a citified way. He looks more like he should be in Austin in the state government. Most of the men here are cowboys and ranchers." One thing for certain, he'd have the attention of all the young ladies in town.

"We'll have to add him to our guest list, of course. It

wouldn't be right to have a party and not invite our newest resident."

Hannah blinked her eyes and frowned. That thought hadn't even occurred to her. The guest list already ran to most people in town, but the hall where the exhibits were now displayed had plenty of room. The expense is what worried her, but it didn't appear to bother Sallie or Manfred.

"Yes, it will be nice to have an extra man as a guest." Hannah bunched her eyebrows in a frown. "If he's to be the county attorney, who do you have for a lawyer for the people?"

"That would be Justin Murphy. He and his family are out of town now, so that's why you haven't met them. They should be back in time to attend the party."

Why had she thought Stoney Creek to be some tiny little western town in Texas? It had a doctor with an infirmary, lawyers to take care of needs, and plenty of stores and businesses in town to accommodate anyone and everything. So much for what she'd heard about the Wild West state of Texas.

Manfred strode toward them with the new attorney in tow. "Sallie, Hannah, I'd like you to meet Mr. Alex Hightower. He's going to be a great asset for Stoney Creek. Mr. Hightower, this is my wife, Sallie Whiteman, and her sister, Hannah Dyer, who is also my nurse."

Dark blue eyes twinkled and a dimple flashed as Mr. Hightower smiled and greeted them. "It's a pleasure to meet you, Mrs. Whiteman, and you too, Miss Dyer."

"My dear, I took the liberty of inviting Mr. Hightower to our welcome party for Hannah. I explained she's a newcomer too."

"That's lovely, Manfred. Hannah and I were discussing

doing that very thing. It's always nice to have another young man at these affairs."

Heat burned in Hannah's cheeks at the scrutiny of the attorney. She ran moist palms down the sides of her skirt. "I'm sure you're accustomed to attending such affairs, but it'll be a pleasure to welcome you to ours, Mr. Hightower."

"I'm looking forward to it, but now if you'll excuse me, I promised to join Mr. Swenson to watch the horse race this afternoon. He told me of a Mr. Gordon who has some of the best horses to be found in these parts of Texas. I hope to purchase one from him soon."

He tipped his hat and strode toward the area where Mr. Swenson, Camilla, and Micah were standing. Hannah blinked her eyes and swallowed hard. Mr. Hightower was going to meet Camilla, and with her beauty, she'd have him charmed right out of his boots. Even if Camilla and Micah were known to be courting, a twinge of jealousy poked at Hannah. Why did girls like Camilla get the notice of all men who met them? How nice it would be to have someone like Alex Hightower pay her the same attention.

While Manfred and Sallie talked, Hannah's gaze followed Mr. Hightower. A minute before he joined them, Micah turned and left. When Mr. Swenson introduced Camilla to Mr. Hightower, she became all smiles and offered her hand to the new attorney. By his posture and the way he held Camilla's hand a tad longer than necessary, the man was already smitten by her charms.

Hannah sighed and bit her lip. If Micah truly loved Camilla, she didn't want to see anyone come between them and cause him pain. She shook herself. It was absolutely none of her business, and she'd best remember that.

Movement toward the alley caught her eye. She peered

in that direction and gasped. That looked like Levi Gordon. She'd only seen him in church, but those broad shoulders on a man as tall as Micah could only belong to his brother. He disappeared behind one of the buildings, and Hannah stared in that direction. Perhaps she'd been mistaken since she'd only seen Levi once. If it was him, for whatever reason, he appeared to be hiding and didn't want others to see him. Far be it from her to reveal the whereabouts of someone who wished to remain hidden.

Micah strode back to the Swenson home where he'd left Smokey. Being away from the crowds kept the horse calm and ready for the big race. Now he'd find out if Smokey could match Red Dawn's accomplishments five years ago. Most of the competition came from neighboring ranches, and Micah had no opportunity to size up any opponents.

If the gray quarter horse ran like he did with Micah across open pasture, they'd stand a very good chance of winning. He regretted not having Levi to race against in a friendly competition, because whichever one of them won, it would bring accolades to the ranch.

After checking all the straps and reins, Micah stroked the horse's forehead and pressed his against it. "You're going to show off your stuff today and make all of us proud, but even if you don't, you're a fine horse, and I'm proud to be riding you."

A new saddle replaced the one he'd sold with Red Dawn, and that was good. A new saddle for a new ride meant he and the horse would be breaking in the same thing. Micah caressed the sleek leather and checked the strap once again. Smokey jerked his head and pulled at the reins.

"Looks like you're as ready for action as I am." He swung up and over Smokey's back and settled his feet in the stirrups. "All right, boy, time to see what we're made of." A nudge sent Smokey prancing and heading up the street for the starting point.

Each contestant had been given a copy of the route so there'd be no mistaking the boundaries and distances. Every quarter mile would be manned by judges who would determine any cause for disqualification. The prize of fifty dollars had grown since the last race he'd been in. Someone must have donated the purse since the entry fees hadn't risen since the last time he'd raced.

Crowds began to gather around the starting point, and Micah had his first good look at the other racers. He spotted two riders from the Hudson spread and one each from other outfits. He recognized the Hudson and Carlyle brands, but the others were unfamiliar to him. In all, seven riders would compete for the prize.

He searched the crowd looking for Camilla. When he found her with her father and that new attorney, the beast of jealousy snatched a bite from his heart. He'd heard Mayor Thornton introduce the lawyer, but he didn't remember the name. Having a county attorney would be good for the town, but not so good for Micah if he captured Camilla's interest.

The announcer called for the racers to position themselves behind the starting line. Micah joined the other riders and found a place between Leroy Gains and a Carlyle cowhand. "Good afternoon, Gains. I see you're still riding Captain Sam. Smokey's as good as Red Dawn, so you'll be eating our dust."

"We'll see about that, Gordon. I haven't lost since you took outta here five years ago. Don't know why these other fellows think they can beat me today." Gains straightened in his saddle and spit out a stream of tobacco onto the road.

Micah cringed. Such a nasty habit, one he'd never take up. The other men laughed and said they'd prove the Hudson and Gordon horses weren't the only fast ones in the area. Micah hoped not, but Captain Sam had some years on Smokey, and he was counting on youth overcoming age.

Finally all the horses stilled long enough for the starter to hold up his pistol. Micah braced himself for the shot with his heels ready to dig into Smokey. One and a quarter miles now loomed as an eternity of running, but Smokey could do that and more if he had to, and that's what Micah counted on now.

The starter began his countdown, and as the count of one rang in the air, the pistol fired and the race was on. Smokey leaped from the starting line like a bolt of lightning, and Micah let him have his lead. They galloped straight north to the boulder at the mouth of the canyon then west for a half mile before turning south, all riders bunched together. Smokey held his own and had the edge over all but Gains, matching the roan stride for stride. Clouds rolled in to cover the sun, but the heat still bore down on Micah.

In less time than Micah thought possible, the others dropped far behind, and he and Gains still rode neck and neck at the turn east back toward town. The hooves thundered over the hard-packed dirt, and just as Micah thought Smokey would pull ahead, Gains shouted something and waved his hat over his head.

Captain Sam took off like he'd been spooked and reached the finish line a good foot ahead of Micah. He pulled up the reins and patted Smokey's neck. "All right, fellow, Captain Sam is one fast horse. We'll get him next time."

Gains grinned at Micah and pushed his hat back on his head. "Now who's eating whose dust?" Then he stuck out his hand. "Smokey's a good horse, and he gave us a good race."

Micah grasped the outstretched hand. "Thanks, and we'll be back next year."

"Oh, I'm sure you will. Now I'm going to collect my prize. Too bad Levi didn't come in and make the race a real competition."

Micah narrowed his eyes at Gains's departing back. Everyone knew Levi had left the Circle G. Did Gains's remark mean Levi had holed up at the Hudson spread? Maybe he should mention that to Pa.

Micah didn't wait for the awarding but headed Smokey to the livery. He wanted to cool him down and brush out some of that dust collected on the trail. Camilla waved at him, and he turned in her direction.

She waited on the boardwalk in front of the bank. "That was some race, Micah. Sorry you had to lose."

"Gains and Captain Sam have the experience now, but wait until next year and see what this beauty can do."

Camilla's laugh rang in the air and lifted Micah's spirits. "Oh, I'm sure you will win next year, Micah Gordon, I'm sure you will."

"I'm taking Smokey to the livery, and then I'll be back to finish our tour of the celebration." He tipped his hat back, and her smile reassured him that she still preferred him.

"I'll be waiting down at the bandstand so we can get a good seat for the concert."

That would be the perfect ending for a little less than perfect day. "I'll see you then."

Across the street at the livery he unsaddled Smokey and began brushing him down. He'd come back and saddle him up again for the ride home, but the horse needed the rest now. Micah bore as much respect for his animals as he did any man. Treat them right, and they'd do whatever he asked of them.

Willy commented on the race and offered condolences before he disappeared to the back of the stables. Burt wasn't anywhere around, so he must be enjoying the festivities with his family. Micah finished with Smokey and stepped out to the street at the same moment a rider rounded the corner of the street up ahead and headed out of town.

Levi. He'd recognize that horse anywhere. Micah turned back for Smokey but realized by the time he'd saddled his horse, Levi would be long gone. What was that fool boy doing now? Micah slapped his hat against his thigh in anger. All he wanted to do now was to wring his brother's neck, but he'd have to find him first. At least Levi had stayed close, but where in thunder was he staying? Maybe it was time to check out the Hudson ranch.

CHAPTER 13

HANNAH DONNED THE one party dress Mama had insisted she have made for her trip to Texas. Mrs. Tenney had copied a design from *Leslie's Ladies' Magazine*, but she had modified the bustle because Sallie had warned that bustles were not the common fashion for the women of Stoney Creek. True to Sallie's words, the only elaborate dresses Hannah had seen were worn by Camilla Swenson and Mrs. Thornton, the mayor's wife.

That suited Hannah just fine. She'd never cared for the corsets and hoops she'd worn in her younger years, and she certainly didn't desire to have all that fabric bunched up behind and fashioned over a silly-looking cage device. Such lengths some women would go to look what they considered their very best. Thankfully Sallie shared some of the same opinions as to fashion, but Mama went by the rules.

The lighter blue ruffles about the neckline and the sleeve edges set off the deeper royal blue of the bodice and over-skirt draped over the lighter blue underskirt. Mama had cringed when she saw how small Mrs. Tenney had made the bustle, but Hannah had hugged the woman and whispered a thank-you.

The dress might be all right for tonight's party, but Hannah didn't see herself wearing it on very many occasions in the future. Life in Stoney Brook ran to the simpler things, although narrow waists were still the rage and corsets made them even more so. Either Camilla Swenson had a small waist to begin with, or she laced herself up tight to make it that way. And if she laced up, how on earth was she able to breathe at all?

Camilla and her tiny waist had certainly won the attentions of both Micah and that Hightower fellow. They'd be polite and ask Hannah for at least one dance tonight, but maybe they'd be surprised that she could dance so well. She had Benjamin Elliot to thank for that. He courted Jenny Harper while she lived with the Dyer family after Sallie's marriage, and he'd helped Hannah master the steps to several dances, including the quadrille.

"Hannah, are you about ready? It's time for us to be at the town hall."

Sallie's voice brought her back from her memories. "Yes, I'll be down in a minute." With a last glance at the three blue bows adorning the skirt under the bustle, Hannah reached for her reticule and gloves. If none of the other girls her age wore gloves, she'd be happy to ditch hers for comfort in the Texas heat.

Manfred waited out front with the carriage, and Lettie stood in the parlor with her arms about her young charges for the evening. She and Burt had offered to take care of the younger children while Sallie and Manfred enjoyed the party.

When Hannah reached the hallway, Sallie clapped her hands. "Perfect! You look absolutely beautiful in that dress, and it's not too extreme to show up some of the other ladies. The young men of Stoney Brook are going to be quite smitten with you tonight. I imagine your dance card will be full before you know it."

"Thank you. I had to really argue with Mama to keep from having a huge bustle with lots of ruffles and bows." Hannah didn't know about attracting young men, but several would ask her to dance because she was the honoree. At least that was the etiquette back home. Perhaps it would be the same here, and if so, it meant Micah Gordon or that new attorney, Alexander Hightower, would ask her to dance.

Sallie laughed. "That sounds like Mama." Then she turned to Lettie. "Are you sure you want to stay here with these young ones and not come to the party?"

"Now you know we don't need to be at that party. It's for Miss Hannah to get to know more folks, and we already know her, and longer than anyone else here." She gave Sallie a little push. "Get on out of here and go enjoy the party. The children will be fine."

Molly stood proud and tall at the fact she was being allowed to attend the party. Since she'd be twelve soon, Sallie deemed it a good thing for her daughter to learn social graces and take part in the event. Hannah grinned at her niece and remembered Sallie's nineteenth birthday party back in St. Francisville. That had been a memorable evening for Hannah. She hoped the same would happen for Molly tonight.

Sallie laughed and waved to Lettie. "You heard the lady, let's go." Sallie's love for social events had not changed.

Hannah followed her sister and niece to the carriage and climbed up beside Molly in the second seat. As they rode to town, Hannah reached over and covered Molly's hands to still her twisting fingers. "Don't be nervous, Molly. It'll be fine. I remember my first grown-up party, and it was your mother's birthday. I was a year older than you are now, but I had a wonderful time. You will too."

"Oh, I hope so, Auntie Han—I mean, Aunt Hannah."

Hannah wrapped her arm about her niece's shoulders and leaned close. "I don't mind if you call me Auntie Hannah. It rather suits me here in Texas." Then she winked.

That brought a giggle from Molly, and she relaxed beside

Hannah as Manfred stopped the carriage and jumped down. He hurried around to help Sallie alight while Molly clambered down on her own. Manfred reached up for Hannah. She grasped his shoulders, and he lifted her up then down to the ground with a firm hand.

When they entered the hall, a huge sign covered one end behind the stage: WELCOME TO STONEY CREEK HANNAH DYER. Three musicians with a fiddle, a guitar, and a bass viol warmed up their instruments as they discussed the selections for the evening. The whine of the violin and twang of the bass strings foretold of the fun to come later in the evening. A long table against a side wall held a large punch bowl and platters of pastries and cakes from the bakery shop.

The baker's wife, Irene Delmont, pushed through the door from the hallway carrying a tray of cookies. She grinned when she spotted Sallie and Hannah. "Good evening, ladies. We're about ready for your guests to arrive."

Sallie rushed over and hugged the slender woman with gray hair in a neat bun atop her head. "It looks wonderful, Irene. You and Gus have done a beautiful job."

"Thank you, Sallie. I love baking for parties, and we don't have near enough of them around here." Irene set the silver tray on the table and stepped back to admire the effect. "It does look nice even if I do say so myself."

Indeed it looked nice, and it was all Hannah could do to keep from snitching one of the miniature pecan pastries right now. How did Mrs. Delmont stay so nice and slim with all these goodies around her? If it had been Hannah, she'd be as round as a pot-bellied stove.

Moments later guests began arriving. Sallie opted not to have a formal receiving line, but she asked Hannah to stay near the stage so that when the music began, she'd be there to start the first dance.

Most of the faces greeting Hannah had become familiar in the nearly four weeks she'd been in town and attending church. Their friendliness and acceptance warmed Hannah's heart and gave her a feeling of home that warded off a longing for her parents. So far Sallie had kept things too busy for any homesickness to linger.

Hannah let go of Mrs. Hempstead's hand and turned to the next guest who had strolled up. Dark brown eyes met hers, and she went weak in the knees. Her heart hammered, and she fought to catch her breath until she realized Camilla Swenson stood at the side of Micah.

A hard swallow pushed back the sharp pang of jealousy. "Mister Gordon, how nice of you to come to my party, and you too, Miss Swenson."

Why had he dreaded coming to this party for Miss Dyer? Camilla hadn't been enthusiastic about it herself, but Ma had insisted, and now Micah was glad she had. "Good evening, Miss Dyer. Your sister must be very pleased with the turnout tonight."

"Oh, she is. Sallie's over there now making sure we have plenty of refreshments. Thank you for coming."

"It's our pleasure, Miss Dyer. Isn't that right, Camilla." He turned to the woman beside him, who wore a smile that didn't reflect itself in her eyes or in any other part of her face.

"Of course it is." She extended a hand encased in a lacy glove to Hannah. "These get-togethers for our townspeople are good for bringing people together. Nothing like the Mayor's Winter Ball, but nice all the same."

At the disappointment now tracing itself across Miss Dyer's face, Micah wanted to scold Camilla for her rudeness. Instead he smiled again and said, "I do hope you will save a dance for me later."

As soon as the words left his mouth, he wanted to snatch them back. What if Hannah didn't dance because of her foot? But her smile erased any fears about that.

"I most certainly will, Mr. Gordon. Thank you for asking."

He stared into those incredible blue eyes for a moment longer. No doubt about it, Hannah Dyer was a beautiful young woman.

Camilla nudged his arm. "Come, Micah, others are waiting to speak with Miss Dyer."

He cleared his throat and turned to Camilla. "Of course, excuse us for taking so much of your time, Miss Dyer." He led Camilla over to the refreshment table. A cup of cold punch would suit him fine now as he needed it in the worst way. Here he had one of if not the most beautiful woman in town on his arm, and he'd been mesmerized by Hannah with hair that flamed with red amidst the gold. He'd never seen anything quite like it.

"I must say, Micah, that was quite an act of kindness to ask Miss Dyer for a dance later."

Micah clenched his teeth at Camilla's comment. Her condescending tone toward the guest of honor had no place at the gathering. "It wasn't kindness, Camilla. Miss Dyer is a very nice young woman, and I met her the first day of her arrival. In fact, we were on the train together."

"I'm sure she is quite sweet, but with that limp and

strange shoe of hers, she might not be able to keep up with the dance steps."

He needed that punch now more than ever or his disappointment in Camilla may very well turn into anger over that last statement, even though he'd considered the same thing. The red punch sloshed over the edge of the cup as he filled it. He reached for a napkin to wipe off the liquid before handing the cup to Camilla and almost spilled it again, this time on her. "I'm so sorry, Camilla. I don't know why I'm so clumsy."

"Ladling punch is not as easy as it looks." She peered at him over the edge of the cup as she took her first sip.

"No, it isn't, and I can't say that I've had much practice at the art." He ladled another cup with almost the same results. More like no practice at all since he hadn't been to any events like this in the past five years. Beer and whiskey didn't have to be ladled, only poured, and that was usually by the bartender or someone else. He sipped his punch and scanned the room. Many people he'd known since childhood filled the room. The number of people in attendance gave testimony that they admired and respected the doctor and his wife.

His gaze landed on Hannah, still greeting guests. A surprisingly intense longing tugged at his heartstrings and sent his emotions on a wave of desire. He gripped the handle of the punch cup and gulped down the cool liquid.

The sugary sweetness slipped down his throat and cooled his emotions to the point he could now speak with Camilla without betraying where his thoughts had strayed.

People milled about the room laughing and conversing with one another. Although they lived in the same small town, the only contact some of these people had with each other came on Saturday at the store or Sunday at church. Most of them had grown accustomed to seeing Micah back in town and greeted him with smiles and handshakes.

No sign of Levi, but then Micah hadn't expected him to make an appearance. Pa had checked with Hudson, and, as he'd suspected, Levi was there. Micah wanted to go out and drag him home, but Pa said no. Levi had to make that decision himself.

Ten minutes later the trio of musicians climbed up on the stage and took their places. Manfred headed to the platform then stood center stage, where he called for everyone's attention.

After welcoming the guests, he called Hannah to come up and stand beside him. He held out his hand toward her and helped her up. With her royal blue dress and her hair piled on her head and curls dangling at her neck, she looked like a queen.

Manfred grabbed her hand and held it. "Ladies and gentlemen, most of you have now met my wife's sister, Hannah Grace Dyer. Mrs. Whiteman and I are honored to have her living with us, and I am especially grateful for her nursing skills. She's already become a most important part of my practice."

The crowd applauded their appreciation until Manfred turned to the trio. "Let the dance begin, and I am honored to have the first one with Miss Dyer." He grinned with a quirk of amusement in his voice. "Eat your hearts out, young men, and get in line for the next one. Shall we, Miss Hannah?" He helped her down from the platform and nodded for the musicians to begin.

After watching Hannah's first few turns, Camilla leaned over and spoke behind the fan she carried. "Well, I do believe our little cripple can dance, although I don't see how with that heavy shoe on her foot."

Yes, indeed, Miss Dyer knew her way around the dance floor. She didn't even look winded. He watched her every move while Camilla stood at his side talking with one of her friends. Hannah never missed a step, and when the music ended, he clapped as hard if not harder than anyone else there.

He turned to Camilla, who eyed him with disdain and said, "It appears she surprised everyone with her dancing. Maybe it won't be so bad for you after all when you take your obligatory turn."

No, it wouldn't, and he could hardly wait until he could claim that honor. The music started up again, and this time he swirled Camilla to the center of the floor. He hadn't forgotten how to lead a lady around in dance, but all the time he spent with Camilla, he cast an eye on the beautiful woman in the blue dress.

CHAPTER 14

MAY I HAVE this dance, Miss Dyer?"

Hannah swirled around at the unfamiliar voice and gulped when she discovered Alexander Hightower standing by her side. Her heart pounded, and she swallowed hard before answering to keep her voice from cracking. "I'd be delighted, Mr. Hightower." She set her punch cup on the table.

The music began, and he swept her across the floor to the center. "I must say I was quite surprised to find this type of party in Stoney Brook. I expected a country shindig with cowboys everywhere. This almost reminds me of back home."

"And where would that be?" Although she'd already heard it from Manfred, her brain refused to think of anything else to say, and she certainly didn't want to discuss the weather.

"I'm from Dallas originally, but I finished my schooling and went into a partnership with a lawyer in New Orleans." He spun her around and grinned in a way that made his eyes sparkle.

That grin sent Hannah's heart into overtime, and she almost missed a step. Then where he'd been registered and she gasped. "New Orleans? That's just down the road from St. Francisville, where my grandparents live. I've only been to New Orleans once, and that was after the war when Mama wanted to go down and visit some friends. It's a beautiful old city."

"Yes, it is. It's nice to know someone here has been there and recognizes her charms."

She'd only been there once, but that had been enough to see

why so many people, including Mama, loved the town. "That wasn't hard to do. We have several homes in St. Francisville that were fashioned after some of the homes there. I love the wrought-iron balconies and French-style windows. Mama made sure Sallie and I learned to speak French, and hearing the language there only added to our delight."

As the music came to an end, everyone clapped, and Mr. Hightower led her back to the side of the room with chairs. "Thank you, Miss Dyer. Perhaps we shall do this again later."

"My pleasure, Mr. Hightower. I'd be delighted to dance with you again." As he walked away, her hand went to her heart to still its rapid beat. That had been the most delightful few minutes.

When Micah suddenly appeared at her side, she started. "Mr. Gordon, I didn't see you come up."

"I didn't mean to startle you. Are you all right?"

Before she had a chance to answer, the leader of the trio stepped forward. "Now that you've enjoyed your traditional social dances, let's get down and have some fun. First will be the Virginia reel. Grab your partner then line up, gents on one side, ladies on the other, and away we'll go."

Micah frowned when Mr. Hightower grabbed Camilla, but he turned to Hannah with a smile. "Looks like we're partners in the reel. Do you want to give it a try?"

Hannah could only nod as her blood raced with anticipation. She wanted so much to dance with Micah, but would she be able to manage all the steps in her bustle skirt? Most of the other women except Camilla and Mrs. Thornton had worn plain homespun fabric full skirts over petticoats and had much more freedom of movement. But if Camilla could do this, then Hannah decided she could too.

The music started, and Micah winked at her as he came

across and bowed. She curtsied, then they locked arms to dance in a circle. It had been much easier to perform the steps in her hoops a few years ago, but she managed to keep from tripping and losing her balance as they promenaded with her arm locked onto Micah's. Her heart pounded with pleasure at the pressure of his arm against hers. She'd never experienced such a feeling with a man before. Micah may be way out of her reach, but his attention tonight was more than she dared hope.

When the music ended, Hannah, out of breath, joined with the others in applauding, but she wanted it to go on and on so she could be near Micah, who still stood by her side. She glanced up at him, but he narrowed his eyes toward Camilla as she laughed and batted her eyes at something Mr. Hightower said.

How could Camilla ignore the man who'd brought her to the dance? Hannah wanted to yell at the woman for her behavior. If Micah had been Hannah's escort, her only thoughts would be of him and how he'd held her as they danced. She certainly wouldn't be spending so much time with another man.

Micah touched her arm. "Would you care for refreshment? My throat's somewhat dry after that last dance."

"Thank you, Micah. I would enjoy a cup of punch." Joy filled her soul to be spending a few more minutes with him. She may not have his admiration, but every moment with him would be a blessing.

They strolled over to the table where Sallie controlled the ladle. Micah grinned at her and picked up two cups. "I'm glad to see someone else handling that ladle. All I did was to spill more than I put in the cup."

Sallie laughed and filled the cups. "Yes, I noticed several of the men with that problem, so that's why I took over the job."

Micah handed Hannah a filled cup. "Would you like to sit down?" He nodded to the side of the room where she'd been earlier.

Although somewhat tired, she had no desire to sit and have Micah leave her alone. Standing here with him was so much better. "I'm fine, but that dance did take some effort."

"Yes, but it was fun. Have you seen our square dances? They're fashioned after the quadrille, but with a few more steps and calls. Sam up there has been our caller almost since I can remember."

"No, I haven't, but Sallie told me about them and even tried to show me a few moves and turns, but I think I'll have to watch awhile to really catch on." The reel had been bad enough, but she'd never be able to make all the quick moves of the squares with her heavy shoe even if she practiced with Manfred and Sallie.

Micah set his punch cup down. "If you'll excuse me, I believe I'll go over and see if Molly would like to join me for the next dance. She's quite the young lady now. Besides, I remember how excited Margaret was at her first dance."

His kindness touched her heart. What a wonderful treat for Molly. His gesture brought back the memory of Benjamin Elliot and his kindness at Sallie's party. After the music started up again and Micah swung Molly out onto the floor, she turned her gaze to other guests. Mr. Hightower still claimed Camilla Swenson as his partner, and they made a very nice-looking couple. However, if Micah was truly interested in Camilla, Hannah would much rather see someone else with Mr. Hightower. After the way Levi had snubbed

Micah and run off, Micah didn't need to be disappointed in love as well.

"This is a lovely party, Hannah. Your sister is a wonderful hostess."

Hannah turned her head at the comment and found Eleanor Bradshaw, the local schoolteacher, standing at the table. "Thank you, she is. Miss Bradshaw, isn't it? I've seen you at church, but haven't had much opportunity to become better acquainted."

"Yes, that's right, and please call me Ellie. I've been to church each Sunday you were there, but with your being busy at the doctor's place, we haven't had much opportunity to get to know one another. I'd like to remedy that and hope we can become friends."

Her brown eyes sparkled, and even though Ellie might be a few years younger, she'd be a nice person to have as a friend in the days ahead. "I'd like that too, Ellie. It's always good to have another woman to talk to now and again."

"I saw you with Micah Gordon a bit ago. I remember when he left Stoney Creek. I was just out of school and preparing to go on to learn to be a teacher. He seems to have changed a lot since then."

"Seeing as how I haven't known him very long, I can't say much about him except that he's been extremely polite to me and to my niece Molly."

"I'm glad. I'm so sorry Levi couldn't accept Micah's return. All I know is that Micah was never interested in running the ranch, but their pa always believed he'd come back and take over. Meanwhile, Levi worked hard to prove himself to his pa, but his pa never seemed to notice his efforts."

So that's what was at the root of the trouble between the brothers. Sallie had told her that Levi had been courting

Ellie before he disappeared, so she must know the two men very well. How tragic for their mother. She couldn't begin to imagine how much it must hurt Mrs. Gordon to have her two boys at odds with each other. She'd have to make their reconciliation a prayer priority.

Ellie's eyebrows raised, and then she frowned. "Please excuse me, Hannah. I must go do something. Maybe we can talk again later." Without another word of good-bye, Ellie turned and hurried toward the back of the building and the room where the food was being prepared.

Hannah bit her lip. What could have happened to make Ellie leave so suddenly? Nothing that had been said could possibly have hurt her feelings. Tempted to follow and find the cause of the sudden departure, Hannah realized it was none of her business, but curiosity nibbled at her. Poking her nose where it didn't belong only led to trouble, as she'd learned from experiences with her brothers. She turned her attention back to the music and dancers.

Levi stepped into the shadows and made his way to the back of the town hall. He'd taken a chance coming here, but he had to see Ellie and explain his reason for abandoning her. At least she hadn't reacted in a way to arouse suspicion when she finally noticed him at the window.

He had breathed in relief when she turned and headed toward the exit. She should be at the door by now. A moment later the door opened then closed. A whispered voice called out, "Levi? Are you here?"

"Yes, over here in the shadows." He kept a close eye trained on the back door to make sure no one followed as she hurried toward him.

He grabbed her in his arms. "I'm so glad you came. I was afraid you'd be too mad to come." Levi led her across the alley and into the shadows of another building.

"I am angry, but you owe me an explanation. What in the world is going on with you? Your ma is worried sick."

"I know, but I had to leave. I tried to see you at the celebration on July Fourth, but never did find you. I'm so sorry I didn't." He held her against his chest and rested his cheek on her head. "Micah coming back and taking over ruined all my hopes and dreams for having the Circle G for you and me one day. I've been doing it all for Pa these past five years, but Micah was always his favorite."

She pulled back away from him to look him straight in the eye. "Levi Gordon, that's the craziest thing I ever heard. Your ma and pa don't have favorites. Micah is the oldest, and the ranch would rightfully belong to him unless your pa wrote a will saying different."

Anger intensified the brown in her eyes, making them almost black, but he couldn't let that change his mind. "You sound like that new highfalutin lawyer they hired for the town. I know what Micah's rights are, but giving your own sweat and blood should count for something. Besides, Micah abandoned us—including the ranch—for five years, with never so much as a good-bye or a note of his whereabouts. Then he comes prancing home without apology, and Pa falls all over himself welcoming Micah home." He didn't want to contradict Ellie directly, but Pa did favor Micah, and that was a fact. Pa would never let Levi run the ranch, at least not as long as Micah stayed around and probably not even if he was gone again.

"Where are you staying?" Ellie asked.

He shrugged and tried to put a note of cheer in his voice. "Out at the Hudson ranch. Turns out I make more money working with the Hudson outfit than I did working for Pa. I already have a spot picked out for my own spread, and soon as I can manage it, I'll ask for my inheritance and strike out on my own."

Ellie said nothing, but the look in her eyes displayed the disappointment. The last thing he wanted to do was to hurt her feelings or cause her any more pain and unhappiness.

He placed his hands on her arms now wrapped around her middle then lifted a hand to finger the chestnut curls teasing her cheek. How he longed to undo all the pins and watch it cascade to her shoulders and down her back. "Ellie, I love you, and I want to marry you, but that can't happen until I have my own ranch and herd. It may take a few years, but can you wait for me?"

"Why should I? How do I know you wouldn't run away from me like you have your ma and pa? One little thing makes you unhappy or angry, and off you go."

"Because I love you and want to spend the rest of my life with you. I had the notion you felt the same about me." He stared into her eyes now filling with tears. Had he been wrong all these months?

"Oh, Levi, I do care, but I can't lie to your parents and not let them know you're close by. How can I wait for you like that?"

"That doesn't matter. Pa knows where I am." He pulled her close to his chest. "I love you, Ellie. You have to believe me."

She pulled back again and stared into his face, blinking her eyes to keep the tears at bay. Then he leaned down and pressed his lips against hers. At first she didn't respond, but then her arms went around his neck, and she kissed him back with a love that matched that swelling in his chest.

Then he stepped back. "I have to go. Someone might see me and tell Pa or Ma. I'll find a way to see you again soon." He released her and turned to leave.

"All right, Levi, for now. I'll be praying for you to come to your senses and make the right decisions. I'll be waiting until next time."

Her words filled him with hope, and he welcomed her prayers. Maybe God would listen to her, because He sure had been silent in answering any prayers Levi had sent up. He swung up onto his horse and headed back for the Hudson ranch.

CHAPTER 15

ICAH STUDIED THE ledgers and then reworked the columns with the same results. July would end in the red unless something could be done in the next few weeks. If this trend kept up, the ranch would go under by the end of September. They had nothing left to put into the expenses of running the Circle G. And the month of work he'd promised would be ending soon with no apparent change in Pa's mind about the will, even after Levi's departure.

How could it have come to this? Micah leaned back in his chair. He couldn't leave now with things in such a mess. Even if Mr. Swenson approved another bank loan, it would only put them further behind. However, at this point a loan appeared to be the only choice. If they could get enough money to tide them over until the cattle drive in the fall, then the ranch could be saved.

If Pa found out Micah had been going through the finances again, he'd be furious, but at least now Micah could see and understand the true situation. Pa still expected him to be out on the range every day with the others. That wouldn't be so bad if Levi were here to share the burden.

Micah's concern ran to more than the figures on the page. Pa didn't have the energy he once had, and many times he had gone home with some excuse for not completing his job. Pa had been close mouthed and unwilling to share anything with Micah. Micah remembered that first night and Pa's rubbing his chest when he didn't know Micah watched him.

Micah slammed the books shut and shoved them back

into the drawer then locked it. He'd have a talk with Pa right now before they went out to join the wranglers for the day. He shoved away from the desk, but the door opened and Pa entered before Micah could stand.

Pa's eyes filled with lightning and his voice thundered. "I thought I told you to mind your own business, and my office isn't a part of your business."

Micah grabbed the edge of the desk to calm his nerves. "I know, Pa, but I've been worried about you and the ranch. I was coming to look for you just now. We need to talk before heading out for the day."

"So you think you have all the answers. I told you I'd take care of it."

"But Pa, we're in trouble. You need my help." If he couldn't get Pa to understand and seek help now, all would be lost.

"I know it doesn't look good, but I plan to go into town later and talk with Mr. Swenson about the loan we discussed last week. It'll take care of things until the cattle drive. It's our only chance to survive the drought and come out even. We have a decent group of new calves to keep us going for next year."

"You're mortgaged to the hilt now. Mr. Swenson may not even be willing to grant you another loan. What if he doesn't?" Micah saw no way around the need for more money immediately, but they had to have something to fall back on in case the answer was a no.

"We'll worry about that after I've talked with Mr. Swenson."

Micah clenched his teeth. Pa's stubbornness in facing reality had put them in this position, and it might bring even more trouble down on their heads. He geared himself up for another discussion that would most likely end up in another argument, but he had to try to reason with his father.

Micah opened the drawer and pulled out the ledger book. "If I had been here to take over these, we wouldn't be in the fix we are. I can see so many places where money was wasted or not used in the best way for the ranch. I blame myself for not being here, but if you'd let me handle all this now, I can plan some ways to make it all work."

"I hear you, son, and you can do all this, but you have to take care of the ranch hands, the cattle, and all that other stuff too. You can't just sit here in an office and expect everyone to do your bidding. You gotta get out there and get dirty and sweaty with the rest of us."

"I know that, but you act like no one but you can add or subtract or know a debit from a credit or an asset from a loss. I know all about those, and I can help you here as well as do the other." The riding, roping, and branding wouldn't be so bad to Micah if he could also take care of where and how the money would be spent. Pa's decisions had put them in this situation, and now he needed help, if only he'd admit it.

"And just what makes you think you can do a better job at this than I can?"

Micah's hands clenched into fists. How many times did he have to explain all he'd learned and how he loved to work with numbers? He may not have done well in school in other things, but arithmetic had always fascinated him. "Have you even looked at any of the proposals I worked up for you? They show you what I can do, and you'd see how much sense they make for us. It does take more than bookwork to make a ranch run, but the books are a big part of it, and I'm good at it."

"I haven't had time to look at anything what with Levi gone, and you not carrying your weight in his absence. Besides, it doesn't make any difference right now. We have a problem, and I'm going in to see Mr. Swenson to settle it."

Deep breaths of air failed to ease the frustration at his father's stubbornness. Somehow he had to make Pa see the reality of what they faced in the next few months. A bank loan was only a temporary fix in a very leaky dam. They'd probably come out even with a good sale, but then the same problems would come back if they weren't resolved now.

His father shoved his hat on his head and turned to leave. "I'm going out to get my horse and tell the boys I'm going into town."

"Pa, wait. If you're determined to go through with this, I want to go with you."

"No. I can do this myself, and I don't need your help or anybody else's." He stomped across the room then slammed the door behind him as he left.

Micah slumped into his chair. He didn't want to defy his father, but then he didn't want Pa to face possible rejection alone. He'd wait a little and then follow him into town and be there nearby in case Mr. Swenson didn't come through. On the way in he'd have to come up with another plan if the bank said no.

Ruth cringed at the noise of a door being slammed. Joel and Micah must have had another disagreement. All those two had done since Micah's return was to argue. Why did Joel have to be so stubborn? He refused to acknowledge anything was wrong. Whenever she tried to talk with him about the ranch or money, he'd hush her up real quick and tell her not to worry herself with any of that and take care of the home and their family. That may be fine for him to say, but her husband was a part of her family, and taking care of him was her first priority.

She removed her apron and sat at the table alone. Margaret was in her room, and Rose had gone out to play with pets. That brought a smile. All the animals on the ranch were Rose's "pets." She stood at the edge of the trail and told all the cattle good-bye as they left for market, and even cried a tear or two that they would not come back.

Rose and Margaret were two rays of sunshine in the darkness that hovered over the ranch. The shadow had been there for a while, but it become dark and foreboding when Micah returned and Levi left. Joel's health continued to decline, but he refused to admit it and hadn't been in to see the doctor since he'd been told he had a heart problem. He'd finally shared that with her, but her husband still held too many secrets from her, secrets she'd already discovered with her own intuition.

With her head bowed, Ruth clasped her hands, sadness nibbling at her heart. Why did men have to be so stubborn and not want to admit when something was wrong? The stress of the arguments with Micah, Levi's departure, and the problems with the ranch did nothing to improve Joel's condition. Still he plowed ahead in determination to make things happen on his own.

A shadow appeared across the table, and she raised her head. "Oh, Micah, I heard the door slam. What happened?"

Micah slumped into the chair across from her. "Same old thing. Pa won't listen to anything I have to say. I have some ideas of how to save on costs, but he won't sit still long enough to hear me out."

She reached across the table with both hands and clasped

his. "Pa has a lot on his mind what with Levi being gone and the worry about money as well as his..." She stopped before she let the information about Joel's health slip from her tongue. He'd be angry to know she even said this much.

"You know about the losses and the debt we've accumulated?"

"Of course I do, not in detail, but in general. Joel thinks I don't pay attention to what I see and hear, and he won't tell me himself. He keeps telling me not to worry and take care of things here in the house, but I can read between the lines. We've been together too long for me not to know."

He leaned forward and squeezed her hands. "Ma, you stopped abruptly a few minutes ago. Are you as concerned about Pa's health as I am? I saw him clutch his chest one night while we talked."

How had this fun-loving, irresponsible boy turn into such a smart, observant young man? She blinked back a tear. "It's more serious than he wants to admit or let anyone see. He'd skin me alive if he knew I was telling you this. None of the others are aware of anything wrong, not even Levi, although I have seen Margaret observing him with a keen eye, so she may suspect."

"What is the problem? Has he seen Dr. Whiteman?"

"It's his heart, and yes, he's seen the doctor, but a lot of good it did him. Joel doesn't want to follow directions and be told what he should and shouldn't do to keep from having something even more serious happen."

"And my arguing, Levi's leaving, and the money problems aren't helping any. They only add to the stress he doesn't need."

Ruth could only nod and squeeze her eyes shut. All the strength she had came from the Lord, and even that seemed to be slipping out of her grasp.

"Ma, I'm so sorry for these past five years. I should never

have left without explaining why I had to go, and I should have let you know where I was and what I was doing, but I wasn't proud of those things then and I'm not proud of them now."

"You were just a boy searching for what you wanted from life. God gave you some answers and brought you back to us. It doesn't matter to Him what you've done in the past; it's what you do with the future that makes a difference."

Micah grimaced. "God and I haven't been exactly on speaking terms since I left. I blamed God for all my problems and troubles. When I finally pulled myself together and got out of the mire, I decided I was through with God because He'd given me so much trouble."

In spite of everything Ruth had to chuckle at Micah's obtuseness. "Son, God didn't give you that trouble. You made it for yourself. You made poor choices and took the wrong turns in your decisions. Don't you think it was He who protected you and finally gave you the strength to get out of that mess and then come home?" She pinned him with her gaze.

Micah turned red and looked away. "I don't know. I hadn't really thought of it in that light. All I can say is that I was miserable and blamed God for letting it happen. Now this business with Pa makes me more upset than ever. Why would God do that to Pa?"

"If I had the answer to that, I'd be able to answer the questions of the ages. We don't know why God does things, only that He knows best and whatever happens is for our good." The misery in his face spoke volumes. Micah hurt with a pain for which she had no remedy; only God could heal the hurts of this boy's heart. He needed someone in his life to love him and work beside him. "What are your feelings for Camilla? She's a bright spot in your life right now, isn't she?"

When no light sparked in Micah's eyes, Ruth feared the worst. Once again his face said more than words as he sat in silence before her. After a moment or two he raised his gaze to hers.

"Ma, I don't know what I feel about Camilla. Something is missing. I see the way James treats Margaret and the way he adores her. She looks at him with such love in her eyes that it amazes me that my little sister could feel like that about a man. Camilla is a smart, talented, and beautiful woman, and I had begun to think maybe I could love her and make a life with her."

"And now?"

"I don't know, but I don't want to hurt her. Sometimes her behavior and attitude toward others anger me, and I begin to wonder if I could ever love a woman like that."

Camilla's attitude had concerned Ruth as well, but she'd said nothing against the girl. Most marriages were made up of two flawed creatures, but she wanted the best for her children. Right now she couldn't picture Camilla as a ranch wife.

"I'll pray for you, son. God has a young woman out there already picked for you. If Camilla is the one, you'll know it." She wanted for him what she'd had with Joel from the very beginning. Their love had been strong from the first moment they met and grew stronger the more they were together. She'd die for him if necessary, and that's what she wanted for her sons and daughters.

"It doesn't matter now anyway. I can't ask a woman to share my life when my future is so uncertain. Camilla is accustomed to so much more than I can give her right now." He shoved back from the table. "Pa was going into town to talk with Mr. Swenson, and I want to be there when he gets out. Pa shouldn't be alone if it's bad news."

"You're right, he shouldn't. Go on, and I'll pray for you both. God still works miracles, you know." She smiled, letting him know by her loving gaze that she considered his return one of those miracles.

When the door closed behind him, her heart squeezed with fear, and she hurried upstairs to her bedroom. She sank to her knees on the floor beside the bed she shared with the man she loved. Beneath her, the rag rug had worn thin from years of her praying in that spot. Her men needed prayer, and that's one thing she could give all three of them right now.

CHAPTER 16

MICAH RODE TO town with a heavy heart. Not only was Pa in poor health, but he also ran a chance of losing all he'd worked for, and Micah blamed himself for it all. If only he could take back the last five years of selfishness and be the support his father had needed. Ma may be praying, but it'd take a bigger miracle than Micah had ever seen to resolve the issues at hand. God hadn't been very helpful to this point, so why would He bother with the Gordon family now?

The past could not be returned or relived, but he could help with the future. First, he'd find Levi and make him listen. The two of them could be great partners to take the load off Pa's back if Levi could be convinced. Then he and Levi could help Pa with whatever needed to be done at the ranch, whether it meant roping and branding calves or scouting for stray cattle.

If they could make do until time for the drive to sell the cattle, they could make enough to take care of expenses for this year. He and Levi together could figure out what to do for the next one.

As much as he liked Camilla, he could not in good conscience continue to court her with the ranch in such a state, and with Levi gone, neither could he pursue the idea of working for Camilla's father. He couldn't see Camilla helping to run a ranch anyway. She had good business sense, but the lifestyle to which she was accustomed didn't run to life in the country. She belonged in town where she could mix and mingle with other town folk.

A face with a dimpled cheek, golden hair, and blue eyes that danced with merriment filled his thoughts. Hannah Dyer had talent and spirit, but with her defect, she'd have a hard time with all the responsibilities that came with ranch life. She'd been very agile and smooth on the dance floor, but did she have the stamina needed to take care of a home and family on a ranch?

Why was he even thinking about her in the first place? He had other problems to solve before taking on any more. He didn't need a wife now anyway. Ma took care of things with Margaret's and Rose's help. Of course Margaret would probably leave soon to marry James, but Ma would still be there to take care of him and Levi.

As he neared town, his resolve to do whatever he could to help his father strengthened, and his confidence in his ability to save the ranch grew. The faint sounds of shouts and gunfire drew his attention, and he spurred his horse to action. Something had happened in town.

Several minutes later he rounded the corner to Main Street and found a crowd near the bank. As he rode up, the sheriff saw him and rode to his side. "The bank was robbed. I'm getting up a posse to go after them, but you'd better go in and see to your pa. He and Miss Swenson were injured in the holdup. Doc Whiteman is with them now."

Fear gripped Micah's heart as the sheriff waved at a group of men who then took off out of town after the robbers. With his heart pounding, Micah jumped down from his horse and pushed his way through the crowd. Nothing could happen to Pa now. He had too much to live for.

The scene that greeted Micah sent his head spinning. Pa lay on the floor, his face ashen and his eyes closed. Blood stained the shoulder of his coat, and the doc worked to stop the bleeding. Micah fell to his knees beside his father.

"Pa, Pa, I'm here. The doc will take care of you."

Doctor Whiteman handed Micah a clean cloth. "Here, hold this over the wound. His bleeding is about stopped, so you can handle it. I'm more concerned about his heart than anything else. His pulse is very weak. We'll get him down to my office in a minute, but I need to check on Miss Swenson right now."

Micah could only nod and hold the cloth over the wound. Then he lifted his gaze to see Camilla as Doc knelt to help her. Blood covered her dress at the shoulder, and she lay perfectly still on the floor. The doctor began working on her then hollered for men to help him get the two victims to the infirmary.

When four men stepped forward, Micah noticed that one of them was Burt. He picked up Camilla as though she were a child and carried her from the bank. Micah's gaze followed him for a moment then turned back to his father. His concern lay more with the man lying on the floor.

"We'll take him now, Micah."

Micah looked up into the eyes of Mr. Hempstead, who stood with three other men holding a cot from the jail.

"We'll put him on this and then carry him down to the doc's place."

Micah stood and swallowed hard before nodding and stepping back. Doc touched his arm. "Walk with them and make sure the bleeding doesn't start up again. I'll hurry on to the infirmary and get things ready for him."

The men lifted Pa onto the cot with gentle hands, then each one picked up a handle and headed for the door. Micah followed the doctor's orders and kept his hand and cloth pressed to his father's shoulder just above the heart. A bullet wound to the shoulder shouldn't be all that serious, but Pa had yet to regain consciousness, and that was more disturbing than the gunshot.

Concern for Pa overrode all thoughts of the ranch and money problems. If Pa didn't survive, they'd have more problems than ever. This wasn't what Ma prayed for. Ma. He'd completely forgotten about her.

He gazed about the crowd now lining the streets and spotted Ellie Bradshaw. He shouted her name, and she ran out to him.

"Ride out to the ranch and tell Ma about Pa. And then out to Hudson's to get Levi. He needs to know too." Maybe this would get his brother back into town and by Pa's side where he belonged.

"My horse is already saddled. I'm going now, and I'll say a prayer for your father." She gathered up her skirts and ran back toward the store where her horse stood tethered to the hitching post.

Micah shook his head. Prayers were not going the way they should, so what good would Ellie's do? A moment later she streaked out of town like the posse was after her and not the robbers. She'd get the word to Levi and Ma.

The four men stepped up to the porch at Doc's place, and Mrs. Whiteman swung open the door. "Bring him in and put him in the room over there to the right. Miss Swenson is on the left." The men did as she instructed, and Micah followed. Once they placed him on the examining table, the men left Micah alone with his father.

Mrs. Whiteman placed a hand on Molly's shoulder. "Sweetie, go get Clara and Tommy and take them to Lettie's to play. We're going to be busy here, so I need them away from the house for now. If Lettie has work to do, you watch the children. Now, scoot."

The young girl didn't say a word but rushed out to do her mother's bidding. Then the doctor's wife grabbed an apron from a hook near the door and slipped her arms into it. The doc joined her in the examining room.

He washed his hands in the basin next to the wall and spoke to his wife. "I left Hannah tending Miss Swenson. If you'll go help her, I'll take care of Joel."

She didn't say a word but hurried across the way to help Hannah. Camilla must need extra help if the doctor was sending his wife to assist Hannah, or Pa was in more serious condition than Micah wanted him to be.

The doctor placed the ends of a stethoscope in his ears and the bell-shaped thing on Pa's chest. The furrowed brow of the doctor squeezed Micah's heart and intensified his fears. He held his father's hand, now limp and cold.

The doctor shook his head. "I'm sorry, Micah. Your pa's heart just couldn't stand the attack. He lost a lot of blood to the bullet wound, but it wouldn't have killed him. It was too much for his heart."

Pa couldn't be gone. Doc had to be mistaken. "No, listen again. He can't be dead." A knot formed in Micah's throat, and his chest constricted with a pain he couldn't define.

The doctor placed his arm across Micah's shoulders. "It's over, Micah. There's nothing I could do. Has someone gone for your mother?"

Micah nodded, but he couldn't speak around the lump that blocked his throat. He blinked back a tear. He wouldn't cry. Men didn't cry in public. He clenched his teeth and continued to hold Pa's lifeless hand.

The doctor stepped back. "I'll leave you alone for the

moment. When your mother gets here, she's going to need your strength to help her through this." He left the room.

"Pa, it's too soon. You weren't supposed to die. Now what are we going to do? We can't do this without you." He swallowed hard and lifted his eyes to the ceiling. "This is a fine way to answer a prayer. You don't care one whit what happens to the Gordon family. Leave us alone. You've caused enough pain."

How foolish he'd been to think a few prayers would solve anything.

Hannah heaped Camilla's soiled clothes on the floor. They'd be disposed of later. Sallie had fetched a gown from her home and had redressed Camilla, being careful with the right arm and shoulder where the bullet had lodged. The medicine Manfred had given earlier had eased the pain, but Camilla still groaned.

Manfred came back, and by the look on his face he had bad news to report. Sallie gasped and hugged him. "It's Mr. Gordon, isn't it? He didn't make it."

"No, he didn't. Too much strain for his heart. I left Micah with him. He indicated someone had gone for his mother. If her daughters aren't with her, she'll need another woman to lend support."

Sallie hugged him tight. "Of course, and I'll be there for her and whoever comes with her."

Hannah's heart ached at the news. To lose someone that close to you would be the most awful thing, especially when it came so sudden. She must help Micah through this. She jerked her thoughts to a halt. What right did she have to do that or to expect her help would even be welcomed? Micah had been nice and polite to her, but they certainly hadn't formed any friendship.

She glanced at the girl Manfred now examined. Camilla was the one who should be giving support to Micah. She could have been killed herself.

Camilla's eye lids fluttered then opened. "What happened? Why are you here, Doctor Whiteman?" Camilla frowned and gazed back and forth between Manfred and Hannah.

Hannah grasped Camilla's hand. "There was a bank holdup, and you were shot in the shoulder. You're at the infirmary now. I'm sure your father will be here as soon as he can leave the bank."

Camilla's eyes closed again. "I remember now. Father and I had just finished talking with Mr. Gordon when two gunmen burst through the back door. Another man came in the front and locked that door. They forced Papa to open the vault. They were stuffing money into sacks when Mr. Gordon lunged for one. That was when he was shot, and then when I went to him, they shot me. It was awful." Tears streamed down her cheeks, and her hand squeezed Hannah's.

"You're going to be all right, Camilla. Doc removed the bullet and we bandaged you up then gave you something for the pain." Hannah smoothed the hair from Camilla's forehead.

"What about Mr. Gordon? Is he all right?"

Hannah glanced up at Manfred, who nodded his assent to tell Camilla. "I'm sorry, but he didn't make it. He died only a few minutes ago."

A sob escaped Camilla's throat. "Oh, no. What will Micah do now? Without Mr. Gordon, they'll lose the ranch." She snapped her mouth closed, yanked her hand from Hannah's, and turned to face the wall.

Lose the ranch? What did she mean by that? The Circle G was supposed to be one of the best spreads in this part of Texas, or at least that's what Manfred and Sallie had said. If what Camilla said was true, Micah was going to need more help than even she could give him. She shook her head and looked to Manfred. "Why would she tell us something like that?"

"I think it's the drug."

Camilla intervened. "It's none of your business, so please forget I said anything at all. Papa would be so angry if he knew I revealed private information about one of our customers. I must speak with Micah as soon as possible."

Manfred placed a hand on her arm. "He's grieving his father now, but I'll let him know. He'll come to you as soon as he feels up to it. Of course he was concerned about you too."

A noise in the foyer interrupted their discussion. Hannah turned her head to see Sallie greet two women. "Mrs. Gordon has arrived," Manfred said. "I must go back there. You'll be fine, but I'm going to keep you here overnight to make sure." With that he turned on his heel and rushed from the room.

Hannah straightened the sheets on Camilla's bed. "I'm sure you'll be fine in the morning, and he'll let you go home."

"Good. I don't want to stay here any longer than I must. Papa will need me to help figure out how much those bank robbers took from us."

A loud wailing from across the way sent a chill up Hannah's spine. Who cared how much money the robbers stole? They had stolen something much more important...Mr. Gordon's life.

She closed her eyes and prayed. *Dear Lord, comfort Mrs.*

Gordon and the whole family as they deal with this. I don't know why Mr. Gordon had to die, but I do know that You share in their grief. Give them the strength they need for the weeks ahead, and reunite this family so they can work together to save the ranch.

If Levi would come home and work beside Micah, then one thing good could come from this tragedy.

CHAPTER 17

MICAH WRAPPED HIS arms around his mother. "Ma, I'm so sorry. I was too late to do anything to save him."

Ma clung to him, her fingernails digging into his flesh, but he ignored the pain. It was nothing compared to the pain in his heart. The doctor's wife had her arms around Rose and Margaret as both girls cried. Tears dampened his shirt and muffled Ma's words. "What am I going to do without Joel? It's too soon for him to be gone. We still need him."

"I know we do. He's the lifeblood of the ranch." He swallowed his own sorrow and frowned. Where was Levi? He should be here. Ma needed all her children around her in this time of crisis. If he didn't show up soon, Micah would go out and drag him back to town.

The doctor came in and approached Micah. "We will need to move Mr. Gordon to the mortician's place. He will embalm the body and then bring it out to the ranch if you desire."

Ma shook her head. "No, I don't want to remember Joel that way at home. We'll speak to the preacher and have the services at the church. That's the place Joel loved to be on Sundays. Will he...will he be able to stay at Mr. Morton's until we can arrange services?"

"I'm sure that can be arranged. I'll speak with him when he arrives shortly. Meanwhile, you can sit here with him until Mr. Morton comes."

"Thank you, Doctor Whiteman." Ma pushed back from

Micah. "You take the girls to the other room. I want to sit alone with Joel for a few minutes."

"Sure, Ma, whatever you want." He turned to his sisters. "Let's go outside."

Mrs. Whiteman shook her head. "No, we'll go into the house and have some tea. You and your sisters can talk around the table."

"Thank you. But if you have coffee, I'd prefer that." His sisters may enjoy sipping tea, but he needed a good strong cup of black coffee to settle his insides. He followed the doctor's wife and his sisters through the door and toward the home behind the offices. Hannah came from the other room.

Camilla. He'd forgotten about her. "Miss Dyer, how is Miss Swenson? Were her injuries serious?"

"No, she'll be fine. Doc removed the bullet and bandaged her wound. He wants her to stay overnight here to make sure no infection sets in." She nodded toward the door across the way. "You may go in and see her, but she may be asleep since the doctor gave her something for her pain."

If he wanted to speak with Camilla, now was the time. After the next half hour or so, things would be much too busy to see her, and he needed to know what had happened at the bank before the holdup. "Thank you. I'll peek in, see if she's awake, and visit a few minutes."

He strode across to the other examining room and opened the door a crack to see if Camilla slept. She lay on the bed with her eyes closed, but she didn't appear to be sleeping. He knocked on the door frame. When she opened her eyes and turned her gaze toward his, he asked, "May I come in a few minutes?"

"Yes, do come in. I'm getting rather lonesome with nobody

around." She blinked her eyes and held out her hand. "I'm so sorry about your father."

He walked to her side and stood there with his hat in one hand and her hand in his other one. "I wanted to check on your condition. Miss Dyer says you'll be fine."

"Yes, I was very lucky." She squeezed his hand with hers. "It all happened so fast. First the men came in and wanted all of us to kneel down with our hands on our heads. When the gunman came toward your father, he resisted and the gunman shot him. Then when I bent down to help him, the gun went off again and hit me. The two just grabbed the money and ran out the back before anyone else could do anything."

Pa, trying to be the hero as usual, but this time it'd gotten him killed. "Pa should have just followed orders like everyone else, but that's not the way he was."

"I know, but I think he was trying to protect the money."

"Protect the money? He should have known he couldn't do that."

"I don't mean the bank's money. I mean his own money. Papa had just finished granting a new loan and given him the money. Your pa was holding it in his hands when the robbers came in. The one who shot your father grabbed it and added it to the rest."

So the loan had been secured. That was good news, but now it was gone. What would happen now? What little may be left in the ranch account would be needed to cover the expenses of the funeral services. God had left them in a mess again. If He'd been at all loving, a good man like Pa would have been spared and one of the robbers killed. "So what happens now?"

"I honestly don't know, but you can talk with my father as

soon as he can get things straight at the bank and see what's left." She pulled her hands away from his and crossed her arms over her chest.

"All right. I hope you can rest now." He stepped back. "I'm going to join my sisters while we wait for Ma. She wanted to sit alone with Pa for a few minutes."

Camilla nodded and turned her head away. Micah's shoulders slumped. So much had happened, and it was barely noon yet. He stepped back from Camilla and shook his head. At least she had tried to help Pa. He almost said something to thank her, but her eyes remained closed, so he left the room. This was probably the last time he'd have with her alone. Why would she want a penniless cowboy to court her now?

His head swam with all that must be done in the next few days. He had no time to worry about Camilla or any woman but his mother and his sisters. Whether Camilla decided to end the courtship or he did made no difference. The end result would be the same.

The door to where his mother sat with Pa was open. Her voice drifted out to the waiting room, and Micah drew closer to see if Ma had a visitor. Through the opening he saw her sitting by Pa's side, holding his hand.

He started to back away, but her words stopped him short. He clutched the brim of his hat and listened.

"Joel, I don't know why you were taken from me so soon, but something good has to come from it. Micah and Levi have to find a common ground and work together from now on. I don't want to lose the one thing you had left to give our boys. I know they grew up at odds with each other. Our fun-loving, carefree Micah and our serious boy who worshipped you and followed you around are so different, but they are both stubborn mules, just like you."

Micah whirled around and strode from the room, anger boiling in his gut. What good could come from what happened today? God had played a cruel trick on Ma, yet here she was thinking something good could come from Pa's death. Whatever good happened wouldn't be God's doing. It'd be up to him and Levi to keep the ranch alive, and unless Levi came home now, even that wasn't going to happen.

As soon as the foreman found Levi and told him the news of his father, he raced into town. All the way regret for the past few weeks gnawed at his conscience. How could he have been so cruel to the two people he loved most in the world? It was all Micah's fault. If he hadn't come home, none of this would have happened.

Anger with Micah and himself boiled in the summer heat as he pulled to a halt in front of the infirmary. He shoved through the door to find Dr. Whiteman alone. "Where's Pa? How is he?"

The doctor shook his head. "Levi, I'm so sorry, but your pa died here a while ago. I'm sorry you didn't get here in time."

Levi clenched his fists at his side. Pa couldn't be dead. There had to be a mistake. "That can't be possible. How did it happen? Ellie told me there had been a bank robbery."

"That's right. Your pa was defending his money and got shot, as did Miss Swenson. The ordeal was too much for your father's heart."

"What do you mean? Pa was in great health. He could ride and rope with the best of them."

"Levi, your pa had a weak heart. He's been hiding it for a while. Even though I told him exercise and healthy eating would help, I don't think he listened. Trauma like he experienced today was more than he could stand."

Levi let the words sink in and tried to comprehend life without his father. "Where is the man or men who did this?" He'd go after the man himself if no one else had.

"I don't know. The sheriff took off with a posse to find them. There were three men on horseback, but they didn't have more than a five-minute lead. If he finds them, they'll be brought back for trial and probably hanging."

Hanging wasn't good enough for anyone who killed Pa. Then he looked around the room and frowned. "Didn't Ma and the girls come in? Ellie said she went to the ranch first and told Ma."

"Your ma and the others have left to go back to the ranch so they can make plans for a funeral service. Mr. Morton has already taken your father's body to his place so he can prepare the body for the funeral."

Levi backed up to a chair and slumped into it. He rested his elbows on his knees with his hands hanging down. Pa was dead, and there had been no time for a good-bye or a chance to seek forgiveness for causing him pain by leaving. With Pa gone, the ranch now belonged to Micah. That sent his stomach churning, but he had no time to think about that now.

He jumped up and headed for the door. "I'm going down to Morton's and see Pa."

The three blocks to the mortuary took only minutes, but in that time Levi made up his mind to let Micah have the ranch and do whatever he wanted with it. Levi had no desire to work the ranch with Micah for a boss. Let the ranch hands stick around and do his bidding.

At the mortuary Mr. Morton led him to the room where he prepared bodies for burial. Pa lay on a table with a sheet draped over him. Mr. Morton pulled the sheet back just enough to expose Pa's face. Levi's throat closed and his heart pounded. Pa hadn't looked this peaceful in many months, maybe years. So Micah had been right about Pa's poor health. Levi clamped his mouth shut and ground his teeth against each other. If he'd only paid attention, he might have been more aware of Pa's condition and done things to make life easier for him.

"Pa, why couldn't you have taken a rest and let me run things? I know more about that ranch than Micah ever will. Things could have been so different if only you'd listened to me."

Guilt tore at Levi's heart with a vengeance and sent doubts flooding through his mind like a mighty storm. He should go back to the ranch and do whatever it took to help his sisters and Ma, but if he went back now, Micah would be in charge, and he didn't deserve to be.

The long tentacles of jealousy began inching themselves around Levi's heart to replace the guilt and doubts. He'd played the good son for so many years expecting Pa to reward him with a share of the ranch. It wasn't fair of Pa to keep hoping for Micah's return when Levi stayed right there to do both his work and his brother's.

"God, why did You let this happen? Why did You bring Micah home to take over the ranch when it should have been mine? I've worked five years to earn Pa's approval, and he gave me nothing."

"He loved you, Levi, and was proud of you."

165

Levi spun around at the words of the voice behind him. "Mr. Morton, I didn't know you were there."

"Of course you didn't, and I know you're grieving, as you should be. But I do want you to know your pa was very proud of the way you worked beside him. He was always bragging on you when he came into town."

"He had a funny way of showing it. At home all he ever talked about was when Micah came back. Now Pa's gone and Micah's here, so I'm left with nothing."

Mr. Morton stepped to Levi's side and pressed his hand on Levi's arm. "Son, your pa left you a great legacy of integrity and a great faith in God. People in this town respected him more than you could possibly know. Don't let your anger toward your brother ruin what you and your pa had."

Easy for him to say, but he hadn't been at the ranch day by day. Pa hadn't bragged or shown much appreciation to Levi. Pa could express his love for Ma openly, but he had a hard time showing it to his sons and daughters. Even when they excelled at school, they heard few words of pride. Pa was a stubborn, close-mouthed man who didn't like others knowing his business or his feelings.

"Thank you, Mr. Morton. I'll see you at the services." He headed for the door and then back to the infirmary to get his horse. He'd have to go out to the ranch eventually, and it may as well be now as later. Maybe he could see Ma without having to encounter Micah. That was one fight he really didn't care to have today, and their meeting would turn into a fight. No doubt about it.

He unhitched his horse and looked up to see Ellie standing by the post. She bit her lip and clasped her hands about her middle. "Did you see your pa?"

Levi nodded. "I was at Morton's just now."

She reached over and grasped his arm. "I'm so sorry. Your pa was a wonderful man."

"So I've been told." He covered her hand and pulled her to him in an embrace. "Ellie, what am I going to do now?"

She rested her head against his chest. "I don't know. Your ma needs you, so perhaps you should go back to the ranch. Your sisters need you too. Go, take care of them, and I'll be waiting here in town for you when you return."

Levi rested his chin on her head. This was one girl he wanted to spend the rest of his life with, and as soon as he could get his head and heart straightened out, he'd tell her again to make it official.

"Thank you, Ellie. I do plan to go see Ma now." He bent down and kissed her cheek. "Thank you for saying you'll wait for me. Knowing that you'll be here will get me through this."

He released her and swung up onto his horse. With one last smile and a tip of his hat, Levi left Ellie and headed for home.

CHAPTER 18

ICAH RODE OUT to gather the men and let them know what had happened to Pa. Some of the cowboys had been with the crew for many years and would take the news hard because they loved and respected Pa. Others had only come on board in the past few years, and Micah had no idea as to how they would react.

His head spun with all the details that needed to be worked out in the days and weeks ahead. Pa had a will, and Micah had left Ma to take care of finding it. She planned to take it in to that new lawyer Hightower and let him take care of any legalities that needed to be handled since Mr. Murphy hadn't returned from his trip. One thing for sure, Pa hadn't changed his will in the past few years, so the ranch now became his full responsibility, and one he didn't want to accept.

Any plans for a relationship with Camilla evaporated with the events of the day, but that was just as well since he would have probably ended it soon anyway if she didn't reject him first. He didn't have time for a woman in his life right now.

Once again the image of Hannah Dyer popped into his head. What a contrast to Camilla. Despite her handicap Hannah enjoyed life and had a sincerity about her that Camilla sorely lacked. If he hadn't seen Hannah's odd-looking shoe, he'd have never known she had any kind of deformity.

He shook his shoulders. Lately, every time he thought about Camilla, Hannah managed to make an appearance too. As he rode, the good time they'd had at the dance and her happiness that day crowded his thoughts. It seemed as though everyone in town had come to love Dr. Whiteman's new nurse. When things settled down a bit, maybe he could explore the reasons she kept intruding into his thoughts, but now he had another job to do.

The herd came into view, and the foreman, Roy Bateman, spotted Micah and waved. He rode over to Micah's mount. "Didn't expect to see you here this late in the afternoon. We were about to come on back in."

"I need you to gather everyone here before we head back. I have some things I have to share now that may make a big difference on what happens when we get back to the bunkhouse."

Roy shoved his hat back on his head. "You sound serious. What's up?"

"I'd rather tell everyone at once." Although Roy probably should know first, Micah didn't want to tell the news twice. Once was plenty enough.

Roy turned back to the herd and whistled then waved at the group of men headed his way. In only a few minutes all were gathered around, questions filling their eyes.

"Micah's come out to tell us something, so listen up," Roy commanded.

Micah let his gaze wander over the men. Some he barely knew and others he'd grown up around. A deep breath then letting it go bolstered his courage. "As you might know, Pa went into town this morning to see the banker, Mr. Swenson. While he was there, the bank was robbed, and Pa and Camilla Swenson were shot." The men murmured among themselves then quieted down and looked to him.

A lump once again formed in Micah's throat, and he had to swallow twice to get the next words out. "Pa didn't make it. His heart gave out on him and he died at Doc Whiteman's place."

Frowns and looks of dismay followed the announcement along with more murmurs and questions among the men.

Roy leaned forward in his saddle. "Micah, I'm so sorry. What a terrible thing for your mother to bear. What is this going to mean for you and the ranch?"

"It's too early to tell. The bank granted an extension on the loan before the robbery, but unfortunately the money that Pa was going to use was stolen by the bandits. So to be honest, for now everything is up in the air. I'll be taking Pa's place unless Levi will come home and help. If any of you don't want to stay, then you're free to go." He'd rather find out who was loyal and ready to stay on now under all the uncertainty than lie to them about the future of the ranch.

Shorty said, "You can count on me, son. I've been around here too long to go anywhere else now."

Roy nodded and sat tall in his saddle. "Count on me too. Figure I've done too much with this herd not to stick around and see it to the end."

Micah gazed around the group. "Anybody want to leave? Now's your chance."

They all shook their heads, and their words of encouragement filled Micah with hope that they'd pull through. "All right, we're in this together. Ma's back at the house with the girls, so I'll let her know that you're going to work with us. She'll appreciate that."

Shorty rode up beside Micah. "What about Levi? Will he come back?"

"I have no idea, but I'm going to do everything I can to get him to listen to me and become a partner. We'll know more when we go over the will in the next few days." If he could find Levi, he'd hogtie that boy and make him listen to reason. Now, of all times, he should be home with his family.

Levi pulled his horse to a stop at the corral and dismounted. He stared at the house a few minutes before heading for the porch, praying Micah was off somewhere else. When he entered the house, Rose ran to him and wrapped her arms around him.

"Levi! You came. I'm so glad you're home."

The other women in the room turned, and Ma stood. The look on her face sent guilt mingled with sorrow straight to his soul. She held out her arms, and he took three strides to be enveloped in her hug. "Ma, I'm so sorry. Doc Whiteman told me what happened."

"I'm so glad you're here. We need you."

"Isn't Micah around to take care of things?" He glanced around, but the girls were alone.

"He went out to find Roy and the others to tell them about your pa. I found Pa's will in the safe in his office. We'll take it in to Mr. Hightower and let him take care of whatever needs to be done." Ma gripped Levi's hands. "I'm sorry, Levi, but he never got around to changing it."

She held his arm and led him to the parlor. His sisters left the room and headed upstairs. Levi clenched his teeth. That meant Micah had full control. He'd ruin the ranch in a few months. He couldn't let him do that, but he couldn't work under his brother either. "Then Micah's going to be running things around here without me. I'm going back to Hudson's. He's paying me good wages, and I hope to get a spread of my own next year."

Ma's eyes glistened with tears, and she gripped his arms, her fingers digging into his skin. Pain shot up to his shoulders, but he ignored it and set his jaw in determination to resist her pleas.

"We need you here, Levi. Hudson has plenty of men to run things for him. He doesn't need you like we do. I don't know everything that's going on, but I know the ranch is struggling financially right now."

Levi stiffened. "Did Micah tell you that?"

Ma nodded. "He's looked at the ledgers a few times now. I knew in general we were struggling, but your brother knows more specifics and has ideas that could help."

"Bully for him," Levi muttered.

Ma's voice grew sharper. "Now that your father is gone, this ranch will need both of you to keep it afloat. You've put so much of your life into this ranch. How could you leave it now?"

"That's the problem. I stayed by Pa and helped him after Micah ran off on his own. I played the good son and did everything Pa wanted me to do. For five years I listened to him talk about Micah and how things would be when he returned. I was doing all the work, but he got all the attention. Now I have nothing to show for those years. If the ranch is struggling, then even the bit he planned to give me is gone."

"Son, Pa was proud of you in more ways than one. Yes, you stayed here and worked hard for him, and you deserve some credit for that. He loved you, and he was praying and thinking through how he could change his will. He never got around to it, but he had come to the decision that you and Micah should share in the ranch."

"Maybe so, but it's too late to change things now. I have to start out on my own and earn what I can. I planned to ask Ellie to marry me this fall, but now that will have to wait awhile, maybe a year or more. I don't want to go into marriage with nothing to support her."

Ma loosened her grip and stepped back. "I understand that, and Ellie is a wonderful girl. I know she'll wait for you however long it takes, but it doesn't have to be a year. You can be married and live here on the ranch. Margaret and James will live in town after they're married. This will always be your home."

His heart ached at the hope in Ma's voice. He saw no way he and Ellie could live here as long as Micah lived in the same house. At least if he was alone, he could live in the bunkhouse and leave the house for Micah and the girls. What was he thinking? He had no plans to come back here and live at all.

"I'm sorry, Ma, but that won't work." He bent down to kiss her cheek. "I'll see you at the services. I understand they'll be at the church."

"That's right, on Monday." She clung to him tighter now. "Please don't go. Wait until Micah gets back and talk this out with him."

He removed her hands as gently as possible and shook his head. "No. It's best for me not to see him with all the anger I hold toward him right now." He jammed his hat on his head and turned to leave before she could change his mind.

With a heavy heart he mounted his horse. Then he spurred his horse and rode away, guilt, grief, anger, and jealousy fighting for a place in his soul.

Hannah checked on Camilla one more time to make sure she rested comfortably and had no pain. Her father had left a few minutes earlier, and by the look on her face and her tight lips, their conversation must have upset her.

"Are you all right, Camilla?" Hannah reached for Camilla's wrist to record her pulse, which now raced beneath Hannah's fingers.

"I will be when those thieves are caught and that money is returned. People are running scared and want to take their money out of their accounts. I wish I could be there with Papa to help him."

"Well, that won't happen for a few days, and I'm sure he can convince people to keep their money in the bank. Right now you have to calm down and get your pulse back to normal. It's much too fast at the moment."

Camilla sighed and let her shoulders drop. "All right, but it's hard to be calm when I want to be with Papa."

"Maybe I can bring a smile to your face."

Hannah jumped at the voice from the doorway, but Camilla's face did light up with a smile.

"Mr. Hightower, how good to see you."

He approached the bed with a handful of daisies. "I saw your father a few minutes ago, and he said you were ready for visitors, so here I am." He held out the flowers. "I wish they were roses, but there were none to be found in town, so these will have to do."

Hannah stepped back. "If you'll excuse me, I'll leave you two to visit, and I'll bring a vase for the flowers when I return." Maybe it wasn't good protocol to leave the two of them alone, but Hannah had no desire to listen to their small talk. The way Camilla gazed at Mr. Hightower certainly proved she'd put Micah completely out of her mind and now concentrated on the new lawyer.

How unfair to Micah. He didn't need Camilla's rejection on top of his father's death and Levi's animosity. If Hannah could be with Micah now, she'd give him all the support and love he so desperately needed.

She headed for the kitchen to find a container for the flowers and to prepare a cup of tea for herself. Sallie peeled potatoes by the sink, and Hannah picked up the teapot filled with hot water.

"How's our patient? Does she need anything?"

Hannah reached for the box of tea in the cabinet. "Not that I know of. Alex Hightower is with her now. He came to visit after her father left."

"And you left them alone?" Sallie stopped peeling and raised her eyebrows.

"Yes, and what difference does it make? She's in a hospital, so to speak. I don't think anything will happen to compromise their reputations." All these silly rules of courting were nothing but a pain. She sat down at the table to pour the hot water over the tea leaves in her cup.

Sallie wiped her hands with her apron. "You don't appear to be very happy. What's bothering you?"

"Oh, I don't know. I keep thinking about the Gordon family and how sad it is that Mr. Gordon died. This is going to be a hard time for them."

"Yes, it is." Sallie pulled out a chair and sat across from Hannah. "But I sense there's more to it than that. Are you thinking more of Micah Gordon and how hard it will be for him?"

Hannah dipped her head. "I suppose I am. He hasn't

shown any interest in me, but he's been kind and considerate, especially at my party."

"That must be something he learned while he was away, because it certainly isn't the way he would have acted back before he left. I like and admire the man he's become. I understand he has a good mind and was always smart in school, but he always tended to think of himself and his own pleasure first."

A sign escaped Hannah, and she blinked her eyes to ward off the tears wanting to form there. "I admire him too. And he's about the most handsome man I've seen in a long time. When he held me to dance the other night, something happened like I'd never experienced before, and I didn't want the time to ever end."

"Oh, Hannah, please guard your heart. There's so much we don't know about the five years he was away. He seems like a better person, but with all the problems he's facing right now, he might up and run off again."

Hannah shook her head and then sipped her tea, the warm liquid soothing her spirits. The Micah she'd seen the past few weeks would face whatever came his way. At least that's what she'd pray he'd do.

CHAPTER 19

Ruth boarded the carriage with a heavy heart. Her Joel would be laid to rest today. Friends from church and neighboring ranches had been in and out of her home all weekend, but today she gathered with her children to pay last respects to the man they loved.

Joel's younger brother and his family had come and stayed in town, but his sister lived too far away to make the trip. A cup of loneliness joined her sorrow because her own sister and aunt could not be with them today. If only travel didn't take so long by train from the Northeast.

Margaret climbed into the seat behind Ruth and gripped her shoulder. "Reverend Weatherby will bring a beautiful message. We'll all be there for you."

Rose joined her sister, but she had nothing to say. Her red eyes and splotched cheeks told their own story. Rose gripped Margaret's hands like she planned to never let them go. Ruth smiled at both girls. "I want to see a bit of a smile. Pa wouldn't like for you to be so sad. We'll miss him so much, but he'd tell us he's having a very good time in heaven meeting all his family gone before and all those disciples he read about in the Bible."

Both girls nodded but said nothing as Ruth turned back to the front. Now she had to convince herself of the same words she'd said to her girls.

Micah hoisted himself up beside her and grabbed the reins. He clicked his tongue and flicked the reins over the horses' backs. "Time to go. Don't want to be late."

Ruth settled back to let her elder son drive them to town.

She allowed her thoughts to wander and remembered so many good times of the past twenty-six, almost twenty-seven, years of marriage to the man who had captured her heart the first time she laid eyes on him at a party in honor of his parents' anniversary. Two years older than she had been, he'd already gone west to Texas to raise horses and cattle.

His rugged good looks, height, and Christian faith attracted her attention, and by the end of the evening, she'd decided she'd fallen in love with Joel Gordon. Ruth bit her lip. He still had those rugged good looks even though he'd aged, and she loved him even more now than she had all those years ago. Micah had come along toward the end of their second year of marriage, so they hadn't much time to be alone as a young couple. Responsibilities for the ranch and a family took precedence, but Joel had never failed to let her know how much he loved her.

How would she ever be able to get along without his encouragement, his embraces, his kisses? She'd have her children around to fill the loneliness of the house, but nothing could fill the empty spaces in her heart or the empty space in their bed. Tears rose, and she let one slip down her cheek before wiping them away. She'd cry later when she was alone. Now she had to be strong for her family.

Micah must have sensed her pain because he reached over and squeezed her hand. He drove the carriage into the church yard and stopped by the hitching post. He jumped down then turned to lift Ruth to the ground. When her feet touched earth, he bent slightly and hugged her to his chest. His arms brought great comfort, but she needed Levi's too.

"We'll make it through this day. You have all of us here to love you and support you." Micah leaned his cheek against her head.

She tilted her head to look straight in his eyes. Her hand brushed his cheek. "I know we will. I'm so thankful you came home when you did. Pa was so happy to have you back."

"I'm glad I came back too." He released her and stepped back to offer his arm to escort her into the church.

Friends from all over the area filled the church as a testimony of their respect and love for Joel Gordon. Reverend Weatherby had the family members remain outside for a few minutes before lining them up to proceed into the church. With Micah gripping her arm, Ruth climbed the few steps up to the porch of the church. Reverend Weatherby went inside and down the aisle to the pulpit. When he arrived there, he faced the congregation and lifted his hands, asking them to rise.

Mr. Morton, with Micah and Ruth right behind him, led the family down to the front pew. As they were seated, Ruth spotted Levi coming to join them. He sat at the opposite end from her and Micah, but a little of the sadness lifted to see her younger son with his sisters. If only he'd stay around and visit with the family and come out to the ranch, she could talk with him more and convince him he needed to come home for good.

The services began with the pastor's wife singing "The Lord's Prayer." As her clear soprano voice lifted the last words heavenward, "For Thine is the kingdom, and the power, and the glory, forever," Ruth's heart soared with them. God was forever, and His kingdom awaited all those who called on His Son, Jesus, as their Savior and Lord. She would see Joel again, but the waiting for that day would be hard.

The remainder of the service passed with several friends offering up memories of Joel and Reverend Weatherby's message giving comfort to the grieving family. It had been a blessed day when the Lord had led this young preacher to their town. Ruth prayed he'd be around a long time with his young family and talented wife.

When the service ended, Mr. Morton escorted Ruth to the casket for a final good-bye. She touched Joel's cheeks and blinked her eyes. "Farewell, my love, until I see you again."

Micah then led her back up the aisle to the back of the church and the vestibule where she would greet guests as they offered condolences. As the line came to an end, Micah tensed beside her, his hand tightening its grip on her arm. The reason for the tension appeared before her. Camilla Swenson held out her hand, but behind her, Levi scooted past and bolted for the door.

"It was a lovely service, Mrs. Gordon. I'm sorry for your loss. Papa and I are honored to have been friends with Mr. Gordon."

Ruth listened to Camilla's words, but her eyes followed Levi. Micah released her arm, but Ruth grabbed him to make him stay.

Camilla's next words were aimed at Micah. "I'm sorry, Micah. Your pa was a good man."

Ruth peered up at her son and the firm set of his jaw. He wanted to go after Levi, but now was not the time. He said nothing to Camilla but nodded his head in answer to her words.

Camilla turned and headed down the steps, where she joined Alexander Hightower and linked her arm with his.

Heartache for Micah rose in Ruth, but joy that the relationship had ended shoved the hurt aside. Her son's heart may be broken now, but he'd find another young woman more worthy of his attentions. Not that Camilla wasn't worthy, but she simply wasn't the type Ruth had envisioned for her son, especially after his revelation a few days ago that his feelings for her weren't as strong as they should be.

At that moment Dr. Whiteman and his wife along with Hannah Dyer appeared to offer words of kindness and condolence. Ruth eyed Hannah. Now there was a girl who'd be perfect for Micah, and from the look in her eyes as she spoke with him, her interest in him had already begun. If Ruth could plant the seed in Micah's head, it wouldn't take much to get it growing and blossoming into a fine relationship. Ruth mentally added Hannah's name to her list of prayers for her family.

Wishing he'd gone after Levi, Micah forced himself to listen to all the praises for his father, Ma's gentle pressure on his arm preventing his leaving. The respect and admiration of so many touched Micah, and he now wished he had come home sooner. For years he'd believed his father favored Levi because he loved the ranch and always did what Pa wanted done. Micah had missed out on getting to know his father as a man and not a hotheaded boy bent on independence.

When Camilla had come through the vestibule and paused to give her condolences to Ma, mixed feelings of jealousy and relief had pierced his heart. Then he observed the expression on her face as she spoke her condolences. Nothing she said came from the heart. How could he have been blinded by her beauty? That was easy. He had always looked for beauty before anything else in the women he sought for companionship. When she joined the new lawyer out on the church lawn, relief emerged as the winner and replaced any jealousy he might have had earlier. He didn't need the distraction of Camilla as he worked to keep his family together.

When he turned his attention back to those coming from the church, the doctor and his wife stood before him. Doc Whiteman grasped Micah's hand. "I'm sorry I couldn't do more to save your father. He was a good man, but stubborn. He refused to let his health keep him from doing what he loved."

"You did your best, and we appreciate it. Thank you for spending so much time with him."

Mrs. Whiteman tucked her hand under the doc's arm. "If there's anything you or your mother need, please let us know. Everyone loved and respected your father."

"I'm beginning to find that out."

"Too bad you didn't come home sooner," the doctor commented.

Mrs. Whiteman squeezed her husband's arm and smiled. "Don't go laying guilt on this fine young man. He and his brother will do the ranch good." She gazed about. "Speaking of which, where is Levi? I saw him during the service, but not since then."

Micah wanted to know that himself. "I'm not sure. He was here moments ago, but left the church. We've been busy here talking with folks, so I don't know where he went. I'm sure he's around somewhere." At least Micah hoped so, for the sake of his mother and his sisters.

The couple moved on, and Hannah Dyer stepped in front of him. "Micah, I truly am sorry for your loss. I know it leaves a void in your life that no one else can fill. I wish we could have done more for him."

One look into her clear blue eyes sent her sincere words of condolence straight to his heart. No guile, only honesty shone from her smile as she spoke. The emotion he'd suppressed when he'd been near her before again rose to the surface. She wasn't one of the young ladies he'd be able to woo and then leave and forget.

"Thank you, Miss Dyer. You and the doctor helped Pa all you could." Funny, as he gazed at her, all his misgivings about her disability faded away. She hadn't been at all clumsy when he'd danced with her. He realized there was so much more to her than either her beauty or her disability. She had a depth of love and caring that spread to all those around her, including him. When things looked clearer, he would make the effort to get to know more about this girl from Mississippi.

"Take care, Micah, and if you or your sisters need anything, let us know." Then she joined her sister and the doctor on the steps and left the church.

His gaze followed her to the edge of the lawn and would have tracked her longer, but Ma nudged him. "Micah, I was just telling Mrs. Weatherby how much her singing meant to us. Didn't you think it was beautiful?"

Micah turned his attention to the preacher's wife. "Yes, yes, I did. You have a wonderful voice, and we appreciate your sharing it with us. It was exactly what Pa would have wanted." Indeed, the clear, sweet notes of the song had set the tone for the entire service.

Reverend Weatherby and his wife were the last ones, so Micah assisted Ma down the steps and out to their carriage. His aunt and uncle and cousins were all standing in a small group waiting for him and Ma. Rose was deep in conversation with two of their cousins.

Mr. Morton and six of Pa's ranching friends carried the casket down the steps and over to the cemetery next to the church. A smaller crowd gathered around the freshly dug grave, and Reverend Weatherby spoke.

"Friends and family gather here to say good-bye to a man God has called home. In John chapter fourteen, Jesus tells us, 'Let not your heart be troubled: ye believe in God, believe also in me. In my Father's house are many mansions: if it were not so, I would have told you. I go to prepare a place for you. And if I go and prepare a place for you, I will come again, and receive you unto myself; that where I am, there ye may be also.' Now Jesus has drawn Joel Gordon unto that prepared place. Because He has prepared a place for us, we too can know that one day we will join Joel to live in one of those mansions. Jesus is the way, the truth, and the life, and through Him we have life everlasting."

Micah listened, but the words had no meaning for him. God had played a cruel joke on them all by taking Pa too soon. Ma may think of God as a loving Father, but that would never be the case for Micah. From now on he'd be in charge, and he didn't need God's help. He needed Levi to help and be a part of the business, but his brother had disappeared once again.

Anger and resentment clawed their way into Micah's heart. Another cruel trick of God to take away the one person who knew more about the ranch and Pa's dreams for it than anyone else. If he could get his hands on that little brother now, he might strangle him—or at least try to knock some sense into his head.

Levi stood out of sight at the corner of the church, hidden by an old oak tree. The reverend's words floated over to his spot. He blinked back tears, hot from the resentment flowing through his veins. *Why did you have to leave before giving me a chance? I should be the one running the outfit, not Micah. Why couldn't you have trusted me to take over and relieve some of the burden?*

Pa had never confided the fact that the ranch was in financial trouble. In fact, he'd never shared much of anything about the money end of the ranch. Levi could rope, brand, and herd with the best of them, but that hadn't been good enough. Micah had been back only a few weeks, and in that time he had learned more about the finances than Levi could ever hope to be told. If that's the way Pa wanted it, then that's the way it'd be, and Levi wouldn't be a part of it. Pride reared its ugly head now. He'd never go home and ask Micah to take him back. He'd return as his own man or not at all.

Levi waited until his sisters and mother had all laid a flower on top of the casket before turning away. He didn't care to see the dirt shoveled in to bury the casket. Tomorrow the will would be read, and after that Levi would ride out of their lives and start planning for his own future. He'd have to stand firm and not let his mother or his sisters persuade him to change his course.

Levi mounted his horse and rode out toward the Hudson spread, anger at Micah overtaking the grief that had gripped him only minutes ago. Levi clenched his teeth and spurred his horse to a full gallop. The faster he could get away from the past, the sooner he could get on with his future.

CHAPTER 20

ICAH SAT WITH his mother, his sisters, and Levi across the desk from Alexander Hightower in the lawyer's new office. The mayor had spared no expense in setting up the attorney in fine surroundings. A large window gave a view of Main Street and the hotel across the street. Since the land office had moved into the courthouse, this building had sat vacant until Hightower arrived.

The lawyer shuffled some papers on his desk. "That was a lovely service yesterday, Mrs. Gordon. It paid great honor to your dear departed husband."

"Thank you, Mr. Hightower. Reverend Weatherby offered a wonderful tribute for Joel. My family and I are most grateful for his encouraging words."

Once again the lawyer shuffled the papers then settled on one document. "I have your husband's last will and testament, and it all seems in order." He glanced up at Micah then over to Levi.

Micah's mind raced with the knowledge of what the contents would mean to each one seated around the desk. Did anyone besides Ma and he know how bad the financial situation really was before Pa died? From the expressions on their faces, they had no anxieties about what Mr. Hightower would reveal. Only Levi wore any signs of concern, but that could be because he knew what Pa had written.

The lawyer cleared his throat and gazed at each one of them for a moment. "Besides the ranch being left to his oldest son, Micah, there is little of any value except the contents of the home. The ranch is mortgaged to the maximum allowed."

Ma bit her lip, but the girls gasped and turned their eyes to Micah. Levi shook his head. "I don't believe it. The ranch was doing fine a few months ago."

Micah stared at Levi and sensed the anger building in his brother. "I don't think so. I've looked over the books very carefully, and we owe more than we're taking in. That was why Pa came into town and was at the bank when it was robbed."

"You're lying. Pa would have told me if anything was wrong." Levi slammed his fist on the desk and jumped to his feet. "He talked about how he was going to give each of us enough inheritance to—I still don't believe it."

Ma reached over and grasped Levi's arm. "Mr. Hightower is right. The ranch has been in trouble for a while. Pa didn't want any of you to know it, and the only reason I do is because I knew him so well."

Mr. Hightower stood and placed the will back into a folder. "I've talked to the authorities and to Mr. Swenson. The bank money has not been recovered, but since the loan was granted and the papers signed, the bank will make good on it and give Micah the money he needs to finish the year before roundup." He leaned on his desk and peered at Micah. "The one stipulation is that you pay it back as soon as you sell the cattle you have ready for market. Then the bank will extend the mortgage."

Levi shoved his hat on his head and glared at Micah. "That's going to be a mighty hard agreement for you to keep, brother. Good luck." Then he stood and strode from the room.

The girls whispered among themselves, and Ma turned tear-filled eyes to Micah. "You have to talk to him and make him listen. He needs to understand that he must come back and help you."

"I've tried, but he won't even talk to me. Always heads in

the opposite direction when I try to approach him. Even yesterday he made sure he was never close enough for me to say anything to him, and you stopped me from going after him."

"Then you have to go out to the Hudson place and make him listen." She glanced at Mr. Hightower then stood. "Thank you for letting us know what the bank will do. Come, girls, it's time to go home."

She sent one last plea to Micah as she left. "Go get your brother and work things out."

By the time Micah reached the street, Levi's dust filled the street. Micah clenched his jaw. He would not follow and beg Levi to come home. He may not believe Micah's story about wanting to share the ranch anyway. He grabbed the reins of his horse and washed his hands of any more dealing with his brother. As far as he was concerned, Levi could stay at the Hudson ranch. He would find a way to make things work.

Even as he thought it, his heart told him different. Without Levi, there would be no one to help take care of the herds. Roy was a good foreman, but could he be depended on to do everything for the ranch that needed to be done in the days before the roundup and the drive to market?

Micah glanced across at the bank. Might as well settle that score now. He led his horse across the street and tethered it to the railing at the bank boardwalk. Camilla had been at the funeral service but had left before the burial. Her pale face told the story of her injuries and how much the effort to be at the church had cost her. He had to admire her for that, even if, as he suspected, she'd done it simply to make an appearance and remind others of what happened to her.

He stepped into the bank, now reopened after the robbery. He spotted Mr. Swenson and strode in his direction. "Good day, Mr. Swenson. Thank you for coming to Pa's funeral, and let Camilla know how much we all appreciated her being there. I know it could not have been easy for her, with her injuries."

The banker stood and shook Micah's hand. "We wanted to support you and the family, but it did tire out Camilla. I urged her not to come in to the bank today, so she's home resting. Our housekeeper will take good care of her." He sat down and indicated the chair across from him.

Micah sat and rolled the brim of his hat with his hands. "Have you heard any more about the robbers?"

"Sheriff just left here. Seems they may have made their way to Barksdale. He's going over there now to check it out. Maybe we'll get our money back yet." He reached into his middle drawer and pulled out a slip of paper. "Here's a bank draft for what we agreed to with your father. The bank is prepared to cover the amount so you can prepare your herd for market."

Micah held the draft and stared at the amount. How would they ever be able to pay back that much and take care of the other expenses? He'd have to go over the books even more thoroughly now. "Thank you, Mr. Swenson. I didn't really expect this."

"Your father was an honest man and always took care of his obligations. We feel sure that you will carry on your father's integrity." He extended his hand toward Micah.

"We'll do our best." He shook Mr. Swenson's hand with a firm grip to hide the trembling and uncertainty not only in his heart but also in every fiber of his being. It was one thing to run the ranch, but another thing entirely to keep Pa's reputation intact.

"I'm sure you will."

The confidence in the banker's voice carried Micah out to his horse and rang in his soul all the way home. He glanced toward the heavens. "Well, God, You've done it again. This is a fine mess I'm in, and all You've done is complicate it even more. Why did You have to let Pa die? If You cared about our family at all, You would have spared his life. I don't know why anybody would put any trust into You." The questions he'd asked before still had no answers.

The Gordon family didn't need any more problems, but trying to live a life he didn't want might be the biggest one of all.

Hannah stood on the wraparound front porch of the infirmary and leaned against the railing. Levi left a cloud of dust behind as he thundered away from town. From what she'd heard, he was in town for the reading of the will. That must not have gone well.

She turned her attention toward town and left the porch to walk that way, using a trip to the general store as an excuse to find out what had happened. Not that she was nosy, but concern for Micah and his new responsibilities grew in her heart. She had to find out.

When she turned onto Main Street, she spotted Micah leaving the bank. He mounted his horse and rode toward Hannah, leaving his family behind. She waited at the corner for him to pass her. Hannah winced at the thin line that closed his mouth. When she lifted a hand in greeting, he nodded but didn't look at her. The firm set of his shoulders and that grim expression meant Levi had hurt him again.

Her gaze followed him until he disappeared down the road out to his ranch.

Her heart grew heavy with the grief Micah must feel. He'd lost his father, and his brother appeared to have abandoned his family. Margaret stood by the carriage speaking to her mother and sisters. A moment later she stepped back and turned in Hannah's direction.

She waited for Hannah to reach her. "Hannah, I'm so glad to see you." She glanced at her mother. "You all go on home. James will bring me later. I want to talk with Hannah."

Mrs. Gordon nodded. "Good afternoon, Hannah. Tell your sister I appreciated the family coming to the services yesterday."

"I most certainly will. We all wanted to be there to show our support to your family during this time of loss."

"Thank you." She clicked her tongue and snapped the reins. "We'll see you at the ranch, Margaret. Will you be in time for supper?"

"I'm not sure, but I will ask James if he'd like to come out and have supper with us."

After the carriage rolled away, Margaret grasped Hannah's arm. "Are you in a hurry to go anywhere? I'd like to have a bit of tea and a chance to talk."

"I'm in no hurry at all. The infirmary has been slow today. Doctor Whiteman can manage without me for a while if anything does happen." Nothing else loomed more important than giving Margaret Gordon an opportunity share her feelings. Hannah liked Micah's sister and looked forward to getting to know her better. Besides, she was curious as to what Margaret might have to say.

Hannah inclined her head toward the building across the

street and up the block. "Let's go to the hotel. It's quiet there, and they have wonderful tea."

Margaret walked in silence beside Hannah, not revealing anything about the reason for wanting this visit. Speculation filled Hannah's thoughts as they strolled toward the hotel. Did Margaret want her to intervene in the feud between her brothers? But what could Hannah do?

Once inside the hotel and in the dining room, the serving girl took their order for tea and shortcake. After the girl left, Margaret breathed deeply and leaned forward with her hands on the table.

"I wanted to talk to you because I didn't want to burden Ma with my worries, and I needed some advice. Our family is at an impasse. As you have seen, Levi hasn't been happy with Micah's return to town, and even with Pa's passing he refuses to come home. With him gone from the ranch, I'm worried about how Micah will handle everything, especially since Camilla Swenson has apparently lost interest in him."

Pain for the humiliation Micah must feel to be rejected not only by his brother but also by the girl he courted stabbed Hannah's heart. "I don't know him well, but from what I've observed, Micah seems strong. He'll recover from Camilla's rejection, and he'll do a good job with the ranch."

"If only that could be so. I wish Pa hadn't been taken from us so soon. He was the backbone of the ranch, and I didn't know until today that we had any financial…oh, dear. You don't want to hear all this."

Although rumors had floated around about the bank robbers taking money Mr. Gordon had received as a loan, Hannah had no idea there had been any money problems, and there had been no reason for her to know. It wasn't any of her business.

Hannah reached across the table for Margaret's hands. They were ice cold to the touch and trembled as Hannah grasped them. "I'm so sorry about your father and the rift between your brothers, but you have to be strong for your ma and help her through this. The best thing we can do for Micah and Levi is to pray for them to resolve their differences."

"You're right, but those two boys are so stubborn. They're worse than Pa ever was. Micah's not going to beg Levi to come home, and Levi isn't going to come home and beg for forgiveness when he'll have to take orders from Micah. God has to do something with them, but I don't know what."

"Our Lord will figure it out, but in the meantime, you might try talking with Ellie. From what I've heard, she and Levi are courting. Maybe Ellie can have a little persuasive power to ease his attitude and get him to see the big picture."

The serving girl set their tea and cakes in from of them then disappeared. Hannah released Margaret's hands and sniffed the aroma filling the air, letting the peppermint scent fill her senses. "Tea always makes me feel better, and if it has peppermint, that's even better."

"Yes, it does help." Margaret sipped a bit then set her cup on its saucer and wrapped her hands around it. "I think you're right. Ellie may be our best way to get Levi to soften his attitude. When we leave here, I'll go to Ellie's and speak with her. Perhaps she'll have some ideas as to how to reach that pigheaded brother of mine."

Hannah picked up a tea cake. "That sounds like a very good idea to me."

She sighed. "Then there's Micah. He never really cared about ranching—that's why he went away in the first place. And now he's stuck doing all the work himself, without

Levi's help. I worry if things get bad enough, he'll just up and leave again, and then where will we be?"

Margaret leaned forward again and this time grabbed Hannah's hand. "I know just the thing for Micah. He needs to have someone to care about him like Levi does. It makes such a difference to have someone who cares and gives you support. I think you're the perfect person to do it."

Hannah almost choked on her tea cake. She grabbed her cup of tea and gulped the hot liquid. It burned for a moment, but it helped the cake go down. She swallowed hard then cleared her throat. "Me! Micah hardly speaks to me. He was nice to me at the party, but that's because he's a gentleman and he had to be polite to the guest of honor."

"I don't think so. Camilla is too sophisticated for him and doesn't care one whit about other people. You're down-to-earth, smart, and care about people, and that's what Micah needs."

Hannah winced at the comparison to Camilla, but then realized Margaret's description was meant as a compliment. "I'm not sure about that, but if you think it'll help, I'll try to visit with him and maybe get him to share his feelings." She'd like nothing better than to have a relationship with Micah, but doing so would take a lot more than simply wanting it.

CHAPTER 21

ICAH RODE BACK to the ranch ahead of the others. Another hot, dry, August day had him covered in dust from chasing strays and moving the herd to better grasses that had dwindled to almost nothing. The Circle G wasn't the only ranch suffering from the drought.

The words to curse the God who had put him into this position threatened to spill from his mouth, but he restrained them once again. He had to keep some semblance of respect, or the men would leave. They had no loyalty to Micah, only to the ranch and the memory of his father. How long he'd be able to put up with the heat, the dust, and the smells of a herd he didn't know, but no end appeared to be in sight.

Since his father's funeral two weeks ago, they'd already lost several head to the dry heat, and if he didn't do something about it, more would be lost, and that meant fewer steers to drive to market. So far he had no clue as to how to save the rest of the herd. Roy had offered a few suggestions, but none were feasible at this point. More feed and a better source of water took money, and that was as scarce as the rain.

Levi would know what to do, just like Pa would have, but his brother had no interest in seeing that Micah succeeded. Not that Micah blamed him. He'd be madder than the devil in a snowstorm if he had been in Levi's boots. But it would take a snowstorm in August before Micah would go begging his brother to come home.

At the stables, Micah dismounted and unsaddled his horse. After making sure Smokey had enough water and feed, Micah headed for the house. Time to clean up and cool off. He looked forward to washing away the dirt and grime clinging to his sweat-drenched body.

When he entered the parlor, Rose swept her hand through the air and wrinkled her nose. "Phewy, you smell worse than a polecat."

He grinned and put out his arms as though to hug her, but she darted out of his reach and stood behind the sofa. "Oh, no, you don't. I don't plan to smell like the back end of a cow. Supper will be ready soon, so you'd better get cleaned up, or you'll be eating alone." With that she scampered behind him and into the kitchen.

A chuckle followed her exit, and Micah headed for the room Ma set aside for washing up. He made a turn at the stairway and decided to get his clean clothes and leave the stinky ones down here for Ma to wash later. Then he'd get the water needed for a bath.

The lilt of Ma's voice singing as she prepared supper followed him up the stairs to his room. Ma had lost her husband, but she still sang of God's love. No matter what chore she had to do, her mouth always filled with either singing or humming one of the gospel hymns from church. Her faith held this family together in these days without Pa, but Micah wasn't anywhere near ready to turn everything over to God. Too much work had to be done and decisions to be made to wait on an answer from someone who didn't care anyway.

A good soaking in the hot water Ma had prepared soothed the aches from being in the saddle for so many hours. It also gave him time to think, but no matter from which angle he looked at his problem, no solution presented itself. He still had the loan to repay, a herd of cattle to take to market, and a family to take care of.

After donning his clean clothes, Micah pulled the plug

in the galvanized tub Pa had rigged up to drain through an attached pipe to the outside and into Ma's garden. He believed nothing should be wasted, and now with the water situation, it was an even better idea. With the exception of days like this one, baths were usually a once or maybe twice a week luxury in the summer. So far the well had held steady, but he'd make certain they took more care with conserving water.

He entered a kitchen filled with the aroma of beef cooking on the stove and fresh-baked yeast breads in the oven. "How long 'til supper? I'm starving."

Ma grinned and cocked her head to the side. "That one thing hasn't changed a bit. You still eat like you never had a decent meal in your life."

"What can I say? I'm a growing young man." He kissed her cheek that was still smooth as silk and now warm from the heat of the kitchen as well as the weather.

"That may be, but you'll have to wait about fifteen minutes like the rest of us. Why don't you go help Margaret get the table ready?"

"Think I'd rather check on some things in the office. Margaret and Rose can manage the table." He pecked her cheek again and sauntered out of the kitchen and through the dining room where Margaret and Rose set plates around the table.

Micah grinned and waved then headed for what was now his office. He closed the door behind him and walked over to a locked cabinet. There he grasped the neck of a bottle of liquor he'd bought the last time he'd been in town. This was one of those days when he needed something to get him through the evening.

He placed the bottle and a shot glass on the desk then

slumped down into Pa's old chair. He would have to replace it with one that fit his lanky frame if he stayed around longer. Did he have any other choice? The bottle sat there, beckoning, but Micah hesitated. Did he want to start down that road again?

Finally he poured a little into the glass then gulped it before he could think about it again. There, just that little bit wouldn't hurt.

Suddenly the image of Hannah Dyer danced before his eyes. The look she'd given him when she spotted him coming from the saloon with the bottle of liquor had been anything but cordial. In fact, it had shouted her disapproval. Why did she care? They were barely friends, so it shouldn't make any difference to her what he did. But for some reason it did.

Micah shoved the bottle back into the drawer and under the books. Keep it out of sight and he might forget about it. He pulled off his bandana and started to wipe out the glass, but stopped. Ma would smell the liquor on it. His gaze lit upon a few sheets of paper on his desk. One swipe and the glass was clean. Then he wadded the paper into a small ball and tossed it into the waste can. He'd have to stay clear of Ma until after they ate, or her bloodhound nose would pick up the scent on his breath. That had been a dumb thing to do here at the house.

Ma's voice called out from the dining room letting him know supper was on the table. He strolled out and took his seat. Seeing both Pa and Levi's chairs empty still brought a stab of pain, but it didn't hurt quite as much after several weeks.

Ma stared at him with a gaze that pierced him straight between the eyes. "Micah, please say grace for us."

He hadn't said grace over a meal since he'd been home,

but now she asked him to do just that. He cleared his throat. What could be so hard about saying a few words over some food, even if was to a God he didn't really have faith in anymore? "Yes, ma'am." He bowed his head and searched his mind for what Pa always used to say. "For Thy bountiful blessings, Lord, we give Thee thanks. Bless us with this food as nourishment for our bodies. Amen."

He opened his eyes and raised his head to find Margaret staring at him. What could that mean? He reached across the table to the platter of meat. "This roast looks good enough to eat, Ma." A chuckle followed in an attempt to bring a little laughter to the group.

Ma only smiled and the girls shook their heads. Looked like another meal eaten in mostly silence. He bit into the roast and savored the rich flavor of beef. At least the food was good even if the conversation lacked any flavor at all.

෴

Hannah finished up the bandage on Billy Weatherby's arm. "There. Your arm will be good as new in a few days. But like the doctor suggested, don't go thinking you can jump off the porch again anytime soon. You could have broken your arm like Kenny Davis did."

Billy grinned back at her and touched the bandage. "I won't, Miss Hannah, I promise. I don't want a broken arm."

She helped him down from the examining table and nodded to Doreen Weatherby. "He'll be fine. My two brothers always had scrapes and cuts when they were growing up."

Doreen grabbed her son's hand. "Thank you, Miss Dyer. I'll speak to the doctor on the way out." She leaned down and ruffled Billy's hair. "When we get home, you go straightway to your room and change your clothes. I'll have to mend those torn pants."

Their departure brought a smile to Hannah's heart as she remembered the many times her brothers had torn or ruined their clothing with their antics. At least if the Lord gave her boys of her own one day, she'd know what to expect from them. A sigh escaped her lips. That day most likely would never happen.

While she cleaned up the room, the idea of having children of her own someday bounced through her thoughts again, but it always ended up with Micah's face in the middle. No matter how hard she tried, she couldn't keep him out of her daydreams, much less her thoughts.

Her heart had skipped a beat with disappointment when she'd spotted him coming from the saloon with a bottle of whiskey under his arm. Their gazes had locked, and no doubt he'd seen her look of disapproval by the way he jerked his eyes away from her and hurried off to his horse.

If Micah was anything like some of the other prodigals she'd known, drinking had been part of his rebellion. One thing for certain, if he planned to take that bottle home with him, he'd have to hide it from his mother. Ruth Gordon didn't seem like a woman who'd tolerate that kind of behavior from her son.

As much as Hannah would've liked to be more than friends with Micah, he had stayed clear of her as though she had a plague or worse. Of course he was busy with the ranch, but his rejection of her still hurt. How could she do anything to help if he wouldn't even acknowledge her presence?

With no other patients waiting to see the doctor, Hannah ambled into the kitchen where Sallie and Molly baked cookies. Daniel lay asleep in his cradle, and Clara and Tommy sat at the table drawing pictures. "Hmm, it sure smells good in here. I hope those are cinnamon sugar cookies in the oven. They're my favorite."

Molly giggled and swiped a flour-laden hand across her cheek, leaving a flour mark behind. "That's what Mama said. I like them too, but the molasses ones are my favorite."

"Those are good too, but then I like any kind of cookie." Hannah sat down with Clara and Tommy. She would really like a few minutes to talk with Sallie alone, but Sallie's time with her family meant so much to her that Hannah didn't want to interfere.

Sallie removed a pan of cookies from the oven. "Supper will be delayed a bit because of our baking spree. We got started and couldn't seem to stop. Right, Miss Molly?" She reached over and wiped a smudge of flour from Molly's cheek.

"Right, Mama. This is fun." Even her red hair had a few streaks of flour in it.

Tommy concentrated on his picture, his tongue between his teeth. Then he laid down his pencil and peered at Hannah. "Is Billy all right? He sure had a lot of blood."

"He's fine now. His mother took him home. He does have a few stitches though and will most likely have a scar." She leaned over his shoulder. "That's an excellent drawing of a horse. Looks almost like you could ride him." The muscles of the horse almost throbbed as Tommy had drawn him racing across a field. "Will you color this one in for me and let me hang it in my room?"

Tommy nodded, beaming with pride.

Clara held up a drawing of the schoolhouse, and though good, it had the mark of a six-year-old in its uneven lines and abstract markings. "I like that one too, Clara. You are both good artists."

The two young ones grinned and hopped down to hug Hannah. Tommy eyed his picture. "I'll fix this one just for you." Then he turned to his mother. "May we go and play now?"

"Of course, but play upstairs in your rooms. Have a cookie to take with you."

They each grabbed a cookie and scampered from the kitchen. Sallie finished moving the cookies from the pan to a cooling rack. "This is the last batch, so we'll let them cool before we put them with the others." She set the pan on the counter and wrapped an arm about Molly's shoulders. "We're all done here, so you can go too. I'll get supper started."

"Yes, ma'am." With a twinkle in her eye she snagged a cookie and skipped through the door. She called back over her shoulder, "I'm going to practice the piano if Papa doesn't have any patients."

Sallie pulled up a chair and sat beside Hannah. "I think you have something on your mind. That's why I sent the children on their way. Is there a problem?"

When they were growing up, Sallie always knew when Hannah needed to talk, and now she'd done it again. Strains of music drifted in from the parlor. That meant no patients in the office, so Hannah had more time to talk. "I didn't mean to intrude on your time with the children, and I don't want to take time away from supper preparations."

"You didn't and you won't. All I have to do for supper is cook the meat. Everything else is simmering on the stove, and the children were ready for a different activity." She picked up a cinnamon cookie and crunched down on it.

Being concerned, but not nosy, Sallie wouldn't come right out and ask what troubled Hannah, and for that matter, Hannah wasn't even sure herself except that it concerned Micah. She plunged in, not wanting to waste any of their precious time alone. "I...I saw Micah come out of the saloon the other day carrying a bottle of whiskey. I'm afraid he may be taking to drink because of his pa's death and all the responsibility of the ranch."

"Oh, dear, that doesn't sound good, but then it may mean nothing at all. He may have bought it for medicinal purposes." She reached over and clasped Hannah's hands. "I warned you not to care about him too much. We don't know what happened in those years he was away from his family."

"Yes, I know that, but I also know he never really wanted the ranch. Margaret told me how much he hated ranching. Now with Levi gone, he has all the responsibility on his shoulders." Responsibilities like that when not wanted would be enough to break anyone's spirit, especially someone like Micah Gordon. And from what she had heard from Margaret at church, Ellie had made no headway as yet with Levi either. How could two grown men be so stubborn?

Sallie squeezed Hannah's hands. "All we can do is to pray for them."

Of course she was right, yet Hannah wanted to do so much more. But she had no idea what that could be.

CHAPTER 22

ICAH RODE INTO town after supper. Friday nights would be busy in the saloon as cowboys from the area ranches came in to spend their cash. The busier it got, the better for him to blend in and not be noticed. He could sit in a corner and drown his miseries without bothering anyone else. Ma had found his bottle in the office and disposed of it. At least he figured that's what happened since it had disappeared from where he'd stashed it. His resolve to abstain had dissolved after a few more head had been lost over the last two weeks.

The men had begun to look at him askance when the foreman began issuing most of the orders every day. Micah had told Roy to decide what needed to be done and let the men know their duties for the day. This morning he'd explained his reasons for giving the foreman more of the responsibility, and the men accepted it without question. They'd follow Roy Bateman's orders much more readily than they had Micah's anyway.

No one in the family had heard anything from Levi since the reading of the will over a month ago. Micah hadn't been to church for several weeks, and Levi hadn't made an appearance either. Ma had scolded but stopped short of demanding Micah's attendance with her and his sisters on Sunday. No doubt Ma still prayed for both her boys, but it didn't appear as if God listened.

Micah snorted. Why should God care about him or Levi for that matter? Both had disappointed their family. If the ranch survived, it would be through Micah's determination and Roy's leadership. But sometimes he needed to get away from the problems of the ranch, as he had done the past two weekends.

When he entered the Texas Star Saloon, the bartender reached under the counter and came up with Micah's favorite brand of liquor and a shot glass. "Thanks, Louie." He dropped a few coins on the bar and picked up the bottle and glass.

The place had filled up fast even for a Friday night. The hot days of summer made the trip to the saloon on the weekend even more important to the ranchers and farmers around these parts. Micah sauntered back to a table on the rear wall. From there he could see everything that went on.

A poker game started up a few tables over. At one time in the past the game would have lured him to join, but the loss of a large sum of money and a night in jail a few years back had cured him of the desire to gamble away his hard-earned money. Not that he earned any now. What he had left from his savings had dwindled to almost nothing. He'd used most of it to help the ranch, but it hadn't gone far.

He poured a shot of amber liquid into his glass. Now here he was spending money on what Ma called devil's brew. Maybe it was, but if he had to make it through the next few weeks until the cattle drive, the expense wasn't a luxury but a necessity.

None of the girls bothered to come to his table. They'd learned he wanted no part of them, so they left him alone. They still tried to flirt from a distance, but Micah ignored them and tended to his own business…forgetting his problems.

A hand slapped down on the table. Micah flinched and looked up into the eyes of James Hempstead, Margaret's beau. "Go away. I don't want to talk to anybody."

James pulled out a chair and sat. He leaned his elbows on

the table and narrowed his eyes at Micah. "Then don't talk. Just listen."

Micah opened his mouth to speak, thought better of it, and gulped down the liquid in his glass. He wiped the back of his hand across his mouth. "Talk all you want, but it doesn't mean I'll listen." Margaret had probably put James up to this, otherwise James would never have darkened a saloon's doors.

"Suit yourself. I've seen the hurt in your ma's and sisters' eyes when you act the way you have. Margaret and Rose both want you to be the cheerful big brother they remember and not the scowling, angry man you've become."

Micah pushed his hat back on his head. "Well, now, I take it you've become the voice of my family. Your coming here was most likely Margaret's idea. I'm not the boy they remember from years ago. I'm a man with a job I don't want and hate." He clamped his mouth shut. He'd already said more than he'd planned to say all evening.

"That may be so, and I understand your feelings about the ranch. The thing is, your pa died before he did anything about it. He left you with a debt you have to pay, or your family will be left with nothing. At least now they have a place to live, and my father is more than willing to give them credit at the store for whatever they need."

A sneer and harsh words formed before Micah could think. "And all that's doing is adding to the debt. We don't need to be piling up bills that might not get paid, and we certainly don't want anyone's charity." He downed another swig of liquor. "Go mind your own business."

"Micah, I love your sister and plan to marry her. What you're doing affects her, so it is my business. She's hurting because of what you're doing. She knows you're here at the saloon on Friday nights, and so does your ma. Neither one of them will say anything because they're afraid you'll run off again."

Although Micah had considered doing just that, he sure didn't intend to let James know about it. Even though James had a right to be concerned because of Margaret, he had no right to dictate what Micah did or didn't do with his own time. Maybe he wasn't doing such a good job at the ranch, but he didn't want to find out what he should or shouldn't do from anybody else when he had a hard enough time deciding for himself.

"Look, James, I don't plan to lose the ranch. We'll get those cattle to market no matter how much I hate those drives."

"A cattle drive is no place for a drunk. Pull yourself together and be the man your ma needs right now. Your pa would be disappointed in you, so don't disappoint her too."

That was nothing new. Pa had never approved of anything Micah had done, so why should now be any different? "I think it's time for you to leave. You haven't changed my mind one way or the other, so you may as well go tell Margaret that you failed."

James shook his head and stood. "You are the most hard-headed, stubborn man I've ever met, even worse than your pa. All I can say is, please don't lose the ranch because of your own personal problems. Think of your mother and your sisters." With that he whirled around and marched from the saloon.

Micah stared at the glass before him, its appeal no longer tempting. He shoved it aside and sat with fist clenched on the table. How he'd like to drown himself in the bottle and forget everything James said and everything that needed to be done. Only trouble with that was the fact that no matter how much drowning he did to forget, the problems never went away and always waited for him to come up for air.

Levi stopped and dismounted in front of Ellie's house. He looked forward to these Friday night dinners and her good home cooking. Food at the Hudson ranch wasn't bad, but it couldn't compare to what Ellie could put together. Her mother helped, but for these meals Ellie did most of the preparation.

The front door opened, and Ellie appeared and waved. "Come on in, we've been waiting for you."

He wrapped the reins of Maverick around the rail and waved back. How pretty she looked standing in the doorway with her welcoming smile. It could be like this every night some day when they could marry and have their own home. What a wonderful wife she'd be with all her talents as well as beauty.

Brown eyes that twinkled like the stars greeted him on the porch. She hooked her arm through his and leaned her head against his arm. "I'm so glad you're here. I've been lonesome without you."

"I've missed you more than you know." He'd been lonesome too and didn't mind admitting it. After all, he'd already told her how much he loved her and that he wanted to marry her. Of course they had to wait awhile with Pa's death and all.

A bitter taste filled his throat and mouth. A lot of things didn't happen because of Pa. In life he'd been stubborn and slow to do what needed to be done. If Pa had listened to reason and taken care of his health and his business, none of them would be in this situation.

Mr. and Mrs. Bradshaw greeted him as he joined them in the parlor. Ellie and her mother excused themselves to finish supper preparations and left him with Mr. Bradshaw.

They sat in the parlor with the aroma of roasting meat and baking bread filling the air. Levi's stomach growled with pleasure and hunger. He looked forward to the meal ahead. It would keep him going for the rest of the week.

"Did you know your brother is in town this evening?"

Levi jerked his head. Micah in town? He'd have to be extra careful not to run into him. "No. I don't keep up with what he's doing."

"Oh, that's right. You're at the Hudson spread now." He tamped down the tobacco in his pipe and peered at Levi. "Seems to me you should be helping your brother with your own herd. From what your mother told my wife, she misses you, and Micah needs you."

If Micah needed him, then why didn't he come and say so? Not that it would make any difference, but at least Micah would be admitting he didn't know what to do with the ranch. "My brother is in charge and owns it all now, so he's the one to make the decisions. I'd only be in the way."

Mr. Bradshaw puffed a few times on his pipe and nodded his head. He said nothing, and a completely unreadable expression filled his round face. As county clerk he probably knew more about what went on in this town than any of its other citizens, even the banker Swenson. The thought chilled Levi, and an unsettling sense of disapproval from Mr. Bradshaw wove its way through his body.

Dinner conversation revolved mostly around the extreme heat and lack of rain. This suited Levi until Mrs. Bradshaw mentioned she'd missed him at church since he'd rarely missed a Sunday in days past. She set a plate with a slice of buttermilk pound cake for dessert before him as she spoke.

"I've missed being there, but I had other things to do." He had missed being there and hearing Reverend Weatherby. He missed his family too, but he'd never admit it to anyone but Ma.

Mrs. Bradshaw made no further comment, but the silence grew more uncomfortable by the minute. Ellie pushed back from the table. "I think it's time to clean up. Levi and I have some things we need to talk about."

"You don't have to help me, dear." Mrs. Bradshaw reached for her husband's hand. "Come, Herman, it'll be like old times for you to help me with the dishes. You two go on and enjoy the evening."

Ellie headed for the front door. "Let's take a walk over by the church."

Since she was now standing on the porch, Levi had no choice but to follow. They strolled in silence for a few minutes with her hand tucked under his elbow, but from the set of her mouth, Ellie had something on her mind.

"Why not just say what you're thinking? I can see it in your face. You're not happy with me for some reason."

"Oh, Levi, I just hate what's happening with your family. With your father's death, it's hard on them to keep going."

"They have Micah. He came home just in time to take over for Pa. They don't need me." Even if they did, he couldn't tuck tail and return like a wounded animal. He had too much pride for that.

"But they do need you. Margaret has said so often. Micah needs you too. He's been away for too many years to come back and step into the role of boss on such short notice. And your ma is afraid he might run off again."

The best thing would be for Micah to leave. Because if he did, then Levi could return and take over, or could he since the ranch belonged to Micah? He'd do it anyway to help Ma if Micah were out of the picture. Since his brother's name was now on the deed, his leaving was not likely to happen.

"Micah won't leave Ma." Levi could concede that much to his brother. "He'll stay around, but he'll probably end up losing the ranch anyway."

Ellie frowned. "If you ask me, you're being stubborn and bullheaded. You ran off just like he did five years ago, but he wasn't needed then like you are now. You refuse to go back, and it's all about your pride and anger at not being at least part owner of the ranch. I think it's high time you asked the Lord for a whole lot of forgiveness for that pride."

Anger flared at her words, but guilt prevented his responding with harsh words. "You don't understand, Ellie. You grew up with a loving family and sister. Your father dotes on both of you. You didn't spend your life trying to please a father who had eyes and ears only for his older son who did nothing but get into trouble and cause grief."

"I'm so sorry you feel that way, because I've heard your father talk about you with pride in his voice and love in his heart."

"He sure had a strange way of showing me any kind of love."

They had made their way back from the church and now stood in front of her house. Ellie turned to face him. Tears glistened in her eyes. "I love you, Levi Gordon, but until you settle things with your family, I cannot consider marriage to you." She spun around and hastened up the walk.

"Ellie, wait. Please." But his voice fell on deaf ears as she entered the house and closed the door. His heart pounded and a lump rose in his throat. Ellie was the best thing to happen to him, and now Micah had even stolen her from him.

With clenched teeth he mounted Maverick and reined him toward the edge of town. Music from the saloon wafted in the air, and resentment took up residence in Levi's heart once again. Knowing his brother, he'd be down there at the Texas Star having a good time despite knowing how it grieved their mother. Levi dug his heels into his horse and raced toward the Hudson ranch, anger roiling in his gut.

CHAPTER 23

MICAH RODE BACK to the ranch with Roy and the others after a hard day of rounding up strays and checking brands. They'd lost more than he'd liked, but they still had a substantial herd to drive to market next month. That is, if the weather cooperated and they didn't lose many more head.

Roy rode up beside him and reined in to keep pace. "We'll have to move the herd to the upper pasture soon and give them the extra feed to fatten them up for the trail ride."

"How does it look there? Will there be enough grass to keep them going?" He hated to admit he hadn't been over all of the ranch to scout out conditions, but he hadn't had the time.

Roy pushed the brim of his hat back and peered at Micah. He looked none too pleased with the question. "You haven't been up to those parts yet, have you? Joel ordered the extra feed for the herd early in the summer because of the predicted dry summer. He wanted to be prepared for those last days before heading out."

Micah should have known Pa would take care of things like that. If only he'd been willing to share the information and let Micah know what had been done. Pa had planned for the herd but not for his family, but then he'd no idea his life would be cut short. "Your brother helped us get everything ready. I'm sorry he's not here to help and let you know what was done before he left."

Micah's jaw hardened. "Any reason why you haven't kept me informed?"

"No. I guess I assumed you knew what was going on. All that should be listed in the ledgers your pa kept on the ranch business."

Entries for purchases and other expenses had been there, but after Pa's death Micah had no time to do more than glance over them. His anger at Levi's leaving and Pa's failure to change his will had blinded him so that he'd not paid as much attention as he should have. If he didn't have to spend so much time out in the pastures, he'd have more time to look at the books more closely. Excuses and more excuses; he could come up with a long list of them, but none of them justified what he'd neglected to do.

When they rode up to the ranch house, Roy pulled his horse up beside Micah. "I see Doc Whiteman is still here. Hope nothing serious is wrong with Rose."

This morning Rose had a high fever from a sunburn she'd suffered yesterday, and Ma sent Margaret into town for the doctor. His young sister may be sicker than he first thought.

Micah dismounted and hurried inside. Instead of Doc Whiteman, Hannah Dyer sat in the parlor talking with Ma.

Ma jumped up and greeted them. "Oh, I'm glad you're home. Doc was here this morning and Rose is fine now. Hannah just came back to check on her, and her fever's already gone down to almost normal."

Micah nodded toward Hannah. "I'm glad to hear that. Thank you for coming all the way out here."

Hannah's smile lit up her face, and Micah's heart tap-danced. She had been beautiful when he noticed her on the train almost two months ago, but the weeks in Texas had given her face a rosy glow that only enhanced her beauty.

"I didn't mind a bit. I'd been wanting to visit with your mother anyway, and now seemed like as good a time as any."

Ma pushed Micah toward a chair. "Sit down and keep Miss Dyer company while I go out and check on supper. Miss Dyer has accepted my invitation to dine with us."

Micah sat, but he kept an eye on Hannah. Ever since that first day, he'd thought of her as Hannah, but out of respect, he'd never call her that in front of others. Her dark green dress intensified the depth of color in her eyes, but it was the peace he saw continually in her face that drew her to him. Unlike Camilla, she was always so full of love and caring for others. He searched his brain for something to say, but his tongue grew thicker than a side of beef. No other woman from his past, not even Camilla, had this effect on him, and for once he didn't know what to say or do.

Finally she smiled at him again and inclined her head toward the stairway. "Rose had a little too much sun yesterday and burned her skin, which left her dehydrated as well. Your mother made sure she had plenty of water today, and I brought out some salve for the tenderness on her face and arms. She'll be uncomfortable for a day or so, and then it'll fade away and she'll be fine. I don't think the burn on her arms will blister, just be tender to the touch."

"Ma tells her to wear her hat and protect her face and arms all the time, but she never listens very well."

"I don't think Rose will stay out in the sun in the future now that she knows how painful it can be."

Micah had no response as Ma came back. He jumped up and grabbed his hat from the table. "If supper's about ready, I need to go and wash up. You don't need a smelly cowboy at the table." He headed for the stairs and took them two at a time. The faster he could get away from Hannah, the better off he'd be. He had no business feeling like he did for her, or any other girl for that matter. Until he took care of

Pa's unfinished business, he didn't need Hannah around to distract him.

He selected a clean shirt with extra care and made sure his hair was well combed. Knowing she'd be seated either across from him or next to him sent his heart to pounding. He pulled his boots up over clean socks. Time to get a grip on himself. He didn't have time for a woman in his life, and he'd better remember that.

Minutes later he sat next to her at the table. When his sisters extended their hands to clasp each other's for the prayer, Micah reached over and grasped Hannah's. When her hand rested in his, a wave of heat flooded his arm and swept straight to his heart. Ma squeezed his other one and then lifted her voice in praise and thanksgiving for the meal before them.

Caught between the two women, he held the hand of one he loved with all his heart and the hand of one he could come to love. When Ma finished, he dropped Hannah's hand like a hot coal. He had to get his mind going another direction right now.

Fortunately the women at the table took over the conversation, and Micah ate in relative solitude, but the turmoil in his heart barred any peace or comfort from filling it.

After dinner Ma insisted that he accompany Hannah back to town as the evening would turn dark before she could make it back alone. Both wanting and dreading the next half hour or so alone, he tied Smokey to the back of the buggy and then assisted Hannah up onto the seat. Unlike that first day, this time she stepped up with no hesitancy or awkwardness.

He joined her then flicked the reins to head the horse toward town. The setting sun painted the sky with an array of colors that grabbed at Micah like a clamp on his soul. Nowhere else had he ever found a sunset quite like those here in Stoney Creek. A heart that had hardened against a God because of problems and sorrows couldn't help but admit that God did exist and had made a beautiful world.

"Beautiful, isn't it? God really knows how to put on a show in Texas. Don't believe I ever saw anything quite as colorful back in Mississippi."

Micah jerked his head at Hannah's words. Had she been reading his mind? He stared at the woman beside him, and warmth he couldn't describe filled his being from the inside out.

She cleared her throat, glanced away, then said, "You don't really care about taking care of the ranch, do you? If Levi were doing it, you'd be off doing something else." She turned to gaze into his eyes.

With those incredible eyes staring at him, Micah could no more hide his feelings than he could lasso the moon. "No, I don't like being in charge at the ranch, and yes, I do wish Levi would come home, but that's not going to happen anytime soon."

She said nothing in response but continued to stare at him. Suddenly all he wanted to do was confess everything to her. He swallowed hard then blurted out an apology. "About seeing me coming out of the saloon, I'm sorry you had to know that."

Surprise and gratification filled her eyes, but she shook her head. "I'm not the one you should be apologizing to, since you're only hurting yourself. I think I understand what might be driving you to drink, but it isn't the way to solve your problem. Only God can help."

A snort burst forth before he could stop it. "That's a good

one. God sure hasn't been much help so far." How could he be confiding so much in this girl already? Camilla and he had never talked this way.

"I think Levi is as miserable as you are, especially since Ellie said she couldn't consider marrying him if he didn't set things right with you and your family."

Micah allowed Hannah's words to sink in. Remorse for all the trouble he'd caused nibbled at his conscience, but he merely frowned and shrugged. "If my brother is fool enough to let a girl like Ellie slip through his fingers all because of his pride and refusal to come home, then he deserves every bit of misery he might encounter."

Looking up, he encountered Hannah's disbelieving stare. She sighed, and he could tell she was choosing her words carefully. "I have two brothers, and all I know is, I would move heaven and earth to fix things if I knew that something stood between us."

"I'm afraid you are a better person than I, Miss Dyer."

"I highly doubt that, Mr. Gordon."

Micah was unexpectedly gratified at her response but dared not contradict or confirm it. They rode the rest of the way in silence, and when they entered town and arrived at the Whiteman home, Micah breathed a sigh of great relief. How much longer he could sit beside this woman and not say more things he'd regret, he didn't know, but now it was almost over.

"You can leave the horse and buggy out back. Manfred will come out and take care of it."

He pulled around the house as she had instructed then jumped down. He helped her down, and as he did so, his hands lingered longer at her waist than they should have.

Once again Hannah gazed up at him. To his surprise,

tears in her eyes glistened in the fading light. She lifted a hand to his face. "Micah, I'm praying for you and Levi to come to an understanding. Two brothers should be working together, not against each other."

Then she reached up and kissed his cheek. "Take care, Micah Gordon." With that she whirled around and rushed into the house.

Micah fingered his cheek. A hard place in his heart softened, and he opened his mouth to call her back, but his throat closed up and no sound came. Despite his growing attraction to Hannah, he couldn't become involved with another woman. He untied Smokey and swung himself up into the saddle.

No matter how long she prayed, if his brother wouldn't come home, it'd all be for naught. In another day, another time, they might have had a relationship, but not now, and most likely never.

The bright lights from the saloon beckoned. Maybe he needed one shot for the long ride back home. He shook his head and turned Smokey to the road. Not tonight. He needed a clear head to go over Pa's books once again. Why he'd neglected the one aspect of ranching he did enjoy was beyond him. Whatever the reason, from now on he wouldn't have to ask Roy; he'd know for himself.

In an effort to avoid her sister, Hannah raced up the back stairs and to her room where she threw her body across her bed. Her lips still tingled from the kiss she'd given Micah, and her cheeks burned from humiliation at being so forward. What must he think of her now? Bad enough he pitied her because of her bad leg, but now he must believe her to be desperate for affection since she'd been so bold as to kiss him when they weren't even courting.

Tears stung her eyelids, but she forced them back and swallowed a sob. Now she'd ruined everything, but it had seemed like such a natural thing to do. The sadness in his eyes had gripped her heart, and all she wanted was to help it disappear.

She rolled over and stared at the ceiling. "Hannah Dyer, you are such an idiot. It'll take a lot more than a peck on the cheek to make that kind of sadness disappear." In fact, nobody would be or could be happy until the Gordon brothers worked out their differences.

"Auntie Annie, you are not an idiot, and Papa says we shouldn't ever call anybody one either. It's not polite."

Hannah sat up to find Clara standing in the doorway in her nightdress and clutching a rag doll to her chest. "Of course it's not polite. I'm angry with myself, that's all." She swiped her fingers across her cheeks to erase the tears that had escaped her eyes.

Clara padded in bare feet over to Hannah and climbed up on the bed beside her. She lifted her fingers and touched Hannah's face. "Your cheeks are wet. Were you crying?"

Hannah reached over and hugged Clara close. "Yes, I was, sweetie. I did something very foolish, and it made me unhappy." She tickled the girl's ribs. "But now that you're here, I can't help but be happy."

Clara's giggles warmed Hannah's heart and did bring back some joy, but no amount of laughter from her niece could erase the embarrassment brought on by her impulsive behavior. How would she ever be able to look Micah in the face again?

CHAPTER 24

HANNAH CLOSED THE door behind Ellie and leaned against it. Her heart sank to her toes at the news Ellie had brought that Micah had come to town again and gone immediately to the saloon. The chasm between the brothers had grown deeper and Micah's problems multiplied. She touched her fingers to her lips, remembering the kiss she'd planted on his cheek a few nights ago.

The voices of Manfred and Sallie drifted from the dining room. Hannah bit her lip. They'd know what to do, but she hesitated in going to them. She hadn't told Sallie about the kiss, and even now heat rose in her cheeks at the brazenness of such an act. She straightened up and breathed deeply to gain courage to speak with her sister.

When she entered the dining room, they stopped their discussion, but not before she caught the end of Sallie's words. "This chasm he and Levi have created will be the death of the Circle G yet. We have to do something to help. Mrs. Gordon is under great stress, and I didn't like the dark circles under her eyes when I saw her earlier this week."

Manfred nodded to Hannah. "Come in and sit down." He leaned on the table, his arms crossed. "We're concerned about Mrs. Gordon and her health."

Concern had already consumed Hannah's thoughts too. "This is a battle those two have to fight between themselves. No one has been able to break through the barrier they created."

Sallie nodded her agreement. "We've both prayed and prayed for those two young men, but so far the Lord hasn't answered. Ellie has tried to reason with Levi and James has tried with Micah, but neither accomplished much except to make both men angrier."

"I wish I could do something," Hannah said. She didn't want to reveal that she'd already tried too and failed miserably.

The side of Micah she'd seen at the depot on her arrival and the man who'd danced with her were entirely different from the man she'd seen these past weeks with misery in his eyes. Now he sat in that saloon trying to forget it all in a bottle of liquor. That couldn't do anything but make matters worse. Why couldn't Micah see that? She sank into a chair next to Sallie.

Sallie reached over and grasped Hannah's hands. "Oh, Hannah, you can't mend people's lives like you can a broken arm or a bad cut. They have to want to be helped, and apparently these two young men don't want to be helped."

"But it hurts so to see the sadness I saw in him and his mother the other night at the ranch. I know how deeply wounded Mrs. Gordon is by her sons' behavior. Imagine how you would feel if it happened with two of your own." Although she had no children of her own, Hannah could think of nothing worse than to have two people who were a part of her and whom she loved with all her heart to turn against each other.

"We all care about him, and we don't like to see what is happening either, but it's not our family and none of our business. All we can and should do is to pray for God to resolve the issues and bring the two brothers back together." Sallie squeezed Hannah's hands once again then stood. "I'm going up to check on the children."

She leaned over and kissed the top of her husband's head. "I'll be back down, and then we can have tea and some of that pecan bread you like so much."

Manfred patted her hand. "Thank you, dear. I'll be in my office looking over a few charts. I may need to go back out to the Hensley place to check on Jonah." He rose from his chair and wrapped his arm about Sallie's waist as they left the kitchen.

Hannah swallowed the lump in her throat. If only she could have a love like that with Micah. Her heart constricted with pain at the picture of him drinking himself to a stupor at the saloon.

An idea leaped into her head, and before she had a chance to reject it, she pushed back from the table. The feud between Micah and Levi may not be her business, but God wouldn't mind if she meddled just a little. Sometimes a little help along the way made God's job easier. At least she hoped it would in this case.

Hannah called out to Manfred to let him know she was going for a walk then stepped out onto the porch. The summer sun left streaks and streams of purple and orange across the evening sky. In a short time darkness would cover the town with only light from a few gas lamps to give any illumination. She hurried down the walk then turned toward the center of town. If she walked fast, she'd get to the lights on Main Street before complete darkness enveloped everything. She increased her pace and ignored the extra weight of her boot.

Music from the piano in the saloon filled the still night air, and Hannah stopped short. She'd never been in a saloon before. What had she been thinking? She couldn't simply march in and confront Micah in front of all those people. She'd embarrass herself as well as Micah. There had to be some other way.

She inched her way along the wall outside the saloon

229

before venturing a peek inside. Cowboys and townsmen filled the tables, and their laughter rang out with the tinny piano as background. Micah sat toward the back at a table by himself. A lone bottle of whiskey and a small glass sat before him on the table.

Hannah's heart ached at the sight. Even from here the set of his shoulders and the angle of his head told a story of sadness and defeat. How she longed to wrap her arms around him and cradle his head against her chest as a mother would a hurt child. However, her emotions were not that of a mother wanting to comfort a child, but more wanting to comfort a man she loved as a wife would her husband.

That thinking had to stop. She bit down hard on her lip to take her mind away from its wayward path. Then she noticed the table sat near a rear door. Hannah narrowed her eyes and peered again through the window. Maybe if she went around back and investigated, there might be a way in without walking across the middle of the saloon.

When she rounded the corner of the building, the black night wrapped itself around her like a shroud. Icy fear raced through her body, and she turned back. No, she wanted to speak with Micah, so there had to be a way. *Lord, give me courage, but if this isn't what You want me to do, I'll turn back now and leave him alone.*

After a moment she took a step back to the light, but a voice in her heart stopped her. *Talk to him. I'll be with you.* She hesitated only seconds before plunging forth between the two buildings and into the alley. At the back of the saloon light spilled from a window and revealed a doorway. Hannah sidled up to it and tried the knob. It turned, and the door opened into a storage room of sorts.

She stepped inside and closed the door behind her. Across

the room was another door that must lead into the saloon. After tiptoeing her way to the door, she opened it a crack. There sat Micah not more than three feet away with his back toward her.

A floorboard creaked and caused Micah to turn his head to find Hannah Dyer beside the storage room door. His mouth dropped open, and he locked gazes with her for a few seconds. What in thunder was she doing in a saloon?

His first instinct was to yell at her, but he kept his voice low. "Get out of here, Hannah. This is no place for a girl like you." If the doc heard about this, he'd have both their heads on a silver platter.

Instead of leaving, she scurried like a mouse to his table and sat down. "I've come to tell you something, and you'd better listen and listen good."

What in the world? She must be out of her head. "I don't care what you have to say. I've heard it all." Why was his heart pounding so? He couldn't let her have this effect on him. "Get yourself home before you get into trouble." At least no one had noticed her sitting there as yet.

He stared at her as she bit her lip as though considering what he said. With her yellow dress cut high at the neck and trimmed in some kind of fancy lace, she looked as out of place as a lamb in a pigsty.

She squared her shoulders and shook her head. "No, I'm not leaving. It's time for you to find Levi, straighten things out between the two of you, and get on with the business of taking care of your pa's ranch. The ways things are now, neither one of you is going to get what you want. You'll still be saddled with the ranch and all its debt, and Ellie won't marry Levi."

The anger in her eyes flashed fire, but she kept her voice at a level that couldn't be heard beyond his table. What a beautiful face, even in anger. Why hadn't he gone after her instead of Camilla? Oh, wait, yes, her deformed leg and foot. He opened his mouth to tell her that it was none of her business, but she plowed ahead.

"Don't you think you caused your ma enough grief when you ran away the first time? Now you're staying in town but running away again. This time you think you can hide from all your problems with a bottle of whiskey, but you can't hide from it and you can't hide from God. Your father would be sorely disappointed in you right now."

"Hah! You think you have it all figured out." She didn't know the half of it. Pa had never been pleased with anything Micah did. He leaned forward. "Well, let me tell you one thing, Sister Dyer, I do what I want whenever I want, and nobody's going to tell me different. I'm not hurting anybody but myself. As for God, He doesn't care about me anyway." Let her chew on that for a while.

Even that didn't stop her. "Micah Gordon, God cares about you. He wants you to succeed. He wants you to do what needs to be done to take care of what your father left you. You don't want to do it alone, so go get Levi and tell him you need him. You're both too stubborn to see how much you do need each other."

That was enough. Micah slammed his fist on the table, causing the bottle to jump. If not for Hannah's quick hands, it would have fallen and spilled its contents in her lap. His voice rose above the crowd noise. "I don't need your advice now or ever, Hannah Dyer. Go home and leave me alone. You don't belong here in the first place."

The stricken look in her eyes hurt to the core, but he couldn't give in to her. Under other circumstances he might be shutting her up with a kiss, but not now. Silence roared its presence as everyone in the saloon stopped all activity to observe the scene. Red flooded Hannah's cheeks as she jumped up.

Her lower lip trembled and her fists clenched at her sides. "Micah Gordon, you are the most stubborn, pigheaded, blind, and…and…oh, why don't you wake up and see the truth." With that she whirled around and marched across the saloon to the front door with her head held high.

Once the doors closed behind Hannah, the music and conversation resumed, but several men glanced in his direction and shook their heads. Tess, the owner of the saloon, sauntered over and stood at his side with her hands on her hips. "She's only telling you what a lot of others in here would like to. Don't you think this feud has gone on long enough? Go home where you belong and work things out with your family."

She grabbed up the bottle. "And this won't help you solve anything. It'll only make matters worse." Tess stared hard at him for a few seconds then headed back to the bar, where she handed over the bottle he'd already paid for.

He'd only had one sip from it, but then he didn't need it anyway with anger roiling inside and sending bile up through his throat. When he headed for the door, the bartender held out the money spent on the whiskey. Micah waved him off. "Keep it. I may need it later."

When the warm night air hit his face, he breathed deeply and untied his horse. He swung his leg up over Smokey's back. "Might as well go home, my friend. No one seems to want me around here."

Rejection...the story of his life...filled him with a sadness he couldn't stop. It flowed through him like water spilling over a dam after a heavy rain. First his father, then the women he'd wanted while he had been away, and then his father again once he'd returned home. It may not have been Micah himself that Pa rejected this summer, but by not accepting the things Micah wanted to do with the ranch, it may as well have been. He'd even ruined any chances he may have had with Hannah Dyer.

He'd hurt her tonight, and that called up a regret in his heart that he had never experienced before. No woman had ever had this effect on him. Despite her handicap, she was a woman who loved with all her heart and soul. She'd be as faithful as Ma had been to Pa, and that was the kind of love he wanted in his life.

The moon sent beams of light to guide him home, but only darkness surrounded his soul. How could he have been so rude to her? Did she really care that much about him? Even if she did, it would do him no good now. He had ruined any chances he may have had with her.

As he drew closer to home, his thoughts rambled through past years and ended up in the last few weeks. Levi criticized and condemned Micah for leaving home without any thought for anyone else in the family, but now he'd gone and done the same thing. Maybe Levi wasn't wasting his money and time on booze and women, but he was hurting his family just the same.

Micah sat up straighter in the saddle. It was time someone shook some sense into that boy. As the oldest, that job belonged to him. In a flash it all became clear. Hannah's words rang true and pierced his heart. He was head of this family now, and it *was* his place to go after Levi and bring him home no matter how angry he may be. Pride or begging had nothing to do with it. Family meant working things out, no matter what.

He'd do that tomorrow morning. It being a Saturday, he'd be able to leave without having to tell anyone what he planned. Now all he had to do was figure out a way to get Levi to swallow his pride and come home.

With new determination he rode up to the ranch house. A horse stood hitched at the railing. Micah peered through the moonlight. It sure looked like Levi's horse, but what was he doing out here at the ranch?

The front door opened and a figure stood silhouetted in the light. Micah dismounted and strode to the porch. "Levi? What are you doing here?"

CHAPTER 25

L EVI ATTEMPTED TO brush past Micah, but he grabbed his brother's arm. "I want to talk with you, and you're going to listen."

"I'm not listening to anything you have to say." Levi yanked his arm to get away, but Micah tightened his grasp. "Let me go."

"No. You're both staying here." Ma stood in the doorway with her hands on her hips. "You two have been feuding long enough. You come inside now and get this mess sorted out before I take a switch to you both."

Even with all his years away, Micah never forgot that tone of voice. Ma meant business, and he'd best get himself inside. Levi would do the same if he knew what was good for him. Micah dropped his brother's arm. "Yes, ma'am, I'm coming."

He shot a glare at Levi. His brother clenched his teeth and his eyes narrowed, but he followed Micah into the parlor.

"Now, sit yourselves down here and let's get this business cleared up once and for all. It makes no sense for you to be at two different ranches when only one of them really needs you both." She waited until Micah and Levi settled in their chairs.

"I've waited long enough for you boys to come to some agreement. Since neither of you has made a move to talk to the other, I've decided it's time to step in and make it happen. Micah, I reckon you have something to say to Levi, and Levi, you're going to listen. When he's done, it'll be your turn to talk and state your opinion."

This was more like old times. When he and Levi argued,

Ma let them handle things their own way, but if they didn't, she stepped in and did what needed to be done in the situation. He wished she hadn't waited so long this time, but at least Levi would be forced to listen.

"Thank you, Ma." He leaned toward Levi. "I know when we were boys we didn't always get along, but we never let things go this far. We've both made mistakes. Mine was to leave and stay away so long without giving anyone any idea of where I was. Yours was to run off when I did come home."

A frown muddied Levi's face, and he opened his mouth to most likely protest, but Ma stopped him. "Don't say a word, Levi. You wait until he's done, and then you can have your say."

Levi slumped back in his chair still wearing the frown and crossed his arms.

"Levi, I talked with Pa soon as I came home and told him I didn't want this ranch as my own to run. I can't handle it, and I've about proved that with the way things have gone the past month. I begged him to change his will and at least make the ranch half yours. I would gladly have worked with you as a business partner. You know more about running this place than I could ever know. If not for you and Roy, we'd be in even worse condition than we are."

Levi's eyebrows arched and his eyes opened wide. "Why didn't you say so in the first place?"

"You never gave me a chance. Every time I went after you, you ran the opposite direction. And the one time I did try to talk to you, you twisted my words into something I couldn't even recognize."

"Ma, did you know about this?" Levi straightened in his chair and leaned toward Ma.

"Yes, Pa and I talked about it. He was so worried about

losing the ranch completely that he didn't get around to changing his will. He wanted it to be debt free. He figured that one last loan from the bank would tide him over until he got the herd to market. He never planned on dying before he could do that."

Levi sat back and furrowed his brow. He seemed to be trying to digest what had been said. He remained silent then gazed first at Ma and then at Micah. "You really tried to talk Pa into giving me half the ranch?"

"Yes, so we could be partners. I would do the book work, and you would do everything else that you're so good at doing." Hope swelled in Micah's chest. If Levi believed him and decided to come home, they had an even better chance of saving the ranch. Pa's legacy would not be lost.

Levi pondered Micah's words a minute or so. "Where does this put Ma and the girls?"

Micah glanced at Ma, and the joy of what she was hearing spilled from her face like spring rain overflowing the creek banks. "Ma will never have to worry about having a place to live. She'll always have a place with one of us. Margaret will most likely be marrying James next year, and if what I've seen between you and Ellie is the same, we'll have another wedding in the family. That will come later on for Rose too."

Levi grinned and let go a snicker. "Much later, I would hope." Then his face went slack again. "This all sounds good now, but Pa is gone and the ranch is yours. So nothing's really changed."

"But it can. We can go into town and meet with that lawyer Hightower and see how we can do this. Since we're brothers, and the place is in my name now, or will be after we pay off the bank, I should be able to name you as partner."

"I forgot about the bank. That puts things in a different

light." Levi stood and rolled his hat brim through his fingers. "This is a lot to digest right now."

Ma reached out to grasp his arm. "Please don't go yet. Besides, you haven't given your side of the story."

Before Levi could reply, Margaret spoke from the foot of the stairs. "Ma, is it all right if we come down now and join you? We've been sitting up there wondering what was happening with Micah here. We heard your voices but couldn't tell what anyone said."

Ma hurried to Margaret's side. "Of course, come in." She motioned to Rose standing a few steps up. "Both of you come on. This is a family meeting now, and you're a part of the family."

As they trooped in, Margaret's raised eyebrows and questioning glance sent threads of guilt through Levi. If Micah told the truth, then Levi had hurt the family more than he'd ever realized. He loved his sisters and Ma with all his heart, but accepting Micah back into the family had been more than he could take. How could he explain, much less excuse, those feelings of hurt and anger and the actions that had resulted from them?

His sisters sat on the couch, their backs straight as arrows. He swallowed the sudden amusement at the picture they presented. They reminded him of the crows sitting on the back fence of the garden waiting to see what Ma planted. He cleared his throat to compose his thoughts.

"Ma asked me to explain my behavior these past months, but I'm not sure I can." He set the hat he had held all through Micah's speech on the lamp table and stared at it for a minute or so as though he thought it would reveal what he should say. Waves of remorse washed over him to cover the emotions simmering in his heart and soul.

Too much time had been spent in anger and resentment. He had to let them go and allow love for family to fill in the space. Anger had cost him a future with Ellie, but hope rose in his heart that love could bring her back when she learned of this reconciliation with his family. Determination to right his wrong set in and the words became clear.

"I'm sorry for the hurt I caused the family with my attitude. The only excuse I can offer is that for so many years when we were younger, I worked hard to win Pa's approval. He never seemed to notice what I did with him or what I accomplished. He only talked of you, Micah, and how smart you were."

Micah shook his head and his mouth tightened to a firm line. Whether Micah believed it or not, Levi told what he saw to be the truth. "No matter what you did, he never criticized or complained. He just went in and bailed you out and brought you home. When you left, he grieved hard."

Margaret face contorted with pain. "Oh, Levi, I'm so sorry you see it that way, but—"

Ma cut her off. "Hush now. Same rule applies for Levi as it did Micah. We'll hear what he has to say, and then we'll give our opinions. Now, go ahead, son."

Memories of all the times Micah had been in trouble then rescued by Pa swarmed in and threatened to undo the desire to forgive his brother and work with him. Levi couldn't let that happen. He'd been too late to make up with Pa, but he had time now to do it with Ma and the rest of the family.

He stared at Micah, who gazed back without a waver, waiting for Levi to continue. "When you returned, all those old feelings of jealousy rose up and clouded my judgment. All I could see was the repetition of all that had happened before you left. I was tired of being the good son who always did what his parents wanted, so the best thing for me to do was to get away from here before I did something worse."

Micah's gazed remained glued to Levi's. He swallowed hard and prepared for the words he must say next. "I might have killed you, Micah, just to keep you from getting control of the ranch and taking my place."

Ma's gasp and his sisters' murmurs of disbelief tore at Levi and cut his heart into shards. How had he fallen so far away from God that he would even consider taking his brother's life? "My leaving was the best thing for all of us at the time."

Silence now ensued as each one seemed to collect his or her own thoughts about Levi's revelation.

Micah was the first to break the somber mood that had descended on the group like a shroud. "I had no idea you felt that way, Levi. I always thought Pa favored you, and the only way I could get his attention was by being bad."

Ma slapped her hands together. "You're both wrong as sin. Your father loved you both and was so proud of both of his sons. Micah, your grades in school made him almost bust his buttons with praise. And you, Levi, how you rode around after him and dogged his footsteps to learn everything you could about the ranch pleased him no end. You may have disappointed him by your leaving, Micah, and you as well, Levi, but he always knew that you'd be home again, Micah, and he believed with all his heart that you would too, Levi. And he was right."

Margaret wiped away the tears on her cheeks with her fingers. "Pa didn't know how to tell us how much he loved us, but he showed me in all kinds of ways, like teaching me how to ride and how to swim, and encouraging us to read and learn. He did with you too, but you were both too jealous of each other to see it."

Memories of Pa letting him take chances and try new ways of doing things flooded Levi's mind. That was Pa showing his love and pride. He sneaked a peek at Micah, who now wore the beginnings of a smile.

Levi stretched out his hand. "Truce, brother?"

Micah grabbed it and pulled Levi toward him. "Yes, brother, we'll be the partners we should have been from the beginning."

Ma clapped her hands with joy. "I knew we could work these things out if I could ever get you two to sit down and talk with each other." She hooked her hands onto the elbows of her sons. "Now, I think it's time for a little refreshment. There's still some cobbler left from supper, so let me go warm it up and fix some coffee."

That sounded good to Levi, and he kissed her cheek. "Lead the way. My stomach's calling out for that piece with my name on it."

Rose's arms came around his waist. "I'm so glad you're here. I've missed you so much. Micah's been too busy to talk to me. Now maybe I'll have more time with both of you."

Levi leaned down to kiss the top of her head. "You will, little one, I promise."

After they had laughed and reminisced over coffee and cobbler, new contentment filled Levi like he'd never experienced before. Levi rose to leave. "I'll need to go back and let Mr. Hudson know I'm coming back here, although I'm sure he won't be surprised. He's been after me the whole time to come home." Then Ellie came to mind. That was one stop he looked forward to making.

Ma grinned like someone had handed her the moon. "Good for him. I always knew that man had good sense."

"I'll follow you out to your horse. Need to check on Smokey. I just left him standing there when I saw you were here."

Micah walked with him outside. Before Levi mounted his horse, Micah grasped his shoulder. "It's good to have you home. We'll save this place for Pa yet. We'll go into town tomorrow and meet with Hightower. He'll tell us how we can carry out our plans." Then he grinned and slapped Levi's back. "I know of a little gal you need to see pretty quick and let her know what's going on."

"Yeah, I'm thinking the same thing." Now it was his time to grin and give it right back to his brother. "And on that subject, she's the best thing that ever happened to me. Finding the right girl to settle down with can make a big difference. I know things didn't work out with Camilla, but then she's really not for you."

"With more men than women in this town, finding the right girl will be hard to do."

"Oh, I don't think you have to look farther than the doc's office to find one who would be perfect for you." Levi swung up onto his horse before Micah could react except to open his mouth and gape. The expression on his brother's face was priceless.

Levi yanked on the reins and laughed. "I see that's been more than a passing thought with you too. See you tomorrow." Then he spurred Maverick up the road, leaving Micah to ponder that last statement. Tomorrow might turn out to be a more interesting day than any Saturday in recent history.

CHAPTER 26

THE NEXT MORNING Micah took more time to think about Levi's parting words last night as he rode to town to meet Levi. Hannah was a smart, talented woman. He'd heard her playing the piano one Saturday afternoon he'd been in town and passed by the doc's house. Not only that, but she was also pretty to look at. As hard as he tried, he couldn't get the image of her last night at the saloon out of his mind. Feisty and ready to speak her mind described Hannah Dyer perfectly.

God had played a cruel trick on Hannah by giving her that short leg. No one should have a burden like that. He must overlook it and look instead to her heart and her love of people.

His fingers touched the cheek where she had kissed him the other night. Light and soft as a feather her lips had brushed his cheek. The soft spot she had opened grew until he had to admit that the real barrier to a relationship with her was her love of God and her faith. After all he'd been through and all he'd done, he didn't deserve God's love, much less the love of a woman like Hannah.

Micah shook his head to clear it of those thoughts and images of Hannah. A clear head was necessary this morning to talk with Alex Hightower and Mr. Swenson. When Micah turned the corner onto Main Street, he spotted Levi dismounting his horse in front of the lawyer's office. He waved then stepped up to the boardwalk to wait for Micah. Just like his brother to be ahead of time, but then that would be an asset in the future.

Levi had grown into a strong young man, and now that Micah had spent time with him, he saw his brother's deep love for the family and the ranch. If things worked out as Micah hoped, together they could restore the Circle G to its former heights as one of the most successful ranches in the county.

Micah tied Smokey's reins and grinned at his brother. "Right on time as usual."

"This is too important a day to waste time. Before going to Hudson's last night, I stopped and made sure Hightower would have time for us this morning. He's waiting for us in his office, but Mr. Murphy has returned and is there with him."

"Didn't Murphy handle Pa's affairs before he left?"

"Yes, but Ma had the will, so Hightower handled it for us."

"Then let's get to it." Micah followed Levi into the office where Hightower sat with Mr. Murphy going over a folder of papers. He rose and gestured for them to have a seat.

Sitting in the same chair where he'd listened to the attorney read his father's will sent a chill of anticipation down his spine. This would be the beginning of a partnership that would have made Pa proud and would give Ma assurance about her future.

Mr. Hightower cleared his throat. "Levi gave me some idea of what you two are planning with your father's estate, but Mr. Murphy has something from your father you need to hear."

Micah leaned forward in his chair, his hat between his hands. His heart pounded as he stared at the man who had handled the Gordon affairs for so many years. He glanced at Levi and shook his head slightly to indicate he had no more idea of what Murphy had to say than Levi did.

Mr. Murphy cleared his throat. "I'm sorry I was away

when your pa passed away. With my grandparents' death in St. Louis, I had to be there to help settle the estate, and it took much longer than we expected."

He paused and looked from Micah to Levi and back again. "Your father was very much into tradition, and that meant the ranch would go to the oldest son. Micah, he was sure you'd return someday, and he was adamant about leaving the ranch as your legacy. But recently he left a message with the clerk in my office to see him on my return in regards to changing a part of his will concerning Levi. Your mother confirmed that, but unfortunately he did not have a chance to specify the changes before he died."

Micah furrowed his brow. "I want to give at least half of the ranch to Levi. We want to be full partners in the Circle G. Does the will allow that?"

Alex Hightower picked up a folder. "That's what I figured you'd want to do. You do realize that right now the bank owns the ranch and will continue to do so unless you can pay off the loan. If you aren't able to do that, then you can't divide half of nothing."

Hope dissipated like the morning dew in the sunshine. The loan muddied the waters. It had cost Pa his life, and now it may cost Micah and Levi their futures. "But if we pay off the loan?"

"Then we can talk about this again when that happens."

Levi jumped up and paced back and forth along the width of the room. "That means we have to get a full herd to market and get it there ahead of others. The earlier we're there, the higher the prices will be per head."

Micah nodded firmly. "We're getting those cattle to market, and we'll come back and pay the loan. Right, Levi?"

"Right." Levi jammed his hat onto his head. "Maybe we

need to talk to Swenson about this." He turned on his heel and headed out the door.

Micah jumped up to follow but leaned on Alex's desk and addressed the two men. "Know this about the Gordon family. We're not going down without a fight, and with Levi's help, we're going to save everything. You may as well get started on making us both a part of that deed."

"We'll do all we can on our end." Mr. Murphy nodded toward the door. "Right now you'd better go after your brother and see Mr. Swenson together."

"I will." He jammed his hat on his head and strode from the office. Getting the cattle to market and getting a fair price for them now became more important than ever.

A commotion of shouting and running came from the street. Micah stepped onto the boardwalk outside the lawyer's office with Alex right behind him. Mr. Swenson stood in the middle of the street with the sheriff and a small crowd of onlookers.

Had the bank been robbed again? Micah headed toward the group, but Levi spotted him and ran over.

"They finally caught the bank robbers and got back almost all the money. They're over in the next county, and the sheriff there is bringing them back here to stand trial for robbery, assault, and murder. Soon as Mr. Swenson is finished talking with the sheriff, he'll sit down and listen to what we have to say."

That meant with the money being returned, they'd have back the part stolen from Pa too. Their debt would be cut in half. Although Mr. Swenson had not asked it, Micah had planned to pay back what Pa had borrowed plus the amount stolen. "That's the best news I've heard all day. I think I need a drink after all we've found out this morning."

Levi grabbed Micah's shirt sleeve. "You're not going to the saloon. It's too early in the morning for one thing, and drinking is bad for you anyway."

Micah bellowed out a laugh and wrapped his arm around Levi's shoulder. The saloon was the last place he wanted to be. "Right on both counts, little brother, but a cup of coffee and a cinnamon bun from the bakery would sure hit the spot. Don't you think so?"

"That I do. My stomach's rumbling for it now."

They both laughed, and Micah kept his arm on Levi's shoulders as they walked across to the bakery. A few more problems had cropped up, but with the two of them working together, a little understanding from Mr. Swenson, and a successful cattle drive, he and Levi could handle anything that came their way.

Hannah paced the floor in Ellie's parlor. "How long do you think it's going to take them to get through at that lawyer's office? I can't stand the suspense."

"I have no idea, but Levi said they'd come here as soon as they had taken care of business. We'll have to be patient and wait."

"I'm so happy Micah and Levi have made up. I just hope Micah isn't mad at me for showing up at the saloon last night. I was so embarrassed, but I was also determined to make him see how wrong he was in not making a move to reconcile with his brother. But I hadn't planned on making a scene in front of such a crowd." Even now her cheeks burned with the way she had conducted herself last evening. Still, Micah had taken her words to heart and had gone home.

Ellie picked up a piece of cross-stitch work and sat down in a rocking chair. "When Levi came by last night and told me what had happened, I was so happy and cried so hard that it scared him. I had to tell him they were happy tears. When he asked if there was still a chance for us, I said of course."

Hannah had heard this all once if not twice before, but she didn't intend to mar Ellie's happiness by pointing out that little fact. "I'm so glad you asked Levi and Micah to come to dinner at your place today. I only pray that Micah will come. If he doesn't, I'm going home. I'm not about to spoil your time with Levi."

"I think Micah will come, and he'll be surprised you're here, but he'll accept it and we'll have a nice dinner for the four of us. Mama and Papa have already left for Gloria's place. They're always ready to see their grandson."

At first Hannah had worried about two women being alone in the house with two men without a proper chaperone, but Mrs. Bradshaw had assured her that in broad daylight, no one would think anything about it. Still, Hannah remembered how strict her parents were back in Mississippi and her grandparents in Louisiana. Even though she had scorned the idea of chaperones, she hesitated in breaking any rules. Maybe Texas could be more lenient because it was part of what her parents called "the Frontier."

Hannah lifted her skirt and stared down at her elevated shoe. "I'm worried Micah will be upset and won't want to stay. I remember the expression on his face that day at the depot when he first saw my ugly boot." She'd never forget it, and if it meant what it usually did, Micah would never look at her with anything but pity.

"Things can change. Look at how he danced with you at

your party. He seemed to be enjoying your company rather nicely."

"But he was simply being a gentleman and doing his duty with the guest of honor." The kiss the other night hadn't helped any either. He must think her to be rather brazen to do something like that when they weren't even courting. She cringed inside. How many times had she said that to herself in the past few days?

"Hannah, are you all right? You looked a little pained there for the moment."

Heat filled Hannah's face. "I...I was remembering something that happened the other night when Micah brought me home from my visit out to see Rose." Ellie said nothing but cocked her head to one side and raised her eyebrows. Maybe if Ellie knew, she'd help. "I...I kissed Micah. On the cheek, mind you, but it was still a kiss. I'm embarrassed even telling you about it."

Ellie laughed. "Oh, Hannah, that's priceless. I bet Micah was surprised right out of his boots, and I bet he enjoyed every second of it."

"You don't think he'll think I was being too forward?" At least Ellie hadn't disapproved, and it had been enjoyable. Her lips tingled every time she remembered the roughness of the stubble on his face.

The door burst open, and Mr. Bradshaw appeared, out of breath and bent over.

"Papa! What is it? Is Mama all right?"

"Everything's fine, my dear. We just heard the news that the bank robbers have been captured. The sheriff's on his way over here to bring them back for trial. I thought you and Hannah would want to know."

Ellie threw her arms around her father in a hug. "Oh, that

is great news. I imagine that's what's keeping Levi and Micah from being here before now. Thank you for letting us know."

What a blessing for Micah and his brother. Now they would see justice done for the men who had caused the death of their father. With so many witnesses, the trial should be swift and sure. Hannah breathed a prayer of gratitude for the capture of the men.

After Mr. Bradshaw left, Ellie waved her hand. "Come on, let's get things ready. Our men should be here shortly. And we have cause to truly celebrate now."

Hannah wasn't sure they had cause for that yet. She'd save her celebration mood until Micah and Levi arrived. She'd be able to tell from their faces what tone would be set for the afternoon. She prayed it would be a time of happiness for all of them.

The aroma of the roasting chicken and baking bread filled the room as Hannah finished setting the table. So much depended on the outcome of this dinner. Either Micah would be pleased and spend the afternoon with them, or he would be indifferent and leave without eating.

A knock called her attention to the front door. Ellie tugged off her apron and tossed it toward a chair. "They're here."

Hannah's heart thumped and butterflies had a field day in her stomach. She gripped the back of a chair as Ellie opened the door.

Levi stepped through the door first and wrapped his arms around Ellie. "We've had both wonderful news and some not so good, but we're starving and ready for one of your meals."

Micah entered behind Levi. His eyes opened wide, and his brow furrowed. "Miss Dyer, I didn't expect to see you here."

Hannah's heart plummeted, and she wished she could disappear. This had been a really bad idea.

CHAPTER 27

BOTH DISMAY AND delight filled Micah when his gaze locked with Hannah's. Delight to find her here, and dismay that he'd be close to her for the afternoon. How could he sit next to her and have any kind of conversation if he couldn't control his heart and had to admit to himself his growing feelings for her?

Hannah spoke up, breaking the awkward silence. "Ellie invited me to share time with you today. I hope you're not displeased that I'm here."

He removed his hat, continuing to stare at her. Red tinged her cheeks. She must be as embarrassed by this as he was. Perhaps she remembered the other evening and the kiss she'd bestowed upon his cheek. Not to mention the little scene at the saloon last night. "No, I'm glad you're able to join us." And he had to admit that pleasure overrode the dismay.

Levi grinned from ear to ear. "This has been a most productive morning, and I do believe it's going to be an even better afternoon."

"Papa came and told us about the bank robbers being captured. I hope that's not the only good news you have to share." Ellie stood beside Levi and held his arm.

They looked as natural together as Ma and Pa had when he was alive. What would it be like to have that kind of love from a woman? He glanced at Hannah, and something rumbled in his chest. Not hunger pangs, those would be in his stomach. This was different from anything he'd ever experienced, and it took all of his willpower not to touch his cheek where she'd planted that kiss.

Levi squeezed Ellie's hand. "No, we have some things to work out with Pa's will, but Mr. Swenson is so delighted to be getting back almost all the money stolen, that he's willing to work with us to take care of the bank loan."

Hannah clasped her hands and raised them to her lips. "That is good news, but what's the bad?"

They might as well tell the ladies the whole story, so they'd understand why the next month was so important. "If we don't get our herd to market and make a good sale, we won't have the money to pay the loan and the ranch will belong to the bank, not us. Right now, Levi has agreed to come back, and he's to be in charge. I'll handle the books and take care of finances."

"I know the two of you can make the drive and take care of the loan. Levi's being home is what you really wanted, isn't it?" Hannah's eyes sparkled joy and excitement. He hoped some of that happened to be aimed at him and the fact that they would be together for the afternoon.

Levi nodded and hugged Ellie close. "Yes, and now this young lady and I can get on with our plans for a wedding next year."

"That's wonderful. I'm so happy for you and Ellie." Hannah paused, then asked, "It's none of my business, but what did Mr. Hudson say when you told him you were leaving?"

Laughter filled the room. Micah had heard this earlier today. "Mr. Hudson was delighted. He'd been trying to get Levi to come home ever since he arrived there looking for a job."

A spot of red crept into Levi's face. "That's right. He kept after me, but I was too stubborn to see the wisdom of his words. He even gave me a bonus with my pay when I left because he was so happy I'd seen the light."

"Oh, Levi, that's wonderful. Sallie, the doctor, and I have been praying for you every day. We knew the Lord would someday open your eyes to what you needed to do."

There it was again. Hannah's faith. How could she love him when he didn't see God her way? Wait a minute. What did love have to do with it? Was that where this was headed? Even if he did love her, God didn't love him, or was what had happened yesterday and today really an answer to prayer and God's plan? That would take time to digest and was not something he wanted to think about at the moment. Ellie had a dinner prepared.

Micah patted his belly. "I smell good food, and it's calling to me. Can we eat now?"

"Of course; I'll put it on the table. Hannah and I will be right back."

Micah and Levi found their places at the table and stood behind their chairs. A minute or so later Hannah and Ellie returned bearing food that looked fit for a king. Levi was one lucky young man to have a pretty woman like Ellie who could also cook.

After the women set the platters and bowls on the table, Micah held out a chair for Hannah. "If this tastes as good as it looks, I might eat myself into oblivion."

"Hannah helped me. She fixed the potatoes and made the gravy, and she brought over the pie she made this morning."

So the nurse could cook too. "Then I'm more than ready to dig into this feast." He sat down as the others clasped hands and Hannah and Ellie reached for his. He sucked in his breath and hoped Ellie would ask Levi to say grace. Micah would participate and hold hands, but he had no desire to pray aloud.

Levi did offer the prayer, but Micah heard little of it. Why did God have to play such a big part in their lives? These three people had more faith than he had been able to muster in all twenty-four years of his life. No matter how much he wanted to forget God and enjoy life, the faith of those around him kept interfering.

During the meal he and Levi explained to the girls about the cattle drive and the auction at the other end. Then Hannah served the dessert of custard pie that slid down his palate smooth as silk. Admiration for her stepped up another rung on the ladder to his heart.

Ellie stood and began gathering dishes. "Levi will help me in the kitchen. Why don't you two have a seat in the parlor and talk while we work."

Hannah protested, "No, Ellie, let me help you. After all, you did most of the cooking."

"Don't be silly." Then her eyes took on a mischievous gleam. "You're a guest. Besides, I do want some time alone with this cowboy here."

"Oh, of course, I didn't think." Hannah turned to Micah and bit her lip. "I guess you're stuck with me."

That wasn't quite the word he'd use. Pleasure of her company would be more like it. Both Ma and Margaret had told him much about Hannah, but he wanted to know more, and now would be the perfect time.

"Then let's make the most of it. How about a walk? I think I need to do that or else fall asleep from being so full." He held out his hand, and she reached over and took it. The warmth from her hand spread up his arm like butter on hot pancakes and melted away any doubts he might have about a relationship. This woman was special.

Hannah picked up a parasol to shade her face from the afternoon sun. He hadn't considered the heat at this time of day since he was so accustomed to being out in it. "Perhaps it would be better if we stayed inside where it's a little cooler."

"What about sitting on the porch? It's well shaded with the trees around the house, and the chairs there are quite comfortable."

"Then that's what we shall do." He opened the door and bowed. "After you, Miss Dyer."

"Oh, Mr. Gordon, aren't we friends enough to call each other by our first names? Miss Dyer is much too formal for a place like Stoney Creek."

"All right. Hannah it is." He waited until she was seated in one of the wicker chairs before he took the one next to her.

His tongue planted itself against the roof of his mouth and refused to budge. Some company he'd turned out to be. Never had he been so at a loss for conversation with a woman than he was right now. Most of the time words of flattery and small talk flowed from his lips like honey and pleased whoever happened to be with him. But not now. With Hannah all pretense left his lips, but the truth of his growing attraction for her might be too much to reveal just yet.

Finally she turned to him with a serious intent shimmering in her eyes. "I think I need to apologize for two things about my behavior the past week. I had no business kissing you like I did. That was most forward of me."

"I accept your apology, but there's no need to. In fact, I wouldn't be offended if you did it again anytime." He almost choked on the words. What was he doing? Now she'd be embarrassed if not offended. Indeed, her cheeks already bloomed a bright rose pink.

"Now it's my turn to seek apology. I didn't mean to embarrass you. I meant that I enjoyed your company. Um...what was the other thing you wanted to apologize for?" Best to get away from the subject of that kiss, although he'd like nothing better than to lean over and place one on those pretty lips right now.

Her throat moved up and down as she swallowed and licked her lips. "Well, I also owe you an apology for my behavior in the saloon. That was most unladylike, and I had no business accosting you the way I did."

"But it got the job done, Hannah. I left that place and went straight home where Levi was visiting with Ma." That was another thing he'd never be sorry about her doing.

"Then I'm glad I did. Seeing you and Levi laugh at dinner made me so happy. God has truly answered our prayers and brought the two of you back together."

There it was. That God thing again. "I don't think God had much to do with it. We talked and worked things out between us." Of course Ma had a big hand in it by making them obey her first, but he hadn't seen God doing anything.

She leaned toward him and shook her head. "But don't you see, we all prayed for it to happen because we knew the split wasn't what God wanted for you. He loves you too much for that."

He reached over and grasped her hands. "Hannah, God doesn't love me. I've gone too far away, and nothing but pain and misery have come my way for it."

She pulled her shoulders back and got that set look about her like Ma had before she gave him a good scolding. He'd hear another one right now, and he most likely deserved it too.

"Micah Gordon, God didn't give you the pain and misery. You made bad choices and suffered as a result. God still loves you. He sent Jesus to die for you and forgive your sins. It doesn't matter what you did in the past, God wants your heart for the future. He has a wonderful future planned for you and Levi if you'll listen to Him."

The words repeated much of what Ma had said, but how could he believe them after all that had happened in his life? If Pa's dying was part of God's plan, then it wasn't a very good plan. He stared at Hannah, and the peace that shone from her face stabbed him with guilt. Would he ever have peace like that?

"That sounds good, Hannah, but how can it be? He let Pa die, and now we're in danger of losing the ranch because he's not here."

"But your pa is here. The knowledge and skills he gave you and Levi will never leave you. If you and Levi do what you're capable of doing, you won't lose the ranch."

If only he could believe that. "I don't know, Hannah. It's all so confusing right now. The only thing I'm sure of is that Levi and I must save the ranch."

"And you will. We're all praying for you to do just that."

He moved his chair to be directly in front of her and held her hands. "Hannah, your faith is beautiful, but I have none. How could you or God care for someone like me?"

Before she could respond, he leaned forward. "I'm falling in love with you, Miss Hannah Dyer, but I don't deserve someone like you in my life, and you can certainly do better than me." He reached up and pulled her face to his and kissed her. The emotion that washed over him in that kiss scared him, but he couldn't stop, especially when Hannah responded, grasping the sides of his neck with her hands.

He pulled back. "Good-bye, Hannah. Tell Levi I'll see him at the ranch." He reached for his hat then all but ran to Smokey. The sooner he got away from here, the sooner he could forget the young woman still seated on the porch and her God.

Tears flooded Hannah's eyes. Both joy and sorrow flowed down her cheeks as she touched her lips that had been covered by Micah's. He had said he was falling in love with her, but he'd left her. He thought he didn't deserve her love. How could she possibly do any better than to have a man like Micah in love with her?

Somehow she had to make him see that God's love extended to everyone regardless of where they were in life. Micah was not the same man who'd left Stoney Creek five years ago. The man she'd seen was caring and determined to do what was right. Yes, he'd had a few lapses with his drinking, but it hadn't taken over his life again as it could have.

God's love for the prodigal had brought him home to make a better life for himself and his family. Her own love for Micah began to grow anew. He hadn't even mentioned her bad foot. Maybe that meant her deformity didn't matter, but her practical side took over. It could also mean that he had decided he didn't deserve to be burdened down with her problem or her ugly body. Hannah wrapped her arms across her chest and bit her lip. *Lord, please help me know the truth about Micah's love, and bring him back to You. Whatever happens after that, I leave in Your hands.*

CHAPTER 28

HANNAH WORKED AT her nursing duties with a heavy heart. Micah had not been at church Sunday, and now it had been almost a week since she'd last seen him at Ellie's. When he had left last Saturday, she'd gone home and wept and spilled her heart to Sallie.

No logical explanation for Micah's sudden departure could be found by Hannah or her sister. Margaret could tell her nothing at church except that Micah had left the house early, before any of the rest of them had risen. He didn't return until after dinner. Ma had saved him back a plate, but Margaret didn't see him or talk with him.

Manfred opened the door to the examining room a crack and poked his head through. "Mrs. Jarvis will be here shortly for a checkup. When you finish in here, come on over and take notes while I talk with her."

"Of course; I'll be in as soon as she arrives." Mrs. Jarvis was recovering from deep lung congestion, and the doctor wanted to keep a close eye on her because of her age. The elderly woman had recently celebrated her eighty-first birthday, and Manfred wanted to keep her healthy.

That shouldn't be a problem for the feisty woman who still took care of her own home and boarded two young men who'd recently come to town. Hannah stowed the last bandage and smiled. She should look so good and be so active when she reached eighty years of age or more.

With that chore finished, Hannah checked her watch. At least twenty minutes remained before Mrs. Jarvis would be in, but knowing her, ten minutes could be cut from that time.

Mrs. Jarvis always arrived at least ten minutes ahead of her appointment time. A cup of tea would definitely hit the spot right now.

In the kitchen Hannah found the kettle of water always kept hot on the back of the stove. She made her tea, found a cinnamon cookie in the tin, and sat down to enjoy her break. As she sipped her tea, questions and doubts about Micah returned again and again. She pressed her lips together, remembering the kiss last Saturday. Everything had gone so well until the subject of Hannah's faith came up.

Micah either didn't want to believe God could love him, or he didn't want to admit that God's love had kept him safe all the years he'd been away. Either way, until Micah made a decision to accept the Lord back into his life, she doubted he would make any effort to see her or further their relationship. Nor, in truth, could she encourage him to do so.

Sallie came into the kitchen and grabbed her apron from a hook by the door. "Oh, I didn't expect to see you here."

"I'm taking a break before Mrs. Jarvis gets here. I thought maybe a cup of tea would cheer me up a little." Although it did soothe, the herbal brew did nothing for her morale.

"I see." Sallie pulled out a chair and sat across the table from Hannah. "I take it you're still thinking about Micah."

"You're right, I am. Things were going so smoothly as we talked, and I really thought he would come around to seeing God's love for him again. But he hasn't even tried to see me or communicate with me this past week. It's been the longest week of my life."

"I'm sure it has, but you have to give him as much time as it takes for him to work out what he wants. Now that Levi is home and helping out, he has more time to think about his future and the place of God in his life. Our Lord is patient and understanding, so you must be too."

Patience had never been one of Hannah's virtues, and every time she needed it, it eluded her even more. "I know, but waiting is so hard. What if he never comes back to his faith? Where will that leave us?"

"I can't answer that, sweetie. Only the Lord knows what's in Micah's heart and in his future. If that future does include you, it will become clear to him, and he will come to you."

If that never happened, her heart would break. For the first time in her life a man had said he loved her, and she loved him back. She had dreamed of that day, but now it seemed that nothing would come of it. She'd go on being a nurse until she could no longer carry out her duties.

"My head knows that, but my heart wants Micah now. Being in love with him is like nothing I ever imagined. My only concern is for his happiness and well-being. It turns September tomorrow, and soon they'll be leaving with the cattle to take them to auction. If only I could know something before they leave."

Molly burst through the door with all the energy of an eleven-year-old. "Papa said to tell you Mrs. Jarvis is here."

"Oh, my, the time went too fast." Hannah drained the last of her tea and hurried to the front where Manfred stood with Mrs. Jarvis.

"Sorry I'm late. I went back to the kitchen for a cup of tea."

Mrs. Jarvis stood no more than an inch over five feet tall, but her stance made her appear inches taller. "That's quite all right, my dear. I'm a bit early as usual, and a spot of tea in the afternoon always picks up my spirits."

Hannah followed Mrs. Jarvis and Manfred into the

examining room. All thoughts of Micah must be put on hold for the time being. She had a patient who needed her attention.

Micah pulled off his bandana and wiped his forehead. The heat bore down, reminding him that it was the last day of August. In a few days they'd be herding these cattle on a drive to market.

Having Levi back in the fold had eased Micah's burden, but after two days of checking into prices for bulls and wiring around for the best cattle prices, he found he missed riding with his men. Now here he sat on Smokey in the heat and dust checking on his men and the cattle.

In order to drive the cattle the six hundred miles or so to Dodge City and get back before winter set in, they planned to leave next week. If they made ten to fifteen miles a day, they'd get to market and be back before Thanksgiving. With the loan being due the first of December, that would be a good timeline.

Roy Bateman rode to his side. "Levi and I worked out the trail positions for our drive. You and he will be my point men. We'll rotate the others and set up a lottery for first positions. You think that new kid, Jeremy Dobbs, can handle the remuda?"

"Yes. Even though it's not the best job to have and you always give it to the newest boys, with his love of horses, he should do fine." During his seventeenth year that had been Micah's job, and it hadn't been easy.

"All right. We'll take care of the rest of it tonight at the bunkhouse."

Levi rode up to join them. "The herd looks good." Then he grinned at Micah. "I thought you were going to stay away from this until time to leave. Why aren't you back at the house ciphering up numbers?"

"Strange as it may sound, after the past few months on the job, I found I missed it."

"That's a good one. But I tell you right now, I'm ready to get back to the house and get some of Ma's cooking in my belly. It'll be a long while before we have it after we leave."

He waved at Bateman. "I'll see you at the bunkhouse later tonight." He reined his horse around. "If you're coming with me, I'll race you back. Maverick's still faster than anything you can ride." With that he slapped Maverick's rump and took off.

Micah waved his hat. "Yee-haw, little brother, you're on!"

When they arrived back at the ranch house, Levi beat Micah out by only a few feet. As Micah pulled Smokey up at the corral, he noticed a strange horse tied up near the house. "Looks like we have company. Let's check on Ma."

He left his horse at the corral and headed for the house with Levi right behind him. When he entered the parlor, Mr. Murphy sat talking with Ma. She wore a face-splitting grin, and Mr. Murphy appeared a might pleased himself.

"Oh, Micah, Levi, Mr. Murphy has wonderful news."

"Yes, I do. Have a seat and I'll explain it to you."

Micah and Levi exchanged looks and raised eyebrows, but they sat down to hear what the man had to say. "Did you figure a way for us both to have the ranch?" Micah asked.

"Matter of fact I did, and that's the second thing I have to tell you. The first is that in going through Mr. Gordon's papers, I came across an investment he'd made a number of years ago. It was a partnership in a silver mine up in

Colorado. Your mother tells me she remembers him doing it to help a friend get a mine started. I did some checking and contacted the owners. They had lost track of your father and are quite anxious to buy your father's portion."

Micah's mouth dropped open. A silver mine in Colorado? "Is it worth it to sell it?"

Ma could hardly contain her enthusiasm. "That's the best part. You won't believe it."

Murphy grinned. "It's enough to more than pay back the bank loan, take care of the mortgage, and all the other expenses."

Micah glanced at Levi. He wore the same incredulous look as Micah felt deep inside. This was the answer to all their problems with the ranch. Now the money from the cattle sale could be invested back into the ranch. "Then do it. Sell it and take care of the bank."

"I hoped you'd say that because I have the papers all ready for you to sign."

Levi leaned forward. "That's all well and good, but what about the other?"

Again Murphy grinned and extracted another sheet of paper from his carrying case. "As soon as the loans are paid at the bank, Swenson will turn over the deed, and I'll make arrangements to put it in both your names."

Micah shook his head and grinned. "That's even better news than the silver mine." Micah stretched out his hand to Levi. "Looks like we'll be partners, brother."

Levi laughed and shook Micah's hand. "That sounds like the best deal I've ever heard."

If any more good news came his way, Micah's heart might burst clean out of his chest. In less than fifteen minutes all their immediate problems had been solved. Pa had left them more than they ever dreamed. God had answered their prayers. Yes, he'd acknowledge God on this one. No one but Him could ever have put together such a miracle for this family.

With that realization came one more. He had to see Hannah and make things right with her. After he'd neglected her all week, she might not welcome him now, but he had to try. In the midst of the celebrating with his family he sent a plea heavenward. *Lord, You've done this mighty miracle, but can I please ask for one more? Let Your love flow through me and show Hannah how much I love her and how I now understand what she told me about You.*

When God answered that prayer, his life would be complete.

CHAPTER 29

After spending Saturday making final preparations for the cattle drive, Micah had dropped into bed exhausted, but he had fallen asleep with the knowledge he'd be at church and would see Hannah today.

Filled with anticipation, he rose from bed early and dressed in his best black pants, white shirt, and black leather vest. The aroma of bacon and biscuits drifted up the stairs and hastened his last bit of grooming.

When he entered the kitchen, Ma hummed her favorite hymn. He couldn't remember the name, but the familiar sound filled Micah with peace and comfort. He bent over and pecked her cheek with a kiss.

"You sound mighty happy this morning." He reached around to snag a piece of crisp bacon.

She slapped at his hand. "I have every reason to be. Both my boys are back home, and from the looks of you, we're all going to church this morning."

"Yes, we are. That is if my lazy, late-rising brother and sisters can get ready in time."

Margaret slipped through the back door. "Oh, we'll be ready. I've been up a lot longer than you." She handed a basket of eggs to Ma. "If I hadn't, you might have cold grits for breakfast."

A few minutes later Ma poured the beaten eggs into the skillet, and the rest of the family joined them in the kitchen. Rose hugged Micah's waist. "Are you going to church with us today?"

Micah pulled a braid and laughed. "Yes, I am, little one.

We're going to be a family this morning." In addition, he'd get to see Hannah. Now if God answered that one last prayer, it'd be an even better day.

Margaret picked up a stack of plates. "Would your mind also be on Hannah Dyer? She's a fine catch, you know." She winked at him and slipped through the door to the dining room.

Ma simply smiled and stacked biscuits on a platter. Even Rose had a smirk on her face as she poured a glass of milk. His family had ganged up on him this morning, but he didn't care. He'd shout his love for Hannah from the rooftop if it would make a difference.

Later, as they rode up to the church as a family once more, Hannah saw them and waved. The expression on her face lit up his heart like those fireworks he'd seen up in Dallas one July Fourth. She made her way through the gathering crowd to the carriage.

"Oh, my, it's so good to see all of you here this morning." She spoke to Ma and Margaret, but her gaze strayed Micah's way. He touched the brim of his hat in greeting, and her cheeks burned red again as she turned away from him and locked arms with Margaret. When she stumbled going up the steps, Micah frowned. He'd forgotten about her short-ened leg. This time, instead of pity, a sense of wanting to pro-tect her and hold her and make sure she never stumbled or fell again swept over him.

After everyone was seated inside the church, Ma's beaming face made this trip worth the effort of coming. Once, as a child, he'd believed God was good and loved everyone. He remembered the Bible verse he'd proudly said as a five-year-old. "God is love" from chapter four of First John, the sixteenth verse. Of course it wasn't the whole verse, but that's what he remembered.

Reverend Weatherby set his gaze on the Gordon family. "We are full of joy this morning to see the Gordon family with us. God has answered our prayers and brought these two brothers together."

Murmurs and smiles of approval swept the room and surrounded the family, especially Micah, with love. How could he have missed the love in this church? His own selfish pride had blinded him to the truth. He turned his attention to the minister, who began his sermon for the morning.

When Reverend Weatherby began quoting verses from First John, chapter four, a lump grew in Micah's throat as the pastor read from the Bible. "Herein is love, not that we loved God, but that he loved us, and sent his Son to be the propitiation for our sins."

Affirmation of what he'd come to believe sent a shiver through Micah. If he ever believed the Bible, then he had to believe the verses read from the pulpit. Then another verse came to his memory. *We love him, because he first loved us.*

That scripture took on a whole new meaning for Micah, and he couldn't wait to talk with Hannah and tell her what had happened. After what seemed an eternity, the message ended and the last song was sung and the last prayer given.

Micah scooted from the pew and sought Hannah's red-gold hair in the crowd. He spotted her talking with her niece Molly. He approached them and touched Hannah's arm. "May I have a few words with you, please?"

Molly's eyes crinkled at the corners, and she grinned at Micah. "I'll be outside with Mama and Papa." Then she winked at them and hastened up the aisle to the foyer.

Hannah lowered her gaze. "I'm sorry. Molly can be precocious at times."

"That's all right, but can we step outside where it's less crowded?" What he had to say to her wasn't meant for the listening ears of parishioners.

"Of course." She swished her skirt and headed outside.

Micah followed, and at the bottom of the steps nodded toward a few trees to the side of the church. Once they were alone, he stared at her. So much to say, but where could he start? "Hannah, I don't even know where to begin. The reason I left Stoney Creek in the first place was because Pa and I didn't see eye to eye. I always thought he didn't love me or approve of me, so I ran. Not only did I run from Pa, but I ran from God because I believed God must not love me either because nothing I did was right. I blamed God for all my failures and the bad condition I was in. Then I decided I didn't want to live that way, pulled myself together, found a job, made enough money, then came home."

Nothing changed in Hannah's expression. Her clear blue eyes offered no judgment, no condemnation. He went on. "When I returned, everything went from bad to worse, and I blamed God for it all again. He was punishing me, and I didn't like it."

She grasped his arm. "Oh, Micah, God never stopped loving you."

"I know that now, and Reverend Weatherby's message this morning opened my eyes to something else. God's love is always there. He never takes it away. He's loved me all through these years of rebellion." Micah's heart pounded as he spoke the words aloud, words he never dreamed of saying again. Now, with the woman he loved standing before him, he began to understand the deeper side of God's love.

"God protected you all those years. Even in the poor choices you made, He protected your life and kept you safe. Think of the timing for your return. God already knew your pa would die and when, so He made sure you were home to give support to your mother and sisters. He gave you the ranch so you could learn responsibility. His hands have been all over you."

When his mother had said almost the same thing to him, the words had fallen on deaf ears. Now the truth of those words sank deep into his soul. He'd truly come home now, and with God's help, everything would fall into place.

A peace like he'd never experienced came over him. Nothing could keep him from being the son his father wanted to see before his death. Only one thing remained unresolved.

Micah grasped Hannah's hands in his and pulled them to his chest. "Hannah, do you think you could love a prodigal sinner like me? Is there hope for a life with you?"

Her eyes opened wide, and her mouth broadened into the brightest smile he'd ever seen. She leaned in toward him. "That is a most definite possibility. In fact, I'd say it's a sure thing. You're a good man, Micah Gordon, and I love you."

"What do you think they'll say if I kiss you right here at the church?"

"Who cares what they think? If you don't, I'm going to pull your face down to mine and kiss you. Then they will have something to talk about."

He leaned down until his lips were only an inch away from hers. "Can't have that kind of talk about the woman I love." When their lips met, Micah gently pressed her lips until he wanted to burst. His arms went around her, and she lifted her hands to shoulders. He pressed harder, and she returned the kiss with as much love as he had for her.

Hannah drank in the love that flowed between the two of them. In all her dreams of love she could never have imagined such intensity of emotion. This could go on forever, but voices laughing and calling out intervened. She pushed back from Micah. "I think we do have an audience."

She turned her head, as did Micah, to where Levi with Ellie, and Margaret with James, stood clapping their hands. Levi even whistled. Ellie headed toward them with her arms open wide, and Margaret joined in right behind.

Ellie wrapped her arms around Hannah. "I'm so happy to see the two of you work things out. I thought I'd explode if you didn't get together."

Margaret joined her and laughed. "We can't help it. Those in love want everyone else to be too. Ellie and I were cooking up another scheme to get you two alone if necessary."

"Well, it's not necessary, unless we want it that way." She entwined her fingers with Micah's and grinned up at him. "I think we may be able to arrange that later today."

Mrs. Gordon joined the group, as did Levi and James. A minute or so later Sallie and Manfred made their appearance. Everyone talked at once, and Hannah couldn't keep up, but she turned her head from one to the other with a smile. Her heart overflowed with happiness, but one dark spot remained in the corner, pushing to be revealed. She pushed it deep. Nothing could mar the joy of this day and time.

Mrs. Gordon beamed her approval, and Hannah saw in her the mother she'd missed these months away from home. "You children come on out to the ranch for Sunday dinner. This is the greatest day, and I don't want it to end." She didn't wait for an answer but herded Rose with her to the carriage.

Micah started toward his horse still holding Hannah's hand then stopped. "How are we supposed to get out to the ranch? Levi and I both rode our horses into town."

Manfred swept his hand toward his own buggy. "Be our guest. I can ride a horse if I need to make any calls out of town."

"Are you sure, Doctor Whiteman? It would help."

As they walked toward the buggy, that dark spot pushed itself forward again. Was it possible that Micah had forgotten her disability? She had to know for sure what his thoughts were.

They walked toward the buggy with Micah holding her elbow and keeping her close. Before he lifted her up, she placed her hands on his chest. "Micah, there's one thing I have to ask you about, and you must be honest with your answer."

"Of course I will. What do you want to know?" He still held her at the waist, his face only inches above hers.

"That first day at the depot, when you saw my special built-up shoe, your face registered your pity at my deformity. You say you love me, but how do you feel about my distorted body? Will it repulse you each time you look at it?"

Micah's head bent until his forehead touched hers. "My precious Hannah, I must admit it disturbed me when I first saw it, but that was before I came to know you. I love you. Every inch of you. That deformity, as you call it, only makes you more special. I want to love you and cherish you and protect you. God gave me a gift when my eyes were opened to true love and faith. His second gift was to give me your love."

He loved her as she was, inside and out. God had answered her prayer better than she could ever have imagined. Joy erased the last bit of darkness in her soul and allowed the love she had for Micah to sweep in with full force and spread its rays of light throughout her body.

He held her close. "I can't promise what the future will hold, and it won't always be a smooth trip. I only know that God holds our future in His hands, and whatever He's planned is the best for us. I have some wonderful news to share with you on our way to the ranch. It's a miracle what God has done for our family."

"I believe He will give us exactly what we need when we need it. He won't be a minute sooner or a minute later than He wants it to be." She believed that with all her heart and prayed Micah's faith would remain strong and steadfast through the days ahead.

"With you by my side, I can face and conquer whatever comes our way." He tilted her chin and kissed her once again.

Hannah's heart soared to heights she'd never known. The future may be filled with uncertainty, but they would face it together.

Micah leaned close, his mouth only inches from her ear. "I came home to find approval from my pa, but what I found instead is your love, and that love helped me to find the faith I lost along the way."

His soft breath against her cheek sent warmth through her soul. When God started working in His children's lives, the end result would be only the best for them, and God had given her that and so much more.

She slipped her arm through Micah's and rested her head on his shoulder. Their love would be built on a faith that could carry them through whatever came in the days and years ahead. She could hardly wait until their life together began.

Coming in Fall 2014 from Martha Rogers

Book Three in
The Homeward Journey series

CHAPTER 1

MOLLY WAVED GOOD-BYE to her last student and plopped down on the top step of the school's porch. The last day of school always left her with mixed emotions. She loved the idea of three months without her students, but she hated to see the semester end. Just when everyone had truly begun to understand and make so much progress, summer came along. How much would they forget over the summer?

Ellie Gordon, the upper grades teacher, joined her on the steps. "Well, another year gone by. I'm always amazed how much the boys in my classes grow in height during the year, and how much the girls grow into young ladies."

"I know what you mean. When I look at the first graders and then the fifth graders, I can't believe how much they change. You'll be getting a good group from those fifth graders next year." Molly stood and swiped at the dust on her skirt. "It's time for me to get my things and get home."

Old friends of her parents were arriving on the train tomorrow for a visit, and Molly had to help her mother get the house ready. Of course, Mama had been working all week, but she wanted things to be perfect, so Molly had work to do.

She turned to hug Ellie, who now stood on the porch beside her. "I'm so glad you're my teaching partner. If they hadn't decided that married ladies could teach as well as unmarried ones, no telling who I may have ended up with."

Ellie's laughter floated on the warm afternoon air. "Well, I suppose since my own twin boys and Joel are here in school, they figured I would be able to do as good a job as any other. I'm happy you were here to take Miss Crabtree's place two years ago when she left. We were getting more students, and she didn't want to handle that many."

"It's a good thing Levi and Micah and Mr. Hudson decided to enlarge the building and divide into two levels." Molly turned to gaze at the expanded building that had opened last fall. Two larger classrooms were now joined with a coatroom separating them, along with space for storage of materials and supplies. New maps, chalkboards, and pictures adorned the walls, along with new desks that gave the rooms a more comfortable feel, making for a good learning environment the past school year.

Ellie headed back to her classroom. "I'm going to gather my belongings and go down to Margaret's to collect my young'uns. They do love to play together. But they can create a lot of mischief with their cousins too."

Molly laughed and shook her head. How well she understood that since those same cousins occupied her classroom as first and third graders.

After Ellie entered the building, Molly stood on the porch a few minutes longer. How she loved this town where she'd lived since early childhood. It had prospered in those years and now had two doctors to take care of the growing population. Her father had been delighted when one of Stoney Creek's own boys, Andrew Delmont, had returned as a doctor to partner in the practice.

One other thing that had changed happened to be the female population. In those years many more girls had been born than boys, and the female population of Stoney Creek had begun to overtake the males. And that meant very few men her age were single. In addition, younger families made up most of the new people coming into town recently.

Molly sighed, went back inside to collect her belongings, and gazed around her classroom once more before heading for the door. The empty desks and silence surrounded her, and she ran her fingers along the desks as she walked up the center aisle. She'd miss the children this summer, and the months loomed ahead without much activity going on. At least July would be here before she knew it. She loved the celebration for Independence Day.

Once outside, Molly realized she now had to rush to get home and help her sister with the final preparations for the Elliot family's arrival. The last time she'd seen them back in Louisiana had been for her uncle's wedding, and that was over ten years ago. Stefan Elliot was only a few months older, and at the age of twelve, he and a few friends had teased and played jokes on Molly and Clarissa, Stefan's sister.

Clarissa would be with her parents, but Stefan had followed in his father's footsteps and chosen the military as his career, so he most likely wouldn't be with his family. It would be interesting to have a man her age around though. Even though he was an eligible bachelor, her father's partner, Dr. Andrew Delmont, was too much like an older brother to be of much interest other than as a friend.

Molly bounded up the steps to the clinic run by her father and Andrew. She'd never get used to calling him Dr. Delmont. She darted through the waiting area and wiggled her fingers in her father's direction. The examination room's door was closed, which meant Andrew must be with a patient.

Mama's singing echoed from the kitchen where she made last-minute preparations for her guests. The doctor before them had a large family and had built a big house at the back of and over the area that served as an infirmary for the town. They had five bedrooms for the family, plus the infirmary had room for six patients if they needed to stay overnight.

Molly deposited her box of things from school at the bottom of the stairs and joined her mother in the kitchen. "Hi, Mama. I'm sorry I'm late, but it took me longer than I planned to close up for the summer."

Mama continued to roll out the pastry for a pie. "I understand. The last day of school is even more exciting than the first day of a new semester."

"Hmm, maybe, but I love starting the new year, and I will miss the children." She swiped a few berries from the bowl on the counter then grabbed an apron. "What can I do to help?"

"What I need most right now is to see that Alice and Juliet have their things moved into Clara's room so we'll have their room for Mr. and Mrs. Elliot."

"It's nice to have five bedrooms for when we have company. I remember when Aunt Hannah lived with us, and how much fun it was. I'll go up now and check on Alice and Juliet." If Mama's other two babies had lived, the house would be much more crowded, but it suited a family with six children just fine. She and Clarissa would share a room, and what fun they would have catching up on what had happened since their last visit.

At the top of the stairs the voices of her younger sisters reached the hallway. Their giggles meant they were either sharing a funny moment or up to a prank on Clara. Molly opened the door to find the two girls trying on some of Clara's clothes. "What's going on here?"

Their eyes widened and their cheeks burned red. Alice jumped up from the floor and nearly fell over trying to balance in Clara's best shoes. "Molly, we didn't know you were home."

Molly crossed her arms over her chest and tapped her foot on the hardwood floor. "Obviously. I don't think Clara would be happy with what you're doing with her things. Now get out of those clothes and put them back where they belong. You're lucky I found you and not Clara."

"Yes, ma'am, and please don't tell her." Alice pulled off the shoes and put them back in the wardrobe with the others.

Juliet slipped one of Clara's skirts down to her feet and stepped out of it. "Clara has such pretty things, and we just wanted to see how they looked."

"I understand, but it's not nice to pry into someone else's belongings." Molly had to hide the smile that threatened to surface at the sight of the two younger girls scrambling to get things back in order. Alice had been promoted to Ellie's class for next year, but Juliet would still be in Molly's. The two had been fairly well behaved in school, but Alice was one to be watched. That child loved practical jokes and, like other eleven-year-olds, always had fun on her mind.

"Have you moved your clothes and things so Mr. and Mrs. Elliot will have plenty of room?"

Juliet nodded her head. "Yes, we did. Clara was nice and made a space for us in the wardrobe and in the chest."

"And this is how you repay her kindness?" At the remorse in Juliet's big brown eyes, Molly's stern voice turned gentle. "I won't tell on you this time, but Mama and I both expect you two to be on your best behavior while the Elliot family is here."

At their firm nods, Molly wrapped her arms around them and kissed their heads. "I love you girls. Now play with your dolls or something else for a while."

Molly closed the door to their room and made her way to the one to be used by Mr. and Mrs. Elliot. Everything looked in order, even to the empty drawers in the chest and the extra space in the wardrobe. Next she checked on her brothers' rooms. Now twelve and nineteen, they kept their room fairly neat, but Daniel's clothes, discarded after school, lay scattered on the floor.

Molly grinned and shook her head. Mama would have him clean it up later or Tom would force him to. Tom should be off work by now and had probably taken Daniel for a ride. Her youngest brother loved horses and wanted to work on his uncle Micah's ranch one day. No telling where they were riding, but if they stayed true to form, they'd be back soon because suppertime would be along shortly.

By this time tomorrow the house would be full of people. She anticipated seeing Clarissa, but she wished Stefan could join them too. He would certainly make for a more interesting visit.

Stefan rubbed his thumb along the handle of his cane. Two more weeks and he'd be rid of this thing and able to get back to his regiment. At least his injury had not been severe enough to prevent his return, but being off for these past weeks had been boring to say the least. He glanced through the window of the train as it clacked its way across East Texas and the piney woods. Not a whole lot different from the part of Louisiana they'd just come through. Still, it was Texas, and that made the difference.

Tomorrow morning they'd arrive in Stoney Creek to visit old friends of his family. His parents had talked of little else for weeks and then insisted that he join them. After much persuasion and pleading from his sister, Clarissa, he consented. Why, he wasn't sure, except that he did remember back ten years ago when Molly Whiteman visited for her uncle's wedding. If she was as pretty now as she was then, the visit just might prove to be worth the time and effort.

He fingered the brass buttons on his uniform. The blue and gold of the army had attracted more than one young lady, so it should be no different with Molly. She'd be impressed by the medal he'd earned for marksmanship as well as the one from the skirmish with Indians that had caused his injury. Indian uprisings were supposed to be over, but once in a while a renegade band would try to defy the government.

Ever since childhood he'd planned to follow in his father's footsteps and be a high-ranking officer in the United States Army. Now he was well on his way to that goal since his graduation from West Point.

"Are you thinking about when you'll return to your regiment?" Clarissa leaned forward and pressed Stefan's arm.

He patted his sister's hand. "Yes and no. I'll be glad to get rid of this cane and get back to duty, but I was also thinking of our visit with the Whiteman family. Did I understand Mother to say they have six children?"

"Yes, they do. You remember Molly, don't you?"

Heat rose in his face. "Hmm, yes, and I...uh...I was wondering about her. If I remember correctly, she has red hair like her mother."

Clarissa sat back, a smirk filling her face. "You remember correctly, and well you should, with as much grief as you gave us when they were in Louisiana. I was ready to have Father string you up to dry."

"I must have lost that part of the memory." He frowned to

hide the fact that he did indeed remember the teasing. He'd done it all to get Molly's attention and see if he could rouse the anger that was supposed to go along with having red hair. It had worked, and she had been even prettier with her anger riled up.

"I just bet you have." Clarissa's laughter rang out and caused his parents to turn their heads toward them. A few of the other passengers also looked in their direction with curiosity written across their faces.

Stefan frowned at his sister. "Quiet down. You have everyone staring at us."

"And since when did *you* not want all the attention? I've seen you showing off your uniform and telling tall tales enough to know you enjoy it."

"This is different. Now sit back like a young lady and be quiet." What she said had an element of truth, but could he help it if he drew the attention of the young ladies? If Molly didn't take to him, he'd find someone in town who would. After all, they'd be there a fortnight, and that was plenty of time to charm an impressionable young lady or two.

Clarissa shook her head and poked him in that teasing manner of hers. "I can't wait to see Molly again. It's been so long." A sly grin turned up the corners of her lips. "She's not the same little girl she was ten years ago."

"I should hope not. You aren't the same either." He smiled but made no further comment. Under no circumstances would he admit his anticipation of seeing Molly again, and to express disinterest would be a lie. He may embellish the truth, but telling an outright lie was not his way. He'd have to be careful with his comments and reactions around Molly. The hours until the next morning couldn't pass quickly enough.

Can Sallie and Manfred
overcome the distance that the war
has put between them *and* find love?

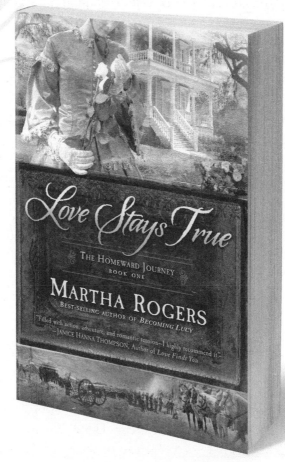

THE HOMEWARD JOURNEY, BOOK ONE
If you enjoyed the adventures of Hannah and Micah,
you'll love the story of Hannah's older sister Sallie as she
waits for her love to return from the Civil War.

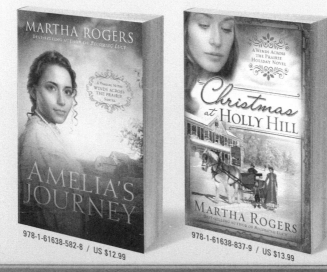
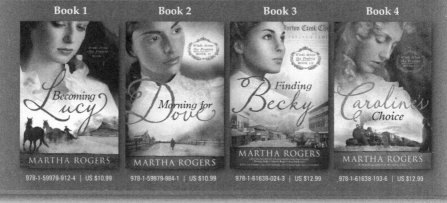